THE KEEPER

A X WILKINSON

MOONTOON PUBLISHING

Cover illustration by A X Wilkinson with Midjourney

First edition 2023

ISBN: 978-0-473-67607-0

AXWilkinson.com

CHAPTER ONE

Nearly half her life was gone, and Martha was with the wrong man in the wrong place.

Her London friends would disagree. They thought she had the perfect life – working as an artist, living in a fancy apartment, being practically married to a gorgeous man who even her parents approved of. But none of it was the way she had imagined her life would turn out.

Carl wasn't the one, no matter how much Martha willed him to be. He was generous, kind and considerate, an easy man to live with most of the time, but there was no profound connection between them. Their friends didn't see that; they saw the act he put on of the loving partner showing her off to the world. They were the golden couple who had witnessed friends' weddings and divorces, become a fixture on the social calendar of parties, then fancy restaurants, and now dinner parties in endless rotation. Sometimes Martha felt she was in a play, acting out some other person's life. It wasn't supposed to be hers. This wasn't the plan. She didn't know what the plan had been, but she knew this wasn't it.

It was all okay. Just okay. She had nothing to want for, but everything to desire from a heart that had been mothballed for years.

She had been seriously in love only once, as a teenager. It hadn't run its course, and those who didn't understand her dismissed it as a schoolgirl crush. Crushes rarely last, but on the brink of middle-age her feelings for him hadn't changed.

Sometimes she wondered if she was looking back with rose-tinted spectacles. But when she reread his letters, her love for him overwhelmed her and the ache of loss cut deep. Time hadn't dulled it, only driven it under. At first, she couldn't accept he had gone. He had planned to start painting again when he left her, and she always thought of him when she was painting. It felt as though she was working with him looking over her shoulder like before. She would look back and, finding he wasn't there, feel his absence like a cold blow to the heart of her.

In the early years, she had tried to find him. She had never given up hope and regularly browsed the art annuals, magazines and gallery brochures, hoping to get a glimpse of his work. There was nothing. Wider searches came up short: no friends reuniting, no death or marriage. It was as if he had never existed.

Just at the point she thought she might never find him, she saw the painting, and it reignited the fire that they had tried to put out. It had smouldered for years, smothered by the ashes of time, yet persisting. An underground fire waiting for oxygen.

The painting was oxygen.

The passion came back to her like the waves she loved on the north Cornish coast, crashing into her and leaving her breathless. As a young woman, she had pursued her dreams, battling through the breakers to put herself in position to ride the waves. Then she had struggled to get to the back and had been idling there for too long, waiting for her ride, losing her nerve, failing to find it. Now she believed she could do it and she knew there was one other person who would believe in her too, as he had all that time ago. She had to find him. The man behind the painting.

CHAPTER TWO

Martha remembered the day she had first seen him. It was January 1990 and she was on the bus, staring out of the window on the bottom deck, listening to her Walkman. Janis Ian was singing from the seventies about not fitting in, not being popular, and being unloved. Martha wanted to reach out down the years to Janis, to offer her friendship. A new decade and a new school didn't hold the same appeal.

Moving house promised an opportunity to reinvent herself, become someone cool, maybe even someone everyone wanted to be with. Martha had told herself this before; it never worked. It's not worth being different when you're seventeen. Far better to dress the same way, listen to the same bands and do all the same boring things as everybody else. That's how you get to have friends. That's how you get to be popular. By selling out and sucking up. It was so stupid. Infantile. She wasn't any good at being a teenager, no matter how hard she tried.

Damn it.

What was the point of even trying? It was a stupid game with stupid rules, and winning meant cheating on herself by betraying her beliefs. Better this time not to make friends. Then there was no one to turn on you and bring you down. It was impossible to be like them, anyway. She had no interest in fashion, she didn't want to talk about the latest TV heartthrob, and she couldn't bear the music that was in the charts. Martha loved listening to singer-songwriters from the seventies; her hobbies were painting and gardening. Her dad laughed at her, saying that if she'd only listen to Radio 4, she would pass for a middle-aged woman. It was a compliment to Martha, who felt more comfortable at home than anywhere else. She had always found it easier to talk to her parents' generation than her own. It would be better to not talk to hers at all.

So that was the plan. Don't talk to anyone. Keep her head down and get through the rest of this school year and the next before she could leave. Nearly two years more. Ugh. This plan wouldn't work. She couldn't be invisible and besides, her life was boring enough as it was without drawing out the months at school into days, hours and minutes of endless clock-watching. Surely she could find one person like her. One person to connect with. One person who didn't think Jason Donovan and Hammer pants were the answer to life, the universe, and everything. A person like no one she had met before.

Maybe it was easier to stick to the plan.

The bus stopped to let the boys out at their school. Martha watched them larking around, swearing at each other, pushing and shoving and spitting out hormones. Boys her age were so immature; it was depressing. She looked around her. Most of the girls left on the lower deck were younger: thirteen- and fourteen-year-olds. Laughter tumbled down the steps from the older girls on the top deck. She turned up the volume on her Walkman and looked back out of the window, watching the terraced houses, corner-shops and pubs pass by. The driver turned into Kingswood Avenue, a straight road lined with horse chestnut trees knitted together overhead like a cathedral nave. Then they were at the gates and the girls spilled out of the bus, chatting and giggling, deep in their own worlds. Martha was invisible to them. Perfect. She waited until the last three bovver-booted girls clomped down the steps. Their hair was brushed straight and pony-tailed, but packet black. Martha followed them off the bus and passed them as they sat on the kerb to change into the uniform's grey, flat shoes. They slipped into the grounds as the prefects shut the large spiked wrought-iron gates before ushering the stragglers up the steps to the main entrance.

Martha wrinkled her nose. The pale green and grey corridors smelled of chemical disinfectant applied by the gallon. She looked at the sun streaming through the east-facing window and visualised where she was on the orientation map the school had sent her, confidently walking through the science block, rounding the corner by the windows that looked out onto the playing fields, then taking the stairs past the art room two at a time. Catching her breath, her memory failed her. She stopped and rifled through her satchel to sneak another look at the map.

"Are you lost?" A deep voice behind her.

Martha fumbled through the satchel and pulled out the welcome pack. "No, I'm – "

"What form are you?"

She turned around and looked up at the man. He struck her as more lumberjack than teacher; a checked flannel shirt was tucked into jeans and matched with a chunky belt and a pair of grunty, lace-up tan boots that seemed overkill for walking up and down concrete-floored corridors. He was tall and slim and his hair was slightly dishevelled, but not carefully; there wasn't a hint of product. It looked as if he hadn't shaved for a few days. His stubble was dotted with grey but his unlined face suggested he couldn't be much more than thirty.

He looked at her, waiting for her answer. And those eyes. Oh boy.

"6B," she said.

His eyes creased as he smiled. "Mrs Madison. History teacher. Stickler for being on time. She runs a tight ship at registration and you're now late. Follow me and I'll get you in."

As he loped away, Martha stuffed the welcome pack back into her satchel and hurried to catch up. He was up another flight of steps and had opened a door to the left to announce, "I found a straggler, Mrs Madison. I think she's new here. Don't let her get away." His hand on her back, guiding her into the classroom, and he was gone.

"Oh, you must be Martha Carson. Hurry up and sit down... Simone Fitzgibbons?"

"Here."

"Catherine Godley?"

"Here."

CHAPTER THREE

After registration, the girls filed into the main hall and sat in plastic chairs facing the stage. Assembly was standard issue. The headteacher, Miss Staverly, introduced herself to the new girls and welcomed the old ones back. There were reminders about the behaviour expected of Stoneview School girls, particularly out of school where they were its representatives in the community: a community that would be sure to contact Miss Staverly if there were transgressions. And then there was the part about the importance of study and hard work and blah blah blah. The usual guff plus a turgid hymn that the girls mumbled along to, accompanied by an out-of-tune piano.

Martha looked out of the window to the rolling fields beyond. The expanse of green calmed her, as it always had. In Somerset, they had lived in a small house with an enormous garden. Martha had loved helping her dad there, getting her hands dirty, planting seeds, weeding and harvesting fruit and vegetables for the kitchen. When her dad's job forced him to move to Cornwall in a hurry, they bought the house in the same rush. The garden was tiny. The previous owners had clearly preferred sitting outside to gardening in it. Martha's family had traded a kitchen garden, fruit bushes, and an orchard for a patio with a built-in barbecue and decorative, but unproductive, flowerbeds.

She was outside looking at the dead flower heads on the following Saturday when a soft voice floated from the neighbour's garden. "It looks lovely in the spring, you know." An impish old lady with bright white curly hair was leaning over the fence.

"Okay. But I prefer growing veggies."

"Me too."

Martha walked to the fence and looked over it at the lawn, small pond and borders of shrubs and perennials. "Where are they?"

"I have an allotment. Why don't you sign up for one, er...?"

"Martha." She smiled. "An allotment would be great."

"Nice to meet you, Martha. I'm Joan. How old are you?"

"Seventeen."

"Oh. You have to be eighteen, though I guess it doesn't matter – there's a two-year wait at the moment."

Martha's smile vanished.

Joan's face crumpled with concern.. "Do you like gardening that much?"

"I love it. Everything tastes better when you've grown it yourself."

"Doesn't it? Yes. Well. This could be perfect."

"What do you mean? I can't grow much here, even if I take up the flower beds and cover the patio in pots."

"True. Which is why you should join me in my allotment."

"Oh, I don't know – "

"Yes, you must. I've got one of the bigger plots and I can't keep on top of it like I used to. Half of it is becoming a jungle. We could share it, if you're keen. Share the work and share the harvest."

"And the cost. How much is it? I don't have a job yet, but I have some savings."

"Don't worry about that. The council charge me peanuts because I'm a pensioner. Come over tomorrow with some gloves and you can see if you want to invest your time and a bit of blood, sweat and tears."

"Blood, sweat and tears?"

"The brambles are vicious."

That was how Martha began working with Joan in her allotment. She spent the next day and would spend the whole of the following weekend hacking away at the briars that grew beyond head height, before digging out their massive roots. But it was a good feeling to look at the ground she had cleared, as she and Joan chatted over a cup of tea and a super-rich chocolate cake.

Time passed quickly in a garden, but it dragged in school. As they stacked all the chairs by the side of the assembly hall, Martha reflected on the nearly two years she would have to endure before her parents would let her start a horticulture course. What a drag. She had picked biology, as she thought it might have some relevance. She was doing Spanish because she wanted to travel and it seemed easier than French. The only A-level that she was likely to do well at was art.

All the art teachers she had had before let her do her own thing, recognising that her talent would carry her through the exams. She hoped the new art teacher would be the same. Martha went into the classroom and found a space at a table near the back. The other girls were chattering as usual, but then the door opened and a rapt quiet smothered the room. The silence dissipated as some girls nudged each other and giggled when the teacher came in. It was the man from the hallway. He wasn't like Martha's previous art teachers. He wasn't like them at all.

CHAPTER FOUR

Dean Finlay ambled into the art room as if he had all the time in the world. Then he dropped his leather shoulder bag on his chair, stacked his books on the desk, and ran his hands through his hair to brush it back from his eyes. Those glacier-blue eyes. It was no wonder all the girls fancied him. When he looked at you, there was an intensity that made most girls look away. Except for Martha, who he was looking at right now.

"I see we have a new victim in this class today."

The girls giggled again. Martha said nothing, but held his gaze. It seemed like minutes, but must have only been a second before he coughed and looked down at the register. All the girls' eyes were now on Martha.

"Martha Carson. Welcome to art and art history. I'm Dean Finlay and you could call me Dean, but the school insists that you call me Mr Finlay, so we're stuck with that."

The other girls giggled some more, but Martha kept quiet.

"Right, let's get back to our use of light, exemplified by the work of the Spanish painters we're studying. Can anyone explain to me what 'chiaroscuro' means?"

A raft of hands shot up, and the class started in earnest. Martha opened her sketchbook and began to draw. She was immersed in capturing the way a beam of sunlight picked out locks of hair in light and shade when she became aware of a presence behind her. She looked up to see Mr Finlay looking at the drawing she had done of him. His smile showed kindness, but his tone was less forgiving.

"Miss Carson, that sketch isn't without merit, but it's not what you're supposed to be working on."

"Chiaroscuro is the use of light and shade. I was demonstrating that, rather than writing about it."

"I'm afraid examiners in art history papers will need writing, Miss Carson. We're out of time now. Here's the textbook and your assignment book. I'd like you to write 500 words or more on what you understand by 'chiaroscuro' and hand it in to me tomorrow."

Martha looked down.

"Can you do that, or do you have a hot date this evening?"

The other girls laughed, and Martha flushed red from ear to ear. She said nothing.

"I'll take that as a yes. And a no," said Mr Finlay, as he walked back to his desk. He put his books and papers in his bag and zipped it shut as the bell rang. "See you all on Thursday."

The girls drifted out of class and Martha tried to blend in between them, desperate to disappear.

"That was a bit harsh," said a lanky girl with long, glossy dark hair, as they flowed through the corridor.

"It's no big deal," said Martha, as the blood rushed back to her face.

"Mr Finlay is normally really nice."

Martha said nothing and hugged her bag to her chest.

"My name's Amy, Amy Chen. And you're... Martha," the girl said, holding out her hand.

Martha let her bag drop to her side, shook her hand, and replied, "I know."

Amy laughed. "Don't let it bother you, Martha. See you later." And she peeled off towards the language block.

But it did bother Martha. She was hoping to cruise through these two years of school, unnoticed. And here she was, first day in the new school and very much noticed.

Martha spent the evening combing through the art history textbook for every mention of chiaroscuro. She rewrote it all in her own words, 501 of them. The next day, she slipped into the art room before registration and left her red assignment book on the desk. As she was leaving, she bumped into Mr Finlay coming in.

"Shit," she said, caught by surprise, and then, "Sorry, sir. I mean, I wasn't expecting you."

"This is the art room and I'm the art teacher."

"Yes, I know, but... never mind. Sorry."

Mr Finlay laughed. "I see you brought your homework. Any problems?"

"No, sir."

"Good. I look forward to reading it." He smiled at her and walked to his desk as Martha bolted out of the door.

CHAPTER FIVE

Thursday's art lesson passed without incident. The class was painting a still life of a collection of objects in the middle of the room. Martha was in her element and relaxed into the work. The bell rang before she realised everyone else had already packed up. She hurriedly put her paint away and went to wash out her brushes.

When she came back, Mr Finlay was holding out her red book. "See you next Tuesday, Miss Carson."

She grabbed the book and left.

Martha waited until she was on the bus home before looking at what Mr Finlay had written. The big, red C startled her. She had never received a C in art before. Yes, in other subjects (and worse), but her grades in art were always As or Bs. She read what Mr Finlay had written:

You have summed up the contents of the textbook adequately. C.

Wasn't that what he wanted? Wasn't that what all teachers wanted? To follow the syllabus, learn the key points in the textbooks, regurgitate it all in the exams? What more did he want? Martha shoved the book in her bag and turned up her music as she watched the countryside go by.

The next assignment was about artists and a sense of place. Martha used the textbook and a book from the library to write her essay. When she got her red book back, she was aghast to see that Mr Finlay had given her a D–. He had written:

Why are you not even trying to think about the art assignments I've set you? You are a competent draughtsperson and talented painter, but you are not using your brain to answer the questions. You are getting someone else to do the thinking for you. Interest and passion in a subject will take you further in life than parroting other people's opinions. It is a lesson worth learning early.

With her next essay, Martha thought she had done a superb job. But Mr Finlay gave her a D–, with the note:

Don't the works of talented artists interest you? The best way to develop your art is to learn from what has gone before you. All the great artists learned from the artists before them. Do you really think you are so different, that you have been delivered to the world with a fully formed, god-like ability?

At first, Martha was furious. She knew she had ticked all the boxes with the essays because she had researched them all thoroughly and copied the work of the best art historians. In her own words, of course. That was more than any other teacher had wanted from her. But not Mr Finlay. He didn't want an analysis of the best in the field. What the hell. Fine. If he wanted her to wing it, she would. She would stop reading her textbook, look at the paintings, and he could read what she really thought of those.

He set the next essay on the development of Picasso. For most of the next week, she spent her lunch hours at the library and studied all his work, from 'Le Picador' to his blue period, through to cubism and beyond. She read everything she could about his life. When she had exhausted all the books, she started the essay, writing about his early years in Malaga and La Coruña, where he learned to paint far better than most working artists today. She described how he broke through impressionism to be one of the founders of cubism. Then she described what happened during the Spanish Civil War, reflecting on how, with 'Guernica', he could communicate the atrocities of war far more than a conventional painting ever could. And then she shot him down in flames:

Picasso squandered his ability. He squandered his talent because of his ego. At first, he pushed boundaries, but then he only sought to get attention for himself. The idea of himself as a genius artist consumed him and he forgot about art. If he had treated women better, his art would have continued to evolve beyond that of a man who became a spoiled brat.

When Mr Finlay handed Martha her red book, she opened it with trepidation. He had written, 'I can't say I agree with your analysis of Picasso's later work. I'm glad it is Picasso who was the target of your vitriol and not me! A–'

In Martha's next essay, she included a slip of paper:

I may have attacked Picasso because he neglected his art, but at least he kept creating it all of his life. Do you create art or only teach it?

When she picked up her red book the next time, Mr Finlay had written, 'Your argument that Salvador Dali was little more than a pale imitation of Hieronymus Bosch was interesting, if a little simplistic. B+'

He had stapled a note within:

Teaching art is sometimes as challenging as practising it. Yes, Picasso kept creating art and didn't become a teacher. He had success early, before life got in the way. It was simple for him to choose his own path and create what he wanted throughout his life. Sometimes events change the path you are on, or the path you might have taken. You can choose anything right now. Why not build on your talent and study art? Miss Staverly says you are planning to study horticulture. I can't imagine you are as good at growing plants as you are at painting them. Your painting, 'Trees Behind Water Treatment Plant', was inspired (even if the title might preclude early commercial success).

No, I don't paint. Not now.

Martha replied:

Surely, if you are keen enough, you can create art any time. Studying horticulture wouldn't stop me painting. And I know there's paid work for me at the end. I don't want to end up like Mum and Dad and never have money for anything but holidays in a tent or leaky caravan. As for early success driving future creativity, van Gogh wasn't recognised in his lifetime, but he didn't stop. He continued until he died.

I guess he wasn't married with children like you. Is that why you don't paint?

M

PS I love those trees and wouldn't want to sell that painting, anyway. Dad says it looks perfect in the downstairs loo!

Dear M

Studying horticulture may not stop you painting, but it will push it to the sidelines. Exactly at the point when you should nurture and develop your talent, you will stagnate. Now is the time to focus on your art, to grasp the opportunities that won't be available to you later. Unlike a horticulture course, which you could do in your thirties, if the art doesn't work out (which it will, I am sure). Where will you be at thirty? In a backwater garden centre, answering endless questions about how to overwinter citrus, prune roses and keep slugs at bay? Or in your studio, preparing for your next exhibition?

You are too young to be worried about what will bring in the money. You don't have a mortgage or kids (or any plans to have either soon, I imagine), so you can work at a nursery part time to pay the bills and put your best time and passion into painting.

I'm married, yes, but I don't have children. I'm not painting because my paintings expressed my sense of self. It is better for me not to do that right now. Seeing how students express themselves is much more rewarding, which is why I would love you to continue to develop your art. I want to see you expressed in that drawing of the winter storm at Maudlin Pool, not in a perfectly potted hydrangea cutting.

D

Dear D

You seem to have a fab life: living in the beautiful countryside with a wife and a good job. Why aren't you painting? What happened to you?

M

Dear M

You are young and until now most of the important decisions in life will have been made for you by other people.

The decisions you have had to make are straightforward (which cereal to have for your breakfast, what outfit to wear on a Friday night, which band's album to buy on a Saturday morning), but you'll see that life becomes more complicated. I was stupid and reckless as a kid and I chose to do the right thing as a grown man. That meant giving up my art to provide for my family. There isn't a single day where I don't think about what might have been if I hadn't. But I know I made the only decision I could as a decent person.

Your choice is your own and doing a horticulture course will get you a job and maybe painting won't do that for you straightaway. But it will. You have a talent rarely seen and an intelligence that can push that forward if nothing substantial gets in your way. Right now, the only thing in your way is you. Sometimes you can be too sensible, especially when you don't have responsibilities to anyone but yourself.

D

In her next assignment, Martha stapled the note:

Goya is part of our course, 'The Spanish Artists of Light'? More like darkness. I've never seen anything so depressing. Enough of war, loss, and doom and gloom! Don't you like anyone whose work brings joy to the world? Does everything have to be refracted through a prism of bitterness? What happened to you to be such a downer?

When she got her red book back, it only had the grade, A. There was no note. She continued to get good grades for her essays about Velázquez, Murillo, and Zurbarán. But she had upset him. Well, tough. He needed to be told. What was so bad about his life, anyway?

CHAPTER SIX

Then he introduced her to Joaquín Sorolla. It was like stepping out of the darkness into the light.

Dear D

Now we're talking. This guy can paint. The paintings show life in a way that photographs never can. This is the reason to be an artist. To supercharge what you see with the way it makes you feel. The joy of children playing on the beach or a mother's love for her baby. Though there is a sadness too, knowing that these moments don't last. But he doesn't dwell on that, doesn't go psycho like Goya.

I look at these paintings and I'm jealous of the life these people led. That newborn baby in the mother's bed didn't grow up with the worries I have about the world. Things were a lot simpler back then.

M

Dear M

I share your opinion of Sorolla. How I would've loved my work to have been a tenth as good as his. He didn't let his ego get in the way of his soul. As for things being simpler then, well, yes, they were. But that meant people didn't have the medical advances we have now. That meant that the baby in the painting only had a 50-50 chance of reaching your age. Make the most of the time you are born into and don't wish for the past. You have a bright future ahead of you. What worries do you have at your age? The world is yours for the taking if you work hard and make the right choices.

D

Dear D

Yes, but one of those choices has to be not to have kids. There are five billion people on the planet right now and there will be a billion more by the end of the century. We are polluting the world by burning coal and oil and cutting down the rainforest. What kind of world would a child of mine grow up in? It doesn't look good!

M

Dear M

You are too young to be deciding something so serious as whether to have children. We don't know how the world will be in twenty or thirty years. Technology and education have made many improvements in society that we couldn't have predicted back in the sixties. The next millennium could be a much better world for the next generation. Keep an open mind.

That said, you will have to decide very soon about your studies. I can't stress enough how rare your talent for painting is. I'm sure you could get into any art college you wanted, so let me know and I will write a personal recommendation for you.

D

Dear D

It's hard to get a job with an art degree and the tuition and materials would cost a fortune. My parents earn just enough for me not to qualify for a grant, but not enough to pay for me without it hurting them financially. If I study horticulture, it will be cheaper and when I graduate I can get a job and pay my parents back. I can always paint in my spare time.

M

Dear M

As I've said before, now is exactly the time you should follow your passions and take risks. You're young enough to do what you want to do. If you don't capitalise on that talent, you'll regret it. You can't paint in your spare time and expect it to be your best work. We'll apply for scholarships, or you'll work to pay your way through college. The time to do it is now, now, NOW.

D

***

Dear D

Why are you so keen for me to paint when you don't?

Why aren't you a working artist?

Why are you teaching art in a school in the back of beyond?

M

***

Dean wrote:

I can't answer those sorts of questions this way, Martha.

***

Martha replied with a letter:

Dear Mr Finlay

I'd really like to know why you aren't a painter. You can't ask me to focus on painting without explaining why you aren't. Why aren't you a full-time painter? When you demonstrate painting techniques in class, I can see you're not an ordinary art teacher. There is something more there, isn't there? Why are you wasting your time teaching us?

Apart from that, I have some other questions for you:

1.What is your favourite book?

2.Who would you like to have round to dinner? What would you cook them?

3.What did you do last weekend?

4.Would you like to go to Mars?

5.When did you last paint something for yourself?

Answer me soon!

Martha

Martha knew better than to staple that letter in her red book. Instead, she stapled the following note:

If you want to persuade me to choose art over horticulture as a career, there is a lot to discuss. We should write to each other properly and honestly. There's a white post in the far corner of the playing field. Nobody goes there, and it's very overgrown. You'll find an envelope wrapped in a plastic bag. You'll have to mind the brambles!

Martha was excited to find a plastic bag at the white post the very next day. At lunchtime, she found a quiet spot in the library, opened the letter and read.

CHAPTER SEVEN

Dear M

I enjoy teaching young people like you to paint more than I enjoy painting myself.

I've been teaching for about a decade and I've seen the work of a lot of students. Many of them have been talented and have gone on to study art at college. I know a few who are working as artists now. But none of them had the raw talent you have. Your unique way of seeing things and your style of drawing and painting are gifts. Like all the best gifts, you should value them and look after them, not discard them or neglect them. If your art tuition ends when you leave school, it will be like pushing an albatross out of the nest before it's ready to fly. Your art is a beautiful thing, but it could be spectacular. I'm afraid that if you only do it as a hobby, you'll never progress. Other people may still enjoy what you do, but you'll be missing a chance to create mean-ingful work that can change how people view the world. The kind of art that can move them and make them connect with concepts that cannot be put into words. The best art does that, and yours isn't there yet. It could be.

Seeing art in books gives you a shadow of the experience of seeing the real work. It's vital that artists see actual great art. I've talked to the headmistress, and she has agreed to a subsidised gallery trip for the class. Details are coming out this week, but I hope you'll come, as we'll visit three of London's best galleries – the National Gallery, the National Portrait Gallery and the Tate.

To your questions:

1. My favourite book is *Brave New World* by Aldous Huxley. He wrote it a long time ago, but it seems just as relevant now.

2. I'm not much of a dinner party person. It's more fun for me to go somewhere I can collect wild mussels to cook on a campfire with a bit of white wine and garlic and a good loaf of bread. I'd invite the Prime Minister and see if I could talk some sense into her.

3. I worked on the drawers for the desk I'm making, went on a couple of long walks and marked a lot of homework. It's an exciting life!

4. No, I wouldn't go to Mars. There are too many beautiful places on Earth I haven't seen.

5. When did I last paint something for myself? A long time ago.

Okay, so I have some questions for you:

1. What do you like to do with your free time? Do you ever paint or draw when it is not an assignment?

2. What would you like to be better at depicting in your art?

3. What are you kids listening to these days?

D

Dear D

In my free time, I love to garden. When I'm working in the garden, I don't know where the time goes. I'm never happier than when I've been planting out seedlings, picking vegetables, or even weeding. Joan (my neighbour who owns the allotment) makes a flask of tea and we sit with our backs to the shed, our faces to the garden, and we talk. Mostly about the plants, but sometimes about the world and politics and so on. She must be in her 80s (whenever I ask her age, she says she is a hundred years old). She met her future husband when she was my age, married him at twenty-one, and he died when she was in her forties. They never had children (I don't know why and don't want to ask, in case she couldn't). I asked why she didn't marry again and she said other men couldn't compare to her husband, that they would fall "so short she couldn't see them any more". Now she says she is happy being on her own. Most of her friends her age have lost their husbands. The others spend too much time moaning about the ones they still have. She knows all sorts of people around here and goes out a lot to clubs, meetings and outings. She has a better social life than any of us! I wish she would come out for a night with me. She would be more fun than the school crowd.

Yes, I draw in my spare time (cheeky question!). I nearly always have a sketchbook with me to draw what's around me. Travelling abroad would give me more to draw and improve my art, I guess. The furthest I've been is France, and it was so cool to be in a different country where they speak a different language and have different food. Mind you, I wasn't that keen on snails!

I don't really know what the 'kids' are listening to these days, as I like to listen to other music, like records I find in Dad's collection. He has loads of great albums from the 1970s. I think that was the best decade for music and that the 1980s was the worst. Let's hope the 1990s get better. I use Dad's records and ones that I've bought from charity shops to make mix tapes. I love Bread and The Carpenters, and James Taylor has the most amazing voice.

1. What do you like doing in your free time?

2. What music do you listen to?

3. Do you play an instrument?

Martha

Dear M

I can see that you love gardening and growing plants. Your paintings of plants are some of your best work. As I said in class, you have a way of making cabbages look like super-models. But, again, now is not the time to take the easy path. You are still marked down for that horticulture course, I see. Why won't you take a TINY risk and test your artistic talent on the world? You have nothing to lose. Try that first and yes, if you don't find the success/life you want doing that, you can return to the security of a career as a nursery woman. I'm sure it wouldn't take much to retrain. But if you do it first and settle for that career, you'll never put your heart into your painting. You won't have the same drive to develop and succeed.

You may think you have little to learn about painting, but there is a mountain of knowledge hidden from view. It's not just a matter of a change of scene. You represent what you see very well, but not what you feel. Your essays (and your writing to me) articulate your feelings far better. If you connect the two, your work will reach another level.

Techniques I can teach you in class (and you are learning them well), but that connection is something you will have to look for. And you will know it when you feel it. The work will become easier in a way, but more demanding too. You should find time flies, it speeds up, but you will be exhausted and spent with the channelling of that emotional energy – art is not for the fainthearted.

I have been asking around, and I am sure that you could study at a great school. St Hibbert's has scholarships for applicants with talent like yours.

You would receive good tuition, of course, but just as valuable would be the fellow students you'd meet. Being immersed in a creative atmosphere like that speeds up the development of your work, your style. And you'd have some fun into the bargain. You have said you are keen to travel and broaden your horizons – well, this is a good first step.

I haven't bought an album in ages, but sometimes I listen to the radio. I guess I'm not into music much anymore, so I'm a bit out of touch, but you may be right about the 1980s. All my music is on vinyl and I am an old fogey, but try Jackson

Browne and Joni Mitchell if you like the seventies, and singer-songwriters like James Taylor. Bread and the Carpenters are a little too schmaltzy for me. You should also dip into the sixties and go through the Beatles back catalogue. It's fascinating to see how they developed from the simplicity of *Please Please Me* to (what was very experimental in 1967) *Sergeant Pepper*. And you have to listen to the White Album. *While My Guitar Gently Weeps* is my favourite Beatles song and it wasn't even written by Lennon and McCartney. Of course I shouldn't write about the Beatles and the White Album without mentioning *Martha My Dear*. It is a sweet tune written by Paul McCartney and he named it after the old English sheepdog he had, though the lyrics are more about his relationship with Jane Asher, which was complicated, as are most relationships. But I'm blathering on now...

I used to play the guitar. I was never in a band or anything like that, but it was fun to head off to a beach at the weekend with my art school mates. We would sit around the fire we had cooked over to sing until the early hours, or until the police came and moved us on. I miss those days.

In answer to your question about what I *like* to do in my free time, apart from a little carpentry, I love to bike. Not to dress up in Lycra and break any records, but to explore. If it looks like a nice day and there is nothing else I have to do, I go for a ride. I pick a place on the Ordnance Survey map, like an Iron Age hillfort or an old castle, and I cycle out there to take a look. Then I find a pub on the way home and stop there for a pint and a bite to eat. Very exciting, I know.

D

Dear D

I cycle a lot too, but it's mainly because we live in the middle of nowhere and I don't want to get lifts from my parents all the time. Mum says that the way I drive, I won't pass my test until I'm 40. Mum and Dad gave up taking me out after I lost the second wing mirror, and lessons cost a fortune. Luckily, I can save up now that I've got a Saturday job at the garden centre. Cycling there takes me about half an hour, but I ride through beautiful countryside and I always notice something new.

Oh my god, Joni Mitchell is amazing. I can't believe Dad doesn't have any of her records. When I talked to him about this, he said it was because her voice was like a dying banshee.

He is so wrong.

Qs. 1. Where are your friends from art school now, and do you still sing with them?

2. What would be your ideal home? Do you already live there?

3. Do you believe in God?

M

Dear M

As. 1. I've lost touch with most of my friends from art school, apart from the odd Christmas card. I do have one good friend I keep in touch with, but Robert loathes singing and winces when I bring out my guitar. So the answer to that is "no way"!

2. I would like to live out in the countryside and immerse myself in nature. It would be nice never to have to drive anywhere, at least not day-to-day. I don't have to drive much now, but I'm not keen on being in town. The truth is, I enjoy time to myself, and space. We live in town because that was the house we could afford when we moved here. My wife, Kristina, also prefers being in town, so it is better for her. At the end of our cul-de-sac there is a public footpath, and it takes ten minutes to walk down that to be out in a field and another ten minutes to get to the forest, so it's not too bad if I want to escape.

I guess what I'm saying is that the house I live in isn't as important as the place. I could live in a palace, or a shed, or a caravan, if it was somewhere I could get away from people (not all people, just the annoying ones!) and be surrounded by nature. Nature is a wild garden and used to provide everything we needed before we decided we needed more than we really do. I'm going down the rabbit hole here. You must think me misanthropic, but it's not that I dislike people, only that I want to choose when I'm with them. Being in a town feels claustrophobic.

3. No. Do you?

Question: Are you going to apply to St Hibbert's? Time is running out.

Dear D

It sounds like you need to escape from your cul-de-sad-sack! Most of the kids at school hate the countryside, think it's boring and believe that town has everything they want. That's fine if all you want is to get shit-faced at the bars that turn a blind eye to underage drinkers, or hang out at the rec centre to do bugger all. I'd rather bike to the beach or find something of interest I can photograph or draw.

Toph (a boy who works at the garden centre) says that I'm a 'throwback weirdo', but I say that's better than being a throw-up weirdo like the kids in town.

I used to believe in God when I was little, but I used to believe in Father Christmas too... I think with all the terrible things that happen in the world, with innocent children getting awful diseases and so on, that there can't be a god. If there was, he or she would work in horrible ways, not mysterious ones!

In answer to your question, if I studied art, it might put me off the painting I enjoy now. Is that what happened to you?

M

Dear M

You are a little cynical for someone so young. Yes, terrible things happen in the world, but amazing things too. Overall, I think people are good and I have often seen (and experienced) the kindness of strangers, especially when travelling.

But no, I don't believe in a god, at least not a religious god, a single being who directs things. Perhaps the universe functions like some kind of super-intelligent consciousness, the way that our consciousness comes out of a collection of interconnected nerve cells. But if that were the case, I'm sure it would be beyond our understanding.

As Arthur C. Clarke said, "Any sufficiently advanced technology is indistinguishable from magic." I think same is true of science. We don't have the science to explain everything yet, and because of this, some people have to ascribe the existence of the world and what happens to a supernatural being. It is interesting that every society, every civilisation, has its own religions, its own god/s, and they are there to serve a purpose, to help people come to terms with things they don't understand. Nowadays, I think science can do that. And there will always be things we don't understand, but that is part of the joy of life. How boring to understand it all!

Science gives us a way to appreciate life, and art gives us the way to show that appreciation. There is a lot of good in the world, a lot of joy too. You should find a way to celebrate that in your art. And no, going to art college didn't put me off painting. Going to art college would make you more passionate about your art, I'm sure.

D

Dear D

I'm so glad that you aren't a religious nut. Yes, there are good religious people in the world but there are also good atheists! Yes, religious people do good, but bad things are done in the name of religion too. And even with science to help us, we appear to go two steps forward and one step back. We fight fewer wars, right, but is it because we have nuclear weapons as a deterrent? What if someone decides to press the button? Bloody terrifying.

Toph asked me out yesterday, but I didn't feel like going into town to kick cans around with the rec centre deadbeats. I'd have liked to bike out to lunch at a pub garden, but it was hosing down. What do you do in bad weather like we've had this weekend? I've been going stir crazy!

M

P.S. I've got the application form for St Hibbert's in front of me. I might fill it in if you fill me in on WHY you stopped painting.

Dear M

Lighten up a little on the home front. You're a teenager and you should enjoy the freedom of those years. Hang out with your friends and talk about whatever is important to teenagers these days. Go out with Toph.

When I was your age, I was so excited about the future and what the world offered. I felt I was just beginning to discover myself and how to express my feelings through my painting, and the possibilities were endless. Don't you feel that way too?

Yes, the weather has been diabolical. You have to have something to do inside in England when it's bucketing down. There are always projects to be done in our old house. It is a 200-year-old survivor of a country estate that Barratt boxes have erased. At the moment, I'm replacing rotten floorboards. All my tools are in a small shed and I work on other projects in there. That's the only indoor space I dream of having – a workshop where I could practise more carpentry. I'd like to get better at making furniture and progress beyond bookshelves, desks and coffee tables. I really hate having to buy furniture that I know I could make if I had the space. My wife dragged me to IKEA once, and walking around there with crowds of people was my idea of a living hell.

I'd also like to have a dog. They make you go out whatever the weather!

D

P.S. If you give me the signed, completed St Hibbert's application, I'll write about why I stopped painting.

Dear D

You don't remember what it's like to be a teenager. There is so much pressure to fit in, and some girls can be really judgemental. The boys aren't as bad. At least they are rude to your face. I've had so-called friends who are lovely when they are around me and then I find them laughing at me behind my back. And all about such superficial things – what clothes you wear, how you have your hair cut, which pop star you fancy, which stupid soap operas you watch on TV! These aren't the important things in life, unless you are a teenager and don't want to be banished to the far corners of the playground. I had enough of that at my last school. Girls blowing hot and cold with me because of something I said (or didn't say) about a new jacket or something they had done with their hair or a LOOK I had given god knows who!

It's easier to keep myself to myself most of the time. There is one girl here (Amy) who seems okay, but I don't want to ruin things with her by saying too much! We mostly talk about school and teachers (not you, of course... well, maybe a little!).

I love dogs! We had a pointer/collie cross called Charlie until a couple of years ago. When Charlie died, I cried for weeks. Dad was really upset, too. Mum says our new house's garden is too small to have a dog, but I don't think dogs care about that as long as you walk them. You could have a dog for sure!

M

P.S. I've nearly finished the form for St Hibbert's, but the essay is hard. It's lucky you've taught me how to write them! In the meantime, tell me what your paintings were like.

Dear M

Kristina is allergic to dogs. When we have stayed with her sister (who has two lovely retired greyhounds) she has been fine, but she insists that living with one would be a problem. I don't know. Maybe she just doesn't like dogs. I grew up with a family that loved them. We had four in total before I left home. All mutts and all completely different apart from their absolute loyalty. Dogs are non-judgemental and never argue with you (unless it is over something revolting they found in the street that you have to wrestle from them...).

I used to paint all kinds of things: portraits, landscapes, abstracts. I was still finding my style, working things out. If I didn't like my paintings, I would paint over the canvases. If you X-rayed some of my old canvases, you'd find a dozen paintings under many of them. Sometimes my friend Robert would take a liking to them and sell them without my knowledge. So I guess there must be a few paintings out there, but I'm finished with painting for now.

D

P.S. I don't mind you talking about me to other students, but you probably shouldn't mention these letters. Other people might get the wrong idea.

Dear D

Don't worry, I don't show these letters to anyone, And I definitely wouldn't talk about them. They are a private thing, our own little world, and I love getting them. The only other person I can have grown-up conversations with is Joan. She's cool, but if we chat too long, she stares at the garden as if the weeds will take over before our very eyes.

I read that book you like, *Brave New World*. It's very bleak! I can't believe he wrote it in 1931 – there are so many things that haven't dated at all. Do you think there is any hope for civilisation, or are we doomed to a bleak future, too?

I haven't read too many other science fiction books. Only *Hitchhiker's Guide to the Galaxy*. Which is hilarious. Have you read it? I love how mice designed planet Earth as the successor to Deep Thought, the computer that found that the answer to life, the universe and everything was 42. And just before it found what the question was, this supercomputer, Earth, was destroyed (oops... I hope you've read the books!). Let's hope we don't destroy our planet before I can work out the meaning of my life.

M

Dear M

I haven't read *Hitchhiker's Guide to the Galaxy*, but I listened to the radio programmes. Funny stuff. Personally, I think the meaning of life is to find happiness and bring happiness to others. Easier said than done, but it's worth a try.

If you want another good science fiction book about our possible future, try *Neuromancer* by William Gibson. A story about living in a computer-linked 'cyberspace', where there is a threat of artificial intelligence taking over. I certainly hope that is a long way off!

D

P.S. Is that application ready and do you know where your towel is?

Dear D

The books you suggested sound a lot more interesting than what I had to read for my English literature GCSE. They stuffed the syllabus with books so old-fashioned it was impossible to relate to them. *Cider with Rosie* was a self-indulgent mess of a novel. Dickens was okay once you got used to the language, but I prefer to see the adaptations on the BBC (I know – my dad says I'm a philistine). I did like *Jane Eyre*. That book was way ahead of its time with its feisty heroine. But then there was Shakespeare. Strip back the language and the stories don't stand up, in my opinion, ha, ha. They would have been entertaining at the time, but now they've dated! Moving into the more modern (ha!) books we read, I loved *To Kill a Mockingbird*, but found *Tess of the D'Urbervilles* way too tragic. I enjoyed the West Country locations though, so I tried a couple of his others, *The Mayor of Casterbridge* and *Jude the Obscure*. They were tragic too! Couldn't Thomas Hardy write happy?

M

P.S. Not quite and yes, I am one hoopy frood.

Dear M

You can't be serious about Shakespeare. I'll have to find a video I can lend you. The plays come to life on the stage.

If you like Thomas Hardy's writing but not the tragic endings, try *Under the Greenwood Tree*. It's an earlier novel that was a little lighter. You might like it more than he would; like many novelists, I don't think Hardy would have enjoyed re-reading his early work.

D

Dear D

Under the Greenwood Tree – thanks for that suggestion – I loved the ending way more than his other stuff. Thomas Hardy can turn in his grave over that.

M

Dear M

That seems appropriate. As a young man, Thomas Hardy was working as an engineer for the railways. When they needed land in north London, he had the job of disinterring many of the graves at St Pancras churchyard. If you go there now, you can see a tree that has grown into the gravestones he moved.

D

Dear D

When I go to London (I've never been!) I'm going to have to check that tree out. In the meantime, exploring is limited to around here. I bought myself a 1 to 25,000 scale Ordnance Survey map. It's incredible how many prehistoric remains there are around this county. Yesterday I cycled out past Porthwinger to the Iron Age hillfort of Long Castle and on towards Karmouth. The map showed a path to a tiny circle of standing stones.

We must have driven past those stones dozens of times and never would have known they were there.

M

———

Dear M

That's the thing about cycling (or walking) – you see so much more than you do from a car window.

I used to take a sketchbook out with me and draw my discoveries. There is something about drawing that helps me to see things properly, and I remember them better than when I have taken a photo.

D

———

Dear D

You 'used to' take a sketchbook out to draw? Why have you given up? I can't imagine anything that would stop me from drawing. It expresses your soul, doesn't it? When the class draws an object, the drawings are all different. There wouldn't be so much of a difference if you asked us to photograph the object.

So why don't you draw or paint in your free time?

Do you think your painting is no good? You could practise and get better. It's never too late to start again. You are always on at me to spend more time painting. Well, why can't you? What's stopping you? I've nearly finished that essay, so tell me!

M

Dear D

Why don't I draw or paint? I guess it is what you said about it expressing your soul. My soul has been in an awful place for a long time. I found my paintings were expressing a side of me I didn't want to see. Not quite Goya, but dark.

It was different when I was your age, when I had my whole life in front of me, when things were less complicated. I wanted to be a great painter. Perhaps I would've been, but sometimes life takes a turn you don't expect. That is why I'm so excited to see your potential, and hope that you can continue with your work and become a brilliant painter.

D

Dear D

Okay, explain that. Why is your soul dark? You're an arts teacher in a sleepy Cornish town! What happened? What was so big that it stopped you from doing the thing you love, the thing you were meant to do?

M

Dear M

That's just it. I didn't want to be an art teacher, and I never wanted to live in a town. Sometimes choices are made for you, though in my case it was my actions that made that choice.

D

———

Dear D

Then choose something different! What is so hard about that? It's the 1990s. You don't even have kids to worry about. What's stopping you from changing your life right now?

The application form and essay are on your desk.

Your turn.

M

———

Dear M

Okay, I'll tell you if you can promise to keep it to yourself.

D

———

Dear D

I promise. Tell me.

M

CHAPTER EIGHT

Dear M

It was the final term of my last year at St Hibbert's. We had done our coursework, and we had just finished our last exams. All we had left to do were interviews with our coursework assessors. But the serious studying was over and we were elated. My mates and I went out on a bit of a bender, going from pub to pub and then on to a club. We bumped into some girls we vaguely knew. My friend Robert fancied the taller, more glamorous one, and I was left with her friend, Kristina. I knew Kristina because she was in my art history class. She had asked me out several times the year before, but I had put her off, saying I already had a girl-friend (that wasn't strictly true, though I had a few friends I went out with who were girls!). She wasn't bad looking, but she disguised the looks she had with a lot of make-up, bleached blond hair and ever-changing outfits that were the fashion, I guess. The few conversations I'd had with her had been cut short because art was the only thing we had in common but she hated 'talking shop'. Robert asked her what she was planning to do when she left college and she laughed and said *she* wasn't planning on doing anything. She looked at me when she said that and a chill ran down my spine, but she probably meant nothing by it back then.

On the night we met up at the club, she seemed more relaxed and easy-going. We were in the club having a good time, drinking and dancing. After an hour or so, Robert disappeared into a corner with Kristina's friend, and Kristina and I were left at the bar. I tried to talk to her, but the music was so loud. She beckoned me closer. As I moved in, so did she. She kissed me, I kissed her back and then I felt a slap on my back. Robert was grinning at me. The club was closing, and he turned to Kristina's friend to invite her back to his room. She said no, but why didn't we both go back to their flat? I knew where that was going and tried to make my excuses to go home, but Robert elbowed me and told the girls we would love to go with them. He whispered in my ear that I'd ruin his chances if I bailed on him.

I'm not proud of what happened next. I could blame the alcohol, but I was well aware of the choice I could make and I made the wrong one. As we walked up the stairs to their flat, I asked if Robert had any condoms, but he only had one for himself. When Kristina said not to worry, she was on the pill, I believed her. Maybe she was. Mistakes happen, and that was one of the biggest mistakes I ever made.

I had paid my way through college by working at a screen printers during term time and on building sites during the summers (my dad had been a bricklayer and got me various jobs). My plan was to work one last summer before I took off for a year to travel and paint. I knew I could make my money go a long way if I lived in Spain or South America, and I had been learning Spanish with books and tapes with that goal in mind. I'd start in Europe, get my Spanish to a good level and then head off to the Americas to immerse myself in their cultures and truly experience something different.

I had avoided seeing Kristina after our brief encounter (that's a film you should watch!) and hoped I could just walk away from the whole affair with no actual harm done. In my mind, it was a one-night stand. Not something I was proud of, but with two consenting adults and hopefully no expectations on either side, I thought I could escape easily enough. Boy, was I wrong about that. About six weeks after our night together, Kristina showed up at the site I was working at. She walked into the Portakabin where I was eating my lunch and announced in front of everyone:

"I'm pregnant and you're the father".

She gave me a slip of paper with her phone number on it and walked out. The guys around me thought this was hilarious. They patted me on the back and were trying to talk to me, but I couldn't hear them. It was as if someone had sledge-hammered me in the guts. A hole opened up in my world: my travel plans, my work, the person I thought I would be. It was all gone.

D

Martha wrote back immediately and dropped the note back at the Post.

Dear D

Wow... You were really, really unlucky there. A one-night stand with someone you weren't even that keen on, and she got pregnant!? That is so unfair. I know you didn't feel as if you had a choice, but you were remarkably kind to do the decent thing and get married. It's not as though it was the 1950s or anything!

She must have liked you something rotten to go through with all of it. Even if she didn't want an abortion, there was always adoption to consider, right? Why did she want to have a baby so young, with a man she hardly knew?

M

Dear M

I didn't know why she wanted me to be a father to her child. I still don't. Whatever the reason, it was her decision to make, to keep the baby. I couldn't argue with that. I had taken the risk and now I had to face up to my responsibility and do the right thing. We got married at a registry office with her friend and Robert as witnesses. Robert had broken up with Kristina's friend about a month before, so to say that things were awkward was an understatement. He tried to talk me out of marrying Kristina 'for all the wrong reasons', but really there was only one reason and that was I had made her pregnant. She was having the baby, and I had to deal with the consequences. That didn't mean I had to be happy about it though, and that wasn't a good way to start a marriage. I didn't invite my parents to the wedding, plus we weren't going to waste the money we needed on any kind of party afterwards. We went to the pub, had one drink, and then Kristina and I went back to the one-bedroom flat I was renting through the summer.

She wanted me to work with her father, who has a building surveying company. I could've worked my way up from over-paid office work to be his right-hand man, she said. That's what she had envisioned for her husband, but I didn't share that vision. I wanted to keep what little independence I had.

I started a teacher training course and kept working on building sites to help pay the bills. We stayed in the tiny flat as Kristina got bigger and bigger. I tried to make the best of the situation, but it didn't seem to matter what I did; we had rows all the time. It was a freezing cold day in the new year when we'd had a particularly nasty argument about where we were going to live (Kristina wanted to move closer to her parents in Surrey) when she stormed out and slipped down the icy pavement out front. That's when she lost the baby.

It was a terrible thing to happen. I felt guilty, because I was relieved I wouldn't become a father so soon, though it wasn't the way I wanted things to be resolved. Kristina was devastated. We couldn't talk about it without arguing and she kept saying there was no reason for me to stay now that she had 'got rid of the baby'. It was exactly how I felt, but I couldn't say that, with her being so vulnerable. She kept crying and lost her appetite to eat anything, do anything. She went to stay with her parents for about a month.

When she came back, she seemed so much better. She was eating normally again and had put on some weight. But we still argued, and when she said I'd be better off leaving her, I made the mistake of saying it would be better for us both. It was as if I had thrown a switch. She went into a deeper depression than before and I had to take time off work because I couldn't trust that she wouldn't hurt herself. Any time I tried to talk to her, she would either look as if she couldn't hear me, or start crying. I called her parents and they took her to see a counsellor. They all felt she needed to be somewhere new, somewhere we could start again. By the time I finished my teacher's training, it was all arranged. We moved to a housing estate in Penhir, where we live now. I was lucky (I guess) that there was a vacancy in the art department at the school, and so by the September of that year my new life as you know it began.

Robert is the only other person I've talked to about this. I'm not sure why I'm telling you so much, but I guess I want you to know that the decisions we make in life are important. I want you to make the right one, continue on the right path.

D

Dear D

Jeesh. That sounds bloody awful. But that must've been years ago... And you are still together. Did you work it out to become happily married?

M

Dear M

Happily married? That's a rare thing, isn't it? No. The truth is, with no baby and with Kristina mostly recovered from the trauma of losing one, I knew it would be better if we went our separate ways. The more time we spent together, the less it seemed we had in common. She wanted a big house in the suburbs, ideally (I stood my ground to nix that) near her parents. I wanted to be in the countryside and to travel. But every time I tried to leave, she would become hysterical and say I had ruined her life and would make it even worse if I left. A few years ago, we were on holiday in Spain and getting along better than normal. As we were eating out one night, I told her I thought it was best for both of us if we went our separate ways. She seemed very calm then, and I thought it might actually work out. The last few days of the holiday were fine and as we took the ferry home, I felt like my life was about to start again. Two days later, I came home from school to find her in bed with a bottle of painkillers and half a bottle of gin gone. I drove her straight to the hospital, her stomach was pumped, and she was fine. That was the last time we talked about separation. She wouldn't let me have what I wanted – my freedom – and I wouldn't give her what she wanted either. There was no way I was going to be a father to another baby. She insists on a pretence of domestic bliss whenever her parents, or anyone else, come round. To the outside world it seems as if we are a normal married couple, but inside the house it is different. I have been sleeping on the sofa bed in the lounge for years!

I guess I got used to a new kind of normal, and it is scary how quickly the years fly by. Robert says I have a 'childish sense of responsibility'. (He would tell you it all goes back to my childhood, but that's another story.) He has tried to talk to me about it, but since I was adamant that things weren't going to change, I always shut him down and talked about something else.

Our lives have become pretty much separate. I get out of the house whenever I can and she has her circle of friends. As I write this, it reminds me how terrible the situation is. I've been distancing myself from it in my mind, though in my life it is oppressively close.

D

Dear D

Sometimes it seems like the only happily married people I know are my parents. But they are weird. It's terrible when they have arguments, not because I'm afraid they'll split up, but because when they make up (always before the end of the day) they get even more lovey-dovey. It's embarrassing. Amy says her parents are always fighting and they are only staying together for her and her brother and she wishes they wouldn't!

I'd be happy if I never got married. But I would like to be with someone for the rest of my life, to be with someone to share the ups and downs with. I'd like to travel together and to have long conversations. I'd like someone to have a laugh with and play games with. A best friend you share a bed with. But I don't see a reason to get married these days, unless it's for legal reasons like who gets all the stuff when the other one dies. But then can't you just write a will, or something? People spend thousands of pounds on one day and there are so many other things I would do with that money.

Would you ever get married again (assuming you weren't still married, of course!)?

It does seem extreme that you stay in such an unhappy marriage.

If Robert thinks it goes back to your childhood, I want to know what on earth happened then? It must've been even worse!

Yours

M

Dear M

The way you described things is certainly what I hoped for in a long-term relationship. I have nothing against marriage itself, but it was never a goal of mine as a young man. I wasn't thinking that far ahead, until I found that far ahead was right up close.

I haven't really thought about what might happen in the future, as I've spent years living in the present and regretting the past. Maybe I'll tell you at some point what happened when I was about your age, but I'm not proud of myself and I don't think that offloading more of my trauma on you is the best way to move forward. However, these letters to you have made me think about what a terrible state of mind I'm in. One that I need to change. In answer to your question, yes, I would be prepared to commit to someone for life if I met the right person and circumstances didn't conspire against us.

I would certainly want to share my life and interests with that person. I enjoy being alone, but there are so many wonderful things I'd like to see and do with someone else who would appreciate them.

Don't let my grumpy old man stories put you off relationships; you are young and should be out having fun. You don't need to find Mr Right right away, and finding a few Mr Wrongs could help you work out what you don't want to have in a partner as much as what you do. Have fun.

D

Dear D

I'm pretty sure I can recognise a good man when I find one, without having to date a bunch of loser boys! The boys who have asked me out in town have all been revolting. They smoke and swear as if that proves how grown-up they are. They're clueless about what's important in life. I guess Toph (who asked me out at the garden centre) is nice and there's a kid on the bus (Greg) who doesn't smoke and behaves kind of normally. I'd consider talking to him if he didn't change into an idiot when his friends get on, when they all become loud and start showing off. The bus driver stopped the bus yesterday to tell them to keep it down. It's not just school kids on our bus, and a young mother complained to him about the swearing etc, and he laughed it off with the rest of them. I think he likes me (he seems to be looking at me whenever I glance over), but I wonder why he hangs out with such dumb brains. What does that say about him?? I don't have the energy to go there.

It's not like with you. I love writing to you because it's more of a conversation, A proper, grown-up conversation. You can't talk to boys my age like that.

M

———

Dear M

I think it's a lot easier to write to someone like you than to talk to them in real life. I am sure that Greg would be able to express himself much better in writing. Perhaps you should be passing *him* notes!

D

———

Dear D

Greg is okay if all you care about is looks, but he's not really my type. He's too immature. Today he came over to my seat, but his friends were laughing at him in the back of the bus and he went all shy. I waited for him to say something, but he mumbled that he should go. He came and went for no reason! Yes, his friends were putting him off, but if he really wanted to talk to me, why didn't he ignore his friends? And who wants to be with someone who has friends like that? When he went back to sit with them, I could hear them talking about me and laughing. So what was he trying to do? Does he like me or not? It's all so pointless. I can't stand it and can't wait to leave school. The only good thing about it is seeing you. Sometimes I feel trapped in a seventeen-year-old body, when really I feel about thirty. I feel like I have more in common with you than those boys on the bus, that's for sure.

M

Dear M

Things are different for boys of your age. I remember feeling that the opinions of my friends mattered far more than they do now. Back then, peer pressure was very important. You want to fit in and it is hard to assert yourself sometimes. Greg is probably a decent lad. That said, the guy should be nice to you if he wants to go out with you!

D

CHAPTER NINE

Martha thought about whether she was being hard on boys like Toph and Greg. She had never been out with anyone and maybe it was because she was setting her sights on men she couldn't possibly have. She was fantasising about 1970s James Taylor, 1940s Gregory Peck, and yes, today's Dean Finlay. All of them just as unattainable. Dean was right; she didn't have to go out with a perfect guy who she would spend the rest of her life with, like some dopey fairy tale. She needed to grow up and get out of her head. Maybe. She would've liked to talk to Amy about it, but she wasn't sure she could completely trust her yet. All hell would break loose if she blabbed to anyone, as Amy often saw Greg and his friends at the rec centre.

When Martha had a tea break at the allotment with Joan, she asked, "Do you think it's a good idea to practise going out with boys?"

"Practise?" Joan laughed. "You can't practise that kind of thing, darling... though it's a nice idea."

"Yes, right... I was just being silly, I suppose."

"Do you like this boy you want to practise with?"

"I don't know. But I thought going out with him would let me find out. He's quite good-looking..."

"I bet he knows it, too."

"Yes, that's true."

"So, what else do you like about him?"

"Er, well... he doesn't smoke."

"That's it? Your criteria for boyfriend material are good-looking boys who don't smoke?"

Martha laughed. "Yes, when you put it like that, it does sound bad. The thing is, there's another guy I really like. He's into painting and the outdoors like me and we've, er... talked a lot. He shares a lot of my opinions on things, and – "

"He sounds more like your kind of boy... if he's good looking and doesn't smoke, of course," said Joan, nudging Martha.

Martha blushed. "Yes, yes, he is."

Joan had a sip of her tea and waited for Martha to continue.

"The trouble is, he's already with someone."

"Well, the good ones are never single for long. If he knows you exist and you have lots in common, you just have to wait until he comes to his senses, gorgeous girl!"

Martha smiled and nodded.

"Now let's get back to the garden – those beans won't plant themselves!"

When Martha got home from the garden, she ate her dinner in a hurry and headed upstairs, leaving her parents to watch their middle-class murder series. She raced through her homework before writing to Dean.

Dear D

Joan gave me some good advice about relationships today and it didn't involve going out with Greg, which is a relief for me (if not for you!). She's great to talk to, as even if I told her anything secret (I haven't), I know I can trust her not to tell anyone, ever (well maybe if my life was endangered, but otherwise, no way). She also knows so much about gardening, it's like hanging out with a walking-talking-digging-weeding-planting encyclopaedia. She says I'm useful because I have youth on my side. I do all the heavy lifting, digging and reading of all the seed packets!

Do you like gardening? You have never talked about it and I realise now that this may be something we don't have in common. I wish you could come to the allotment and meet Joan. You would like her (and maybe the garden).

M

PS: my parents finally signed the gallery trip permission slip and I've paid – I'm so excited about it. Can't we go out to eat, rather than taking a packed lunch? I've saved lots of money from my job because all I spend it on is old records from charity shops. I scored a couple of Jackson Browne ones this weekend and a mint edition of Janis Ian's Between the Lines. That album is me all over.

Dear M

I like some gardens. The regimented neat and tidy formal ones aren't my cup of tea, but I'd love to grow my own food. I've never had a garden of my own. (We have a patio and a lawn. My wife would go berserk if I planted vegetables. They don't form neat lines.) But since I've been writing to you, I've thought about it more and more. So much so, I approached the council about the allotments here. There's a two-year waiting list, but now I'm on it. One step closer to getting my boots muddy.

D

P.S. We made the gallery trip a packed lunch thing so that it is more affordable, but there will be afternoon tea at the Tate. I'm glad to see that only one person isn't going, and I'm glad that person isn't you.

Martha's heart thumped when she read the last line, but perhaps he was only glad because he wanted her to see the art. It was so hard to read between the lines.

Dear D

You won't believe this, but remember I was telling you about that boy on the bus, Greg? He came over to me and actually asked me out. But he just wanted to go to the park! That's where all the kids take the booze that they've stolen from their parents' houses to drink. They just drink and smoke and hang out. Why would I want to do that? What kind of date is that? Anyway, I said no, of course. Well, now he's totally changed. He's openly laughing with his friends and they even throw stuff at me sometimes. It's so stupid and childish. I can't wait for this year to be over.

M

Dear M

Sorry to hear about Greg. What a jerk!

D

P.S. You deserve better.

CHAPTER TEN

Every time Martha found a note at the Post, it filled her heart so much her chest could barely contain it. The envelope smelled of the sandalwood soap he used and she contented herself with the smell alone until she was able to go to her private corner of the library to read it. She relished every word Dean wrote, the prose lifting her into his world. Dean was writing to her and only her. It was as if no one else existed.

She read his last note so many times that a hole began in the folds. She did deserve better than Greg. He was a jerk. But did she deserve Dean? Is that what he meant? She looked for a sign from him in class. But there was no secret smile, no nod, no wink. He barely looked at her, focusing only on her work. When he pointed out perspective errors in her painting, she thought she would faint with the intensity of his closeness. The smell of him was intoxicating then. She agreed with his criticism, looking into his gemstone eyes, but he fixed them on the work, only the work.

When he moved on to the next canvas, Amy nudged her. "You aren't going all moon-faced for Mr Finlay are you?"

"No," said Martha, painting over lines with the white gouache she wanted to cover her face with.

"Hey, no biggie, but you'll have to get to the back of the queue in this class."

Martha thought to herself, *if only you knew. It's just me, Amy, just me and him.* But she said, "Get real, Amy, he's ancient. He must be at least thirty."

"And married."

"Ugh."

"And with kids."

"Double ugh."

"And a teacher. That means he'll be hard up. I want someone who can afford to take me out to nice restaurants every week," said Amy.

"Well, you should give up flirting with Stefan Romano then; he doesn't even have a Saturday job."

"But he's so lush, Martha."

"And he knows it." Martha relaxed now that they were in the familiar territory of working out how Amy could get Stefan Romano to notice her. She glanced up at Dean and found the moment he was looking at her. He quickly looked away, but it was all she needed; what was between the lines wrote itself clear. She deserved him and he deserved her.

When the class ended, Martha dashed to the toilets and wrote a note for the Post.

Dear Dean

I don't know if I deserve better. I certainly want better. There isn't much choice if you limit yourself to the boys around here. I want to be with someone more mature.

Someone like you.

Don't you want to be happy too? Your wife doesn't make you happy. It sounds like she doesn't care about you anymore, even if she once did. How can you be with someone for the rest of your life if you don't care about each other? You deserve better, too.

You write as if your situation is fixed in stone, but it's not. You have the power to change your life, but you don't. If your wife loved you and you loved her, then it would be something worth saving. But she doesn't love you, only the idea of you. And you are with her because you feel responsible for something that happened a long time ago, that she was responsible for, too. You are both holding on to something that's over, right? You're concerned that I don't waste my artistic talent, my opportunities to be with someone, my life... And yet you're wasting yours! Maybe it's time for you to stop living vicariously through me and start living.

If I'd met you later in my life, I know things would be different. I wouldn't be your pupil, just someone who you have a lot in common with. You think I'm a generation away from you, but I was born in the wrong time. Modern music doesn't interest me – I'd rather listen to Jackson Browne, Joni Mitchell and James Taylor than Prince, Madonna and New Kids on the Block. I don't care about fashion. I don't care about anything teenagers fixate on. I don't want to hang out and smoke and drink down at the park or the recreation centre. I'd rather go for a walk in the countryside, or bike to the beach. Like I know you would.

Would you do that with me?

Love

Martha xxx

There was no reply at the Post the next day. In class, Dean gave them a pencil exercise on light and shadow. He didn't look at her. He didn't even look at her drawing. She checked the Post several times before the next class, but there was nothing there. He was definitely avoiding making eye contact. When he returned her homework, he looked at the desk beside her. Martha stopped staring at him long enough to look down at the grade. The handwriting she knew and loved betrayed her. B–. She was dulled to the rest of the lesson and stayed back after the bell, blocking the door before he could leave.

"Are you picking on me, Mr Finlay?" she asked with her eyes ablaze.

"I wouldn't be picking on you if you did the work I know you're capable of," Dean said.

"What have I done wrong?"

"You've become complacent. You're not trying anymore. You think you can cruise by, but there is still work to do."

"That's not what I'm talking about. Why have you stopped writing to me?"

Dean reached into his jacket and handed her an envelope. He moved towards the door as Martha opened the envelope. It was a letter from St Hibbert's, offering her a place, conditional on the results of her exams. That's all it was.

CHAPTER ELEVEN

Martha should have been happy about the letter from St Hibbert's, but she would have traded it in for a note from Dean. She went to the Post on her way home, but there was nothing. She went again the next morning and there was... a note. He had written! Martha's heart flew up in her chest like a skylark. She put the note in the zip front pocket of her backpack and dashed to the library to be in the world of her and Dean, alone.

Dear M

I shouldn't have made fun of that boy. You should go out with boys your age. It's foolish for me to judge your situation, when mine is very different. I may wish I had more freedom in my life to travel, pursue my art and, yes, go out with other women, but I shouldn't transfer that onto you. You're bound to make some bad choices, but that is the joy of being young. You can have fun. It didn't work out for me because I took my eye off the ball and confused being irresponsible with having fun. But you seem far more sensible than I was at your age, and I'm sure you wouldn't get into the same kind of trouble as I did. So, please: have fun. I'm holding you back.

I loved getting your letters, and I enjoyed reading them, but I am afraid that if someone else found them, they might jump to conclusions about what is going on between us. The truth is, I have crossed a line by writing these notes to you. It's not fair to you and I need to let you live your life properly, without meddling in your decisions, without my interference. Apart from in your art, of course, which *needs* my interference! So I won't be writing any more. Please stop writing to me. I won't be going to the Post to check it.

D

P.S. I am going to burn our correspondence and I suggest you destroy your letters from me too.

Martha felt a cold chill run down her spine. She folded the note in her hands and looked up to gather her thoughts. He couldn't be doing this. She deserved him. He deserved her. She'd just pushed him too quickly.

Stupid, stupid, stupid.

She frowned and blinked away a tear. She unfolded the note again to see if she had missed something between the lines.

"Is someone writing you love letters?"

Amy was beside her, peering over her shoulder. Martha quickly folded the note and stashed it at the bottom of her backpack. Her cheeks were impossibly hot. She laughed. "No, it's a joke. Something from one of the boys on the bus." *He was breaking it. He was breaking their perfect world.*

"Let me read it."

"No, it's silly. Hey what are you doing here, anyway? I've never seen you in the library before." *Damn him. Why did he get to decide what was best for her? She knew what was best in her heart. She deserved him.*

"Yeah, well, I figured that's where you were hiding all this time, with your secret notes and all…"

Martha picked up her backpack to leave. "I'm not hiding. If I was hiding, you wouldn't have found me." *How could he do this to her?*

"Hey, why are you so upset? We never do stuff together. And I was just trying to find you to invite you to a party on Saturday. Misha's parents are going to be away and she's got a pool!"

"It's March." *Martha had to get him out of her mind.*

"It's heated."

"I don't know. I've got lots of stuff on." *He was destroying her.*

"Like what? You don't do anything anymore. You never come out. And I need you to stay over at mine, so Mum and Dad will let me go to the party. They think you're a good influence."

"They have a point." *He's pushing me away. He wants me to be a teenager. Fine.*

"So you'll come?" Amy was nodding her head like crazy.

"All right. But I don't want to be out super late."

"Okay, no problem."

"And I don't want to have to hold your hair back as you vomit."

"No hair holding." Martha gave her a hard stare. "And no vomiting."

"Okay."

"Great. I'll pick you up from your place at six and we can get ready at mine together. We are going to have so much fun."

Martha couldn't see that happening, but it was probably better than being home alone.

***

Amy was only fifteen minutes late when she knocked on Martha's door.

"I'm off, Mum! See you tomorrow."

"Does Amy want to come in for a cup of tea first?"

Martha raised her eyes at Amy, who said, "Hello, Mrs Carson. No, we're fine, we don't want to be late."

"Okay, well, don't rush home – we don't want you getting a speeding ticket like Martha's father."

"Thank you, dear. Have fun, girls!" said Martha's dad from the living room.

"We will," chorused Amy and Martha. Then they were out of the front door and at Amy's car. Martha put her bag in the back seat.

"I hope you've got a change of clothes in there," said Amy.

"What's wrong with what I'm wearing?"

"Jeans and a sweater?"

"I'm wearing hot pants and a crop top underneath."

"I wish you weren't joking. Never mind – you can borrow something of mine."

When they got to Amy's, Martha agreed to a sequined strappy top and a jacket. Amy wore a little black dress.

"That's very restrained for you, Amy," said Martha, looking at the hem that touched Amy's knees.

"Don't worry, I've got these to pin it up with later," said Amy, brandishing a handful of safety pins. "Now you can dress like a tomboy, Martha, but you have to put on more make-up than just lip gloss!" Amy pulled the cork out of a bottle of Blue Nun and poured it into two mugs.

"This is warm," said Martha, taking a sip.

Amy gulped hers down and refilled her mug. "Yeah, it tastes better when it's cold, but if I put it on the windowsill, my dad would see it and throw a fit."

Amy pulled mascara, liquid eyeliner and some dark metallic eye shadow out of a drawer and pushed Martha in front of the mirror. Martha swigged some of the sweet wine from the mug and put on the make-up. Amy fast-forwarded the second side of Now That's What I Call Music 16 before flipping over the cassette. She looked at Martha in the mirror. "Better, but…" She came over and drew fine lines along Martha's bottom lashes, darkened the eyeshadow and applied another sweep of mascara. She looked down at Martha's Nike trainers. "It's a shame we're not the same shoe size."

"Thank goodness. I'd fall over if I wore those," said Martha, looking at Amy's two-inch heels.

"These are my sensible shoes!" Amy did a twirl as Tears for Fears blasted out. Martha drained the rest of her mug and danced with Amy. When they had finished the bottle, they checked the contents of their bags. Martha had money, keys, a mirror, lip gloss and a penknife.

"You have a penknife?" said Amy, peering into Martha's bag.

"It has a bottle opener."

"Okay. You win that one."

As soon as they were out of the house, Amy got Martha to help her pin up the hem of her dress so that it barely covered her bottom. The party was a twenty-minute walk across town. They left the neat lawns and hedges of Amy's street and walked down the main road, past the old man's pub, newsagent's and bookies and into the town centre. Amy took a hip flask out of her bag and offered it to Martha.

"Seriously?" said Martha.

"It's Southern Comfort. You like Southern Comfort," said Amy as she held out the hip flask.

"On ice. With lemonade. But don't let me stop you; you'll need it to kill the pain," said Martha, looking at the red weals forming on Amy's heels.

Amy shrugged and tipped back the hip flask.

The town centre pubs were full. Muffled thumping of music and shouted conversations seeped into the street. Amy and Martha cut through a car park and crossed the river to a path overgrown with buddleia and lined with bottles and fish and chip wrappers. It emerged into a housing estate cul-de-sac filled with cars that spilled over pavements onto untidy lawns.

"That's the place," said Amy, pointing to a newish brick box with tiny PVC windows and a conservatory tacked onto the front. The door was open and *Blue Monday* was beckoning them in.

"I love this song," Amy shouted, dragging Martha into the house.

They squeezed their way through the people filling the hallway and followed the music into the lounge. Amy started dancing and then Martha was dancing, too.

Amy nudged Martha and looked towards the stereo. "Stefan Romano is here. And he's brought his cute friend."

Martha looked behind her. "You have got to be kidding. That's Greg. He's such a prick."

"Oh, my god. He's coming over." Martha rolled her eyes as Amy squeezed her hand hard.

"Hello girls, can I get you a drink?"

Amy was speechless for once, but Martha smiled and said, "I'm good, Stefan. But I've got to go to the bathroom – excuse me."

Amy widened her eyes at her, but Martha made her escape. She was back in the hallway, squeezing through the hot bodies holding warm beer that spilled from plastic glasses. Escaping out of the back of the house to a patio and the relief of the cold night air. A blanket of mist cloaked a swimming pool, which was a good twenty metres long, running almost from fence to fence. The guys in the pool were in boxers and most of the girls were in their underwear, though a few of them had come prepared with padded bikinis that pushed their boobs into the guys' faces.

"Are you going in?" said a blond-haired boy through the mist. He sounded familiar.

"I prefer swimming in the sea – that looks like human soup. What about you?"

"No, I prefer it when it's not full of drunks pissing in the water."

"Yeah, gross. I hadn't even thought of that..."

The boy came forward and Martha saw who it was. "Oh, hello, Toph. It's nice to see someone normal here."

"I'll take that as a compliment. So how do you know Brian?"

"Brian? Is this his place? I thought it was Misha's. That's who Amy knows. What about you?"

"Misha is Brian's sister and Brian and I have been mates since we were little. My dad works for his dad's double-glazing company."

"I see..." Martha looked around, wondering how Amy was doing.

"Oh no, I've started to bore you already. That's the end of my double-glazing chat, I promise."

"Sorry. I was just wondering about my friend."

"Where is she?"

"I last saw her in the lounge with Stefan Romano."

"So that's who he was snogging."

"Really? That's brilliant. She'll be happy." Martha wondered when she'd be able to go home now. She sneaked a look at her watch: it was nearly ten thirty.

"Come on, it's still early, and she did look happy. Let's get a drink."

They left the steamy bodies and went to the kitchen. Toph opened the fridge. It was bare but for a tub of margarine, a slimy lettuce, and a door full of condiments. He slammed the fridge shut and whispered to Martha, "Back-up plan – follow me."

Martha hesitated, but the prospect of waiting alone in the party for Amy was less attractive, so she followed Toph. He punched a code into a lock on a brown side door and glanced back to make sure no one would follow but Martha. They went down a few concrete steps, and Toph flipped a light switch. The garage lit up like a stadium under floodlights.

"Wow," said Martha. "I know nothing about cars, but that looks expensive."

Toph open the bar fridge in the corner, got a couple of beers and fished keys from under a golf bag. "1969 E type Jag." He opened the driver's door for Martha.

"I can't drive this. I haven't even got my licence."

Toph laughed and crossed over to the passenger side. "Neither of us are going anywhere. Mr Carter would kill me if he knew I was even in the garage." He sat in the leather seat, looked at the beers and said, "Bugger. I forgot the bottle opener."

Martha took her penknife out of her bag, levered out the bottle opener and gave it to Toph.

"Bloody brilliant." Toph opened a bottle, gave it to Martha, opened his and then gave her back her penknife. "Do you take that everywhere?" They clinked bottles.

"Uh-huh."

"You are different," said Toph, then quickly added, "in a good way. Cheers!" They drank their beers and talked about school, their friends and their parents.

"Brian's dad is loaded, but he spends all his money on the house, car and holidays because Brian's mum doesn't want to move and leave her friends. My parents would move if they had the money, but they spend everything they have on giving me a good education."

"Is it working?"

"Going to St Luke's as a day-boy? I get good grades, and I might even get into Cambridge, but Brian is my only friend.

The rest of them are toffee-nosed snobs who care too much about their cars and what they're going to do when their trust fund matures. Brian is popular because he's good at rugby, but look at me."

Martha looked at Toph. He wore stonewashed jeans with a belt that was punched with extra holes, and his corduroy shirt bagged around chicken-bone arms.

Toph continued. "Even when I try to eat more, I can't put on weight and I have zero hand-eye coordination, so rugby is out." He smiled. He had lovely straight white teeth, though his nose had a bump in it, as if he had a habit of running headlong into walls.

"Lucky you, never being able to put on weight. I can never seem to lose it."

"You don't have to. You're gorgeous." Toph leaned across, dropped his empty bottle, and took Martha's face in his hands to kiss her. Martha held tightly on to her half full bottle of beer. She kissed Toph back, but it felt weird. Wetter than she'd expected. Was this how kissing was supposed to feel?

Toph drew back. "Are you okay?"

"Yes, fine. Sorry... I didn't know what to do with my beer."

Toph took the bottle, knocked it back, and kissed her again. It was really wet. Was it the beer? Could she wipe her mouth off without offending Toph?

"I really like you, Martha."

"I like you too, Toph."

"Will you go out with me? I mean, to somewhere other than a garage?"

Martha laughed. "Yes, of course." She looked at her watch. "But I'd better check on Amy. I'm staying at hers."

"You can stay here if you want. Brian's parents are away."

"No, I'd better go... Look, here's my number." She scribbled her phone number on the back of an old receipt. "Or I'll see you next Saturday at the garden centre." She got out of the car as Toph picked up the bottles.

"I'll call you," he said, as she went up the steps to the door.

"Great," said Martha and she was through the kitchen, heart racing as she hurried down to the lounge. There was no sign of Amy, but she saw a girl they knew in the hallway. "Have you seen Amy?"

"Yes. She's the one hogging the bathroom. She's been in there for hours."

Martha found the bathroom and a locked door. "Amy, are you in there? It's me, Martha."

The door opened and Amy grabbed Martha and pulled her inside before locking it again. "Where have you been? I've been having a total nightmare." Amy's make-up was all over her face and her hair was more back-alley than back-combed.

"Are you okay?" asked Martha.

"I shouldn't have had that last Cinzano. We ran out of lemonade and used some dodgy lemon liqueur we found at the back of the drinks cabinet."

Martha grabbed a flannel and wet it under the tap. "Gross. Is 'we' you and Stefan?" She gave the flannel to Amy to clean up her face. "Where's he?"

Amy scrubbed hard under her eyes. "Don't talk to me about that bastard. He put his tongue down my throat and copped a good feel, but when I came back from the loo, he was gone."

"*Gone* gone?"

"I wish. I went out to his car, and he was in there with Tracy."

Someone hammered on the door.

"Glasses Tracy or big-boobs Tracy?"

"Take a guess."

"Oh. Bugger." All the guys liked big-boobs Tracy. "That was quick."

"I was in the loo a while," said Amy, picking bits out of her hair.

"Oh, you poor thing," said Martha, opening the bathroom door and pushing Amy out, as another girl, who looked even worse than Amy, lurched in.

"I feel better now. But never mind me. What happened to you? You disappeared."

At that moment, Toph appeared in the hallway. He held an imaginary receiver to his ear and mouthed, "I'll call you."

Amy raised her eyebrows and punched Martha on the arm. "No way! Who's that guy?"

"Toph."

"As in Christopher?"

"I guess."

"Tell me all about it."

And Martha told Amy something about it as they stumbled their way home.

CHAPTER TWELVE

Dean couldn't explain why he didn't burn Martha's letters. He'd intended to. Instead, he took the notes from the bag under his workbench and wrapped them carefully in brown paper, tying the bundle with string. He put the bundle back in the bag and stashed it at the bottom of his wooden box of drill bits. It wasn't fair to Martha to keep writing to her. It had catalysed her artistic development at the cost of her emotional one. Teenagers made mistakes, learned from them and moved on. It wasn't up to him to impede that process. She might have needed his artistic encouragement at the start, but she was on the right track now and he was benefiting more from the exchange than she was. He had needed to change his mindset as much as she had. The letters had woken him up after years of hibernation. He shivered in reflection as he locked the shed and went inside to ring his college friend.

Robert had moved to Truro when he got married a second time, leaving his bachelor pad in London solely for work. His house was less than half an hour's drive away, but they hadn't met any more often than when he'd been living in the city.

"Hello, Robert."

"Dean Finlay. Long time no hear."

"Yeah, sorry about that. That's why I'm calling – are you free Saturday night?"

"No, but it's nothing I can't get out of."

"Oh…"

"Relax. Carmen's parents are here this weekend. I'd rather see you than talk about the stock market over a lentil lasagne. Carmen's going through a vegetarian phase."

"Okay, great. Let's meet at the Three Bells at 7 o'clock."

"The Three Bells? That's an old man's pub. Can't we make it the King's Arms?"

"No. My students go there. Besides, the Three Bells has better beer, and it's cheaper."

"Okay, done. See you there."

"Who was that?" Kristina was in the hallway, arms crossed.

"Robert. I'm meeting him for a beer on Saturday."

"I can't believe you're going to see him after the way he talked to me at his wedding."

"You told his wife you were disappointed that his first marriage broke up. What do you expect?"

"I expect you to take my side. I'm your wife, after all."

"I'm not getting into this again. I'm going for a walk."

"Dinner's nearly ready."

"I'll eat it when I get back."

"If you're going to be like that, I'll have it for my lunch tomorrow."

"That's fine with me."

"What are you going to eat?" she yelled at the closing door.

Dean didn't know and didn't care. He walked out of the gate and left it open, walking on through the cul-de-sac and past the grotty housing estate beyond. By the time he reached the forest, he was breathing hard. Slowing his pace, he inhaled deeply. The air was cold and damp and smelled of bonfires, leaves, and dirt. He passed the evening dog walkers who kept mostly to the edges, emptying their pets before turning for home. As he went deeper into the woodland, his eyes adjusted to the darkness. He followed a deer track up through an overgrown hazel coppice until he reached the clearing dominated by an old beech tree. He stopped, listening to the rustle of a rodent in the crisp leaves of the tree's rain shadow. A tawny owl called at the edge of a distant field and spurred Dean to walk onwards. As he emerged from the other side of the forest, a badger dashed across his path. It felt like a lucky omen, demonstrating how nature continues, oblivious to the mad world of men.

When he returned home with a takeaway curry, the lights were out. The car was gone from the garage. There was no note. Normally he would call Kristina's parents and talk to her mother, who would then put on her father to tell him what he had done wrong and what was expected of him. He didn't call. Instead, he pulled a dusty bottle of wine from the bottom of the rack, uncorked it and poured it into one of the fancy crystal glasses from the highest kitchen cupboard. He carefully placed the first side of an old vinyl record on the turntable and turned the volume knob all the way up, savouring the scratches before Joni's voice sang solace to all the cul-de-sad-sacks. Then he tipped out the curry and enjoyed every mouthful. When *A Case of You* came on, he realised he had finished the bottle. It tasted good, but he knew there was better. A case of wine he could never drink.

Dean was standing at the bar and halfway through a pint of beer by the time Robert turned up.

"Sorry I'm late. Carmen made me eat dinner before I left. If I fart out the place, you'll know why."

"No one will notice in here," said Dean, nodding over at the old man and his pair of Labradors sleeping by the fire. "What are you having?"

Robert nodded to the bartender. "Ginger beer, lime and soda."

A withering look from Dean. "Don't you drink beer anymore?"

"Things change, eh? I don't drink anymore and you don't paint. If it were the good old days, I'd be getting trashed, you'd still be painting and I wouldn't have to be out in all weathers looking for painters who have half your talent."

Dean smiled, drank the rest of his pint, and went to the bar to order another.

"Are you in trouble again?" said Robert, sinking into a battered leather armchair as Dean put the drinks on the table.

Dean sat opposite him, scanning the room once more for anyone he knew. "Definitely."

"What have you done now?"

"Nothing. Not really."

"Same as usual, then." Robert leaned back against the head-rest, thought better of it, and perched forward on the chair. "Why the call?"

"I'm sick of it, Robert. I can't keep going on like this."

"Of course not. No sane person would. What I don't understand is why you didn't leave years ago. What's taken you so long to come to your senses?"

"I've been thinking about my life and what I want to do with it. And it's not this."

"What will you do?"

"I don't know. That's why I called you. I want to finish out the school year so it doesn't disrupt the students, and then I need to leave, start afresh. But I'm not sure how. I don't have the foggiest idea where to start. What do you think? You were always the ideas man."

"Yes, but you were the man who followed things through."

"I've followed things through to the end of the road. I'm stuck."

"That's not true. People make their own dead ends and they can reverse out of them if they want to. What I want to know is, what brought about the change of heart? Have you met someone?"

"No. That's not the reason. I want to be on my own." Dean drank the rest of his pint and looked around the room as Robert watched him with a slow smile.

"Mate, you are terrible at lying. You've met someone, haven't you?"

"Can't you drag your brain out of your pants, Robert? It's not all about sex."

"Maybe not, but it's about time you joined the world of us mere mortals. You can't execute a perfectly righteous but appallingly dull life because of something that happened more than a decade ago. If your marriage to Kristina was a penance, you're all paid up. It's over. Done. Move on."

"I don't want to talk about that, Robert."

"You should talk about it. Men can talk all night about football, but we're crap at talking about the real stuff, the serious shit that will eat us up inside. Women talk about it all the time. It drives me crazy, but it's probably the reason they live longer, right? You're not responsible for something that happened to your brother when you were a kid."

"I said I don't want to talk about it."

"Okay, fine. But talk to someone about it, for god's sake. Talk to this new woman of yours."

Dean shot him a look and reached for his coat.

"Okay, okay. Chill. I'll change the subject. If you are going to leave your job, you'll need another source of income. Paint for me again. You know I can sell your work."

Dean relaxed and sat back in his chair, now that the conversation was back on ground he could walk on. "I've got nothing in me. I pulled out a canvas last weekend and stared at it for hours. Sketchbooks are no better. The house is making me impotent."

"More like she is. She could suck the soul out of Death himself."

Dean continued. "I need to get out. I need my own space." He stared down at his empty glass.

"Cheer up, mate. I'll ask around. We'll think of something and get you out of your suburban hell. Now, tell me about your students. Any of them doing anything promising? Anything I could take a look at?"

"I'm not letting you get near any of my young artists. That's a sure way to get you into trouble again."

"That's not fair. I'm only on my second wife."

"So far. Does she know what you got up to during your first marriage?"

Robert laughed, bought more drinks, and the two friends slotted back into tales of old times.

CHAPTER THIRTEEN

Toph was stacking bags of compost when Martha walked into the garden centre. He shoved the trolley out of the way and marched towards her with a giant smile on his face.

"Hello, Martha. How's the hangover?"

"I feel fine, but Amy isn't too flash. She thinks she'll spend the whole day in bed. I thought you weren't rostered on today."

"They called me this morning because John's sick. He was at the party too, remember?"

Martha didn't remember, shrugged and asked, "How are you?"

"Fantastic. I had a great time last night."

"Me too. It was the best party I've been to in yonks."

"Cool. That's great. Um... do you want to go out sometime this week?"

"This week? I've got a lot of work on..."

"Oh, right. Okay. How about at the weekend? Are you free on Friday night?"

"I think so."

"Do you fancy seeing *Dances with Wolves*? It's supposed to be quite good."

"Sure," Martha said. She had wanted to see the film with Amy, but Amy couldn't stand Kevin Costner.

"Great. I'll meet you at the Regent at 8 o'clock." And then: "Er... I can get my mum to pick you up if you like? It's just that I haven't passed my test yet and..."

"Don't worry, Toph. I'll see you there." Martha would rather bike a couple of miles to take the train into town than be picked up by her date's mother. Plus she could meet up with Amy afterwards and have an exit plan.

When Martha told Toph she would be meeting Amy at the King's Arms after the film, he thought it was an excellent idea and arranged to meet his best friend there, too. Brian wasn't anything like Stefan Romano in the looks department, but he had a lot more personality. He was sweet and funny and Amy added him to her roster of nearly-but-not-quite boyfriends.

On the days they weren't at school or working, Martha went round to Toph's house. His parents went overboard, complimenting her on how she looked, her talent for drawing, her manners: anything they could glean about her. He could see her discomfort and brushed them off before they escaped to his room. Every half hour or so, his mum would knock on the door and discreetly ask if they wanted a cup of tea. Toph swatted her away and then turned up the volume of his jazz records. It wasn't Martha's kind of music but he insisted that if she could hear it live it would be different. Not that they could get into jazz clubs at their age, he said, but he was sure she would love it when they did. He was sure they would enjoy all sorts of things in the future. Martha wasn't sure. She wasn't sure about anything. She still wasn't sure about the kissing. And there was more, of course. Toph told her he respected her and would wait for when she was ready, but Martha didn't think she'd ever be ready. Kissing was enough. In fact it was too much. The only time she enjoyed it was when she imagined he was Dean. Toph responded in kind and reached around to undo her bra. She made a break for the bathroom and then said she needed to get home.

Martha's parents thought Toph was 'a delightful young man' and pushed her out of the house to 'have fun' each time he called. Everybody loved Toph. Everybody except Martha. Martha listed his virtues in her diary and filled a page. She should have fancied him. She tried to have fun. At the weekends, they met up at the pub with his friends, Amy and whoever Amy was with at the time. As the spring days warmed, they would bike to the beach and have a dip in the icy cold water before sharing a flask of hot chocolate and shivering under a blanket. She enjoyed having the company for activities Amy had no interest in. Amy would never cycle anywhere or go on a long walk. And it was pleasant to warm up in old pubs with Toph after they had been out. But something was missing.

That something was Dean.

She became used to Toph's attention, but it was as if it was happening to someone else. Her mind was always on Dean. Would it feel the same with Dean? Was she frigid? At times

Martha detached her mind from her body, observing herself from a distance. Doing what a teenager should be doing without enjoying any of it. One day when they were walking through town, Toph took Martha's hand in his. Martha told herself how lucky she was to be with someone so sweet who wanted to be with her. She gave his hand a squeeze and he turned to her and grinned. But then, from the corner of her eye, Martha was aware of someone standing there, of being watched. She turned her head and saw Dean. Instinctively, she let go of Toph's hand, but Dean had seen her. He looked away and ducked into a shop.

Toph turned to Martha and asked, "Are you okay?"

Martha nodded, but felt shaken. She felt as if she was cheating on Dean. Which was ridiculous, but she felt it all the same. After that, she knew she was only going through the motions, ready to be discovered playing a game that she wasn't very good at.

Her dates with Toph, her job, and increasing amounts of homework made Martha neglect the allotment. One evening Joan called round to see if she was sick. She heard her dad say, "Lovesick, maybe. She has a boyfriend…"

Flushing red and feeling guilty, she changed into her gardening gear and plunged down the stairs, past her dad, who was about to close the door. "Wait for me, Joan!" she yelled, and caught up to her friend.

"Well, hello stranger," said Joan. "I've missed you, as has the allotment. I've had a hell of a time tying in the raspberry canes and I'm getting fat eating cake on my own."

"Sorry, Joan."

"Don't apologise, I'm taking the mickey. You must have a busy life; it's gorgeous to be young, with all those fun things to do."

"Nothing's fun right now," said Martha, as they walked onto the allotments.

"I'll put the kettle on, you tie the rest of the canes onto the wires and then we'll chat over a cup of tea."

Martha had finished in the raspberry patch and was digging out bindweed when Joan tapped her on the shoulder to stop for tea.

"You made your ginger biscuits," said Martha, looking at the tray.

"You look like you need them – dig in," said Joan. "No pun intended..."

They sat down on the bench. Martha looked at the garlic shoots edging the muddy furrows as she ate three biscuits in quick succession. She felt more relaxed than she had in ages. But nothing had changed, and she sighed.

"Spit it out," said Joan.

"I'm not spitting out your biscuits..."

"You know what I mean." Joan fixed her eyes on Martha as she topped up the mugs with tea. "I've seen you moping around in your back garden. You're not happy."

"I can't tell you..."

"Yes, you can. There's nothing you can say that will shock an old bird like me. And I'm not one to spill secrets – I'll swear to it on Blue's grave," she said, crossing her heart and nodding towards the pear tree, under which her old Labrador had been buried.

Martha told her about Toph and Dean. It took another couple of cups of tea and it was well past her dinner time when she finished.

Joan gave her a hug. "You poor dear," she said. "First loves are the worst. And he's a silly man."

"It's not his fault, just because he's my teacher."

"I know that; it takes two to tango. But he has ended it badly, with nothing resolved and with no reason to end it but circumstance. I don't know how he could let you go, darling." Joan put her outstretched hands on Martha's shoulders and looked at her tear-stained face.

"What can I do, Joan?"

"Well, you don't want to hear that it's for the best, do you? He could lose his job..."

"He doesn't want his job – he wants to be a painter."

"Yes, but as you said, it's complicated with the situation at his home. I think you'll have to wait this out."

"How long for?"

"Longer than you want. It can't work out for either of you while you are at school. And what about poor Christopher? You have to settle that."

"I know. But I don't want to hurt him."

"The longer you leave that, the worse it will be."

"You're right. I'll find a good time to tell him. But Dean? Do you think he would wait for me?"

"Don't pin your life to him, sweetie. You have so much life to live yet. If you are meant to be together, he'll be there when it's right." Joan looked at her watch. "Heavens! We'd better get home." As they got up to go, Joan winced.

"Are you okay?" asked Martha.

"I'm fine – just a little indigestion – I shouldn't have biscuits for tea!" said Joan, laughing.

They walked back to their street and Martha skipped up the steps to her front door, yelling, "See you tomorrow, Joan!" as she opened it and went inside.

Martha was cross with herself for neglecting the garden and her friendship with Joan. After school the next day, she went straight from the bus stop to the allotment. Joan wasn't there, but Martha put on her gloves and went back to digging out recalcitrant weeds. She enjoyed the warmth from the exercise and the progress made as she worked her way through the garden beds. It was late again when Martha hurried home. She kicked off her muddy shoes at the door and yelled out that she was back. Her dad came to greet her.

"Sorry I'm late, Dad. I lost track of time at the allotment."

Her dad said nothing, but gave her a long, deep hug.

"What? You weren't worried about me, were you?"

"No, Martha. Come and sit down," he said. "Something's happened."

Martha sat on the sofa, and her dad continued. "There was a package that came for Joan today. You know she's a member of that book club?"

"Yes."

"Well, she wasn't answering her door, and the postman gave it to Mum. She called Joan's phone and knocked on the door, but there was no answer."

"That's why she gave us the key – in case she goes out and –"

"Yes... Well... Your mum went in and found her."

"What?"

Her dad put his arm around Martha's shoulder. "Joan died, love."

Martha pulled back." What? No!"

"She looked as if she was asleep in her armchair, but she was gone."

"Joan died?"

"I'm sorry, love."

"I saw her yesterday; she was fine."

"The ambulance crew said she probably had a heart attack. Her bathroom cabinet was full of heart medicine. It looked as if it happened very quickly, too quickly for her to call them."

Martha crumpled into tears and her dad hugged her as she sobbed and sobbed. She was crying for Joan and for everything else, too.

She couldn't eat her dinner, excused herself and went upstairs. The walls of her bedroom closed in around her as the conversation with Joan, her relationship with Toph, and how she felt about Dean thudded around in her head like a bear in a cage. It was all too much. She opened the door and went out past the cup of tea gone cold that her parents had left her. They were in the lounge watching one of their sweet country murder series, so she shouted she was going out for some fresh air. Walking always helped her think, but as she strode past the phone box that marked the edge of the village, things were still muddled.

When she had left Joan at the allotment, her course of action had seemed so clear – break up with Toph and wait for Dean to come to his senses. But now that Joan was gone, Martha faltered. Was that really what Joan meant?

She climbed the hill road and over the stile into the field that led to the forest. What was she going to tell Toph? She couldn't ask Joan's advice now. Who could she talk to?

She plodded along the forest track, not caring that her trainers were getting muddy and the water was seeping through to her socks. Toph was a nice boy. She didn't deserve him. Amy was always saying what a cute couple Martha and Toph were. But she didn't know that Martha was faking it. Trying to be a normal teenager and failing because she wanted nothing to do with the teenage world. She wanted to be in Dean's world, with him alone. It couldn't happen. She knew that. But it left her unhappy in the world she was in and she had no will to keep up the pretence of their teen romance.

Amy would want to know the real reason for Martha splitting up with Toph. Saying that she was in love with another man wasn't an option, never mind who that man was!

Martha sat on the big limb of a beech tree that stretched out over a mossy bank. It gave under her weight a little and she kicked out the litter of leaves, smelling the sweet black dirt of the forest floor. There was only one person who wouldn't judge her or ask her questions she couldn't give the answers to. One person who she knew could keep secrets.

She had to talk to Dean.

CHAPTER FOURTEEN

Time dragged at school before art class. Martha deflected Amy's bubbly chat by telling her it was her time of the month and she wasn't feeling up to talking. Amy put an arm around her in sympathy and then went to ask Brian's sister about their plans for the weekend. Martha kept glancing at Dean, but he looked right through her. She went up to him when the bell rang and began to talk to him.

He cut her off. "Not now, Martha…"

"When are you free? I need to talk to you."

"Martha, please focus on your work. Please. We have a lot to get through this term, especially since we are taking a day out to go up to London. And you've been falling behind on your coursework. Is that what you want to talk about?"

"No, sir."

"Good. I'll see you next class."

Martha blundered out of the classroom, hot tears pricking her eyes. All he cared about was her work. He was treating her like any other student. Lower than that, even – he could barely look at her. He was right about the coursework, but there were other things to think about, like Joan's death, which he would have known about if he hadn't brushed her off. Now that she wasn't a star pupil, he was kicking her away like something nasty that was stuck to his shoe. He even had that expression, the one you have when you need to get rid of dog mess you've trodden in. It was awful. She'd never seen him look at anyone else like that.

She couldn't find comfort in her music on the bus. As soon as she got home, she raced upstairs, grabbed the biscuit tin of letters at the bottom of her wardrobe and went to the allotment. She made a bonfire of old brambles which burned hot enough to dry her tears as she threw in the letters one by one. Watching the flames, she told herself to stop being a silly schoolgirl and grow up. She could work in the garden centre full time if she wanted to, and just let the art go.

She stopped caring about her art, didn't want to go to school and lost her appetite for anything but listening to sad or angry songs in her room. Her dad put it down to the loss of Joan and being a teenager, and her mum brought her endless cups of tea and cakes, which she barely touched.

Toph called for Martha every day, but she didn't want to see anyone.

After a week of being shut away in the house, Martha's mum stormed into her room. "Martha, we all loved Joan, but this has to stop."

"It isn't just Joan. It's everything."

"Well, part of that everything is waiting out on the front step, as he has been every day this week. It's not fair, Martha. Talk to him."

Martha dragged herself out of bed and put on her dressing down, scuffing down the stairs to the door.

She opened it and Toph smiled up at her. "Hello, Martha."

"Hi, Toph."

"I'm sorry about Joan. I really am."

"Thanks."

"This week has been tough for me, too. I've been doing a lot of thinking." Toph shivered on the step and stomped his feet.

"Do you want to come in?"

Toph stayed where he was, looked down, picked at his fingernails. He took a deep breath, looked up at her and said, "You're just not that into me, are you?"

Martha wasn't expecting the question, but couldn't contradict him. "I'm sorry, Toph. You're a great guy, but..."

"Yeah, well, I hope that the guy you are into is into you. I hope he can give you whatever it is you're looking for. I hope he's worth it." He crossed his arms and kicked his trainers against the step. "Take care, okay?" Toph kissed her on the cheek, turned and walked away.

Martha felt absolutely awful. And massively relieved. Everything he said was true, and in the end he had done the right thing, not her. She wanted to call him up, explain things, apologise, but she knew it would only make the situation worse. Martha went to her room and plugged into her music, listening to sad songs through her headphones and crying for Joan, the boy and the man.

On Saturday the sun warmed her back, birds sang their joy along the hedgerows, but Martha still felt terrible as she cycled to the garden centre, intending to quit. Toph had beaten her to it. The hollowness inside her grew. Toph had lost his job as well as her, even if he hadn't really had her completely. She shouldn't have strung him along. He was decent and didn't deserve to be messed around, but she couldn't make herself feel the way about him that she felt about Dean. Bloody Dean.

Martha returned to school. Amy was outside the school gates to meet her off the bus. "Hello Martha. I heard what happened to your friend. I'm really sorry that I didn't get to meet her. She must've been a lovely person."

Martha nodded. "She was, and it's okay. I mean, it wasn't just Joan."

"Why, what is it?"

"It's everything, really." Martha winced. She had said too much.

"What else has happened? What's going on with you and Toph? Are you okay?"

"It just didn't work out."

"But you looked so cuuute together."

"Looks aren't everything, Amy. Anyway, I don't want to talk about it."

Amy could see that tears were forming in the corners of Martha's eyes. "Of course not. Well, don't worry, we'll soon find you someone new. Someone even better. Someone tall, dark and handsome, eh? We've got art today. How about Mr Finlay?"

Martha couldn't hold it together anymore and began to cry.

"Oh shit. I'm sorry Martha. I'm just being silly. Hey, let's go to the common room. We'll get ourselves a nice strong cup of cheap coffee and stir in the finest powdered milk we can find. I've brought Jammy Dodgers. Jammy Dodgers make everything all right."

Amy walked arm in arm with Martha into the school and kept guard all day. She fended off questions from other students who cared more about gossip than Martha's well-being. Martha was happy to have her protection, especially when she went into the art room. She knew she would fall to pieces if she made eye contact with Dean now. They were doing a life drawing class and Martha focused on the canvas, happy that the class's attention was on the folds, fat and wrinkles of the middle-aged woman in the centre of the room.

Martha relaxed, glad to lose herself in the work. It was good to be drawing, creating something out of nothing. She told herself she'd never give it up again. The bell rang, the model left, and Amy tugged at her sleeve, but Martha worked on. It was only when Dean flashed the lights that she realised she was the only one left in the room except him. She grabbed her stuff and dashed towards the door.

Dean intercepted her and his kind eyes met hers. "I'm sorry, Martha." He handed her her exercise book, she grabbed it and rushed out of the classroom, fumbling as she stuffed her paints and brushes into her bag. She dropped her exercise book, and a note fluttered onto the floor.

Check the location.

Location? The homework had been about the meanings of objects in still-life paintings. What had location got to do with it? Martha shoved the note into her bag and hefted it onto her shoulder.

On the bus the next day, she realised what an idiot she had been. She walked from the bus stop towards the school, then dropped back, pretending to check her bag for something. When she was sure no one else was around, she went and looked beside the Post. Sure enough, there was a plastic bag there. Inside it was an envelope. Martha put it in her bag and ran to school. She could barely think about anything else as she waited for break time to read the letter.

CHAPTER FIFTEEN

Dear M

I'm sorry about everything. Miss Staverly told us about Joan. I know she was a good friend of yours and it must have been a shock to lose her.

I'm also sorry if I startled you the other day. It's none of my business, but I was surprised to see you with that boy and I shouldn't be. He looks like a nice lad, and I hope he makes you happy.

Finally, I wanted to apologise for my reaction to your last letter. You probably don't remember, but you wrote about my wife and me. It hurt me because everything you wrote is true. I've spent half my life trying to make up for something that I can never undo, something that is so terrible nothing will ever make it right. It's only fair that I should tell you the thing that happened that changed my life. It doesn't excuse how I behaved, but it might explain it.

When I was eighteen, I had just passed my driving test and took my brother Mike out the next Friday night. He was only fifteen, but we went to the pub for a drink. I wasn't over the limit, but I had a beer and I wasn't as focused on the road as I should've been. It was a winding road home and I must have drifted over the centre line when a van came around the corner. I swerved too far in, lost control of the car and went off the road. The car hit a tree, and I bashed my head on the steering wheel. It may only have been a few seconds, but I blacked out for a while. When I came to, I looked at my brother and he was in a bad way. I can't describe the scene, but it was horrible. The van driver had continued on (maybe he was unaware of what I did – the road was all blind corners at that point). I had to run back to the pub to call 999. By the time someone took me back to the crash site, the ambulance was there, but it was too late for Mike. I killed him and I can never bring him back. It ruined my life and I've been trying to make up for it ever since.

I never wanted to hurt anyone again, but I did, and not a single thing I've done since has fixed it. There's nothing I can do to make things right with my wife, but I can make things right with you.

Thank you for your insight and openness, which has helped me seek a better course in my life. Please don't reply to this letter, as I won't be checking the Post. There's no need for your kindness. I have a hard road ahead, but it's mine to travel alone.

Your boyfriend is lucky to have you. If I'd had a girlfriend like you at seventeen, it would have stopped me from getting into the mess I'm in, I imagine. Well, you never know what might have happened, but you have been a good influence on me in these times. I think the world of you and want nothing more than your happiness and success. You've found someone you can share adventures with and that's fantastic.

Now I will leave you to your personal life. No more letters, no more interference, only my heartfelt apology.

D

Martha folded up the letter and put it away in her school bag. Her heart was racing. It confirmed to her that the way she felt about Dean was on a different level to the way she had felt about Toph. Breaking up with Toph was horrible, but it had been inevitable.

Martha left a quick note at the Post to see whether Dean would collect it. He didn't. She left another and another and another. The forlorn pile remained untouched. He meant what he wrote. But it didn't change how she felt. She couldn't think about anyone but Dean. The letters were a lifeline. There had to be a way to reconnect with him – something that would demand his attention.

When she knew what that was, she raced through every art class assignment and took the time to make sketches for her project. She took them home, to work on a painting small enough to fit in an empty ice cream tub. A painting of him that was truer than a photograph: where you could almost curl the locks of hair around your fingers, or be lost looking into his eyes of many blues. Looking back, she would say it was the first painting she put her heart and soul into. She also put in a note to say that it was over with Toph.

When the bus arrived at school, she was the last to get off. At the Post, she dug a hole for the tub, covering it with grass and three identical pebbles that had no reason to be there. She finished with a note in her homework:

The Post has something important.

The pebbles were undisturbed the following day. The day after, they had been scattered, and the tub was gone. The day after that, there was an envelope there. Inside it was a beautiful drawing of her. There was no note, but the picture said it all. She wrote back immediately.

***

Dearest D

Oh, how I've missed your letters.

I went out with Toph because he was nice and I thought I should. Unlike Greg, he's a sensible boy who doesn't hang out with idiots. He enjoys doing lots of the things I enjoy doing, like cycling to the beach or playing cards (neither of us like cycling to the beach in the rain). I thought I would grow to like him more, and I did, as a friend, but there was never the connection I have with you. He was the brother I'd never had, which wasn't enough. I'm only sorry that we can't continue to be friends, but he says it's too soon to think about that. I've hurt him and I feel terrible about it. All is fair in love and war, right? Or 'in not-in-love and war'. Gah.

Perhaps it is easier to only have friends and never get involved. Will you be my friend again? I'm sorry I was so intense.

I've missed you.

M

Dear M

I have to admit that I have missed your letters, too. They're one of the few things that make me happy in life.

I'm sorry to hear about Toph, but I am sure you will find another boyfriend easily. You are a rare thing, being attractive and intelligent, with a talent to match. Any boy would be lucky to have you.

I need to keep this short, as I have a lot to prepare for the London trip on Monday.

See you then.

D

CHAPTER SIXTEEN

Martha sat at the front of the coach as the popular girls rushed to the back, chattering and giggling as they went, bags banging against the seats.

Amy sat next to her. "Do you get travel sick, too?"

"Uh-huh," replied Martha. If she was going to be on a bus for six hours, the only place she wanted to be was near Dean.

Dean sprang up the steps and did a headcount. "All present and correct. Right, most of our journey is straight along the dual carriageway and motorway, but if anyone does feel sick, let me know, and I'll try to find somewhere to stop, okay? There are seatbelts on the bus. Please wear them. Lastly, and most importantly, we need to vote on what radio station to listen to."

There was a cacophony of noise as girls shouted out their favourites.

"Radio Four? Who here would like Radio Four?" Martha would have liked to put her hand up but she didn't dare, and no one else shared her and Dean's taste in intelligent talk radio.

"Okay, Radio Three?"

No hands.

"You troglodytes! How about Radio Two?"

Amazingly, there were two hands up, and Martha put hers up in support.

"Fine, Radio Southwest it is, then."

The students went ballistic. "Sir!" "That's not fair, sir!" "Come on, sir!"

Dean talked to the driver, and Radio One blared over the loudspeakers.

When Tears For Fears came on, Amy nudged Martha and they joined the others in singing along.

It was a long and noisy trip up to London.

Once the students had drifted away to research their assignment, Dean made his way to the Sorolla room in the National Gallery. Martha was already there, sitting on the seat in the middle, contemplating a large canvas of a woman in bed with her baby. Her favourite Sorolla.

Martha looked up at Dean, but didn't say a word.

"We probably shouldn't be seen together alone. Even if nothing is going on, girls like to gossip," said Dean.

"I read your assignment sheet. I think we have about ten minutes before the others make it through the first few rooms and fudge the rest."

Dean laughed. "You're probably right."

"So let's not waste time." Martha looked at the picture and continued. "You are the most amazing person I have ever met."

Dean said quietly, "You haven't met many people."

"True. But you are the most amazing person I'll ever meet."

"How can you know that?"

"If I felt any more strongly about someone, my heart would explode." Martha turned to look at Dean and their eyes connected, pulling each other in stronger, seconds seeming like hours. Martha moved her hand towards Dean's and put her fingers over his.

He moved his hand away as if he'd touched a live wire. He breathed in sharply and glanced up at the security camera. "Martha, don't." Dean stood up, and moments later, another student came into the room.

"Sir, Julia shoved my sheet behind a sculpture and I'm afraid to get it back..."

"Okay, I'm coming. Show me where your paper is, Andrea..."

Martha was so charged with energy she couldn't stay seated. She got up, walked towards the painting, and looked at the woman in it. "Isn't love a crazy thing?" It wasn't a question for anyone to answer, but when she turned around, she saw she was alone.

Dean didn't look at her for the rest of the trip. He sat well away from Martha at tea at the Tate, and whenever she looked towards him on the coach, he was talking to the driver or staring straight out front. She didn't care. She could float on the cloud of remembering for hours.

CHAPTER SEVENTEEN

Dearest D

I'm so happy. I've never been this happy. It was a life-changing trip in so many ways. I loved seeing all those paintings for real. Now I understand why you were keen for us to go there. You can imagine the artists at work making those actual brushstrokes. Seeing the paintings up close gave me chills, but it was also a little intimidating. When I was in the Sorolla room, I was transfixed. I could never paint that well. Such an incredible feeling.

Driving around London was really interesting. It's unbelievably busy, isn't it? How did our driver keep his cool in that crazy traffic? Would you drive in that? I'd never want to drive there myself. I did love all the old buildings jammed in together, though I wish we'd had more time to go to places like the Natural History Museum, or to explore some of the parks. They looked magnificent.

But none of that came close to how I felt when you came into the Sorolla room and sat beside me. It was amazing to be close to you in the gallery, even though it was only a few minutes. When we touched, it felt like electricity went through me – in a good way! Did you feel it?

We have got to know each other well through these letters, but I want to get to know you for real. The gallery gave me a taste of that and how sweet it could be. Couldn't we meet? There are quiet places nobody goes to. No one would ever know.

I know you will say it is crossing a line and is the wrong thing to do, but how can it be wrong when being together feels so right?

I think that's from a song I've heard, So I'm probably getting too cheesy right now… I'd better sign off!

Mxox

P.S. Say you'll do it. Just tell me where and when and I'll be there.

P.P.S. I love you.

Dear M

You don't need to be as good as those painters. They show you what is possible. If they show you the sky, you can reach for it. That has to be better than always looking at the ground. All the great artists have been inspired by other art they've seen. Art evolves and informs other artists, changing their direction so that they work differently, stretching upwards and outwards. Most artists are never as good as the other art they witness, but that doesn't matter.

The aim is to achieve your potential, to be the best you can be. Then you can forge your own path so that comparison to others isn't even the point. Occupy a unique part of the artistic spectrum. Just as it is subjective whether red is a better colour than blue, it is subjective whether van Gogh is better than Picasso. They were different painters, living different lives, being influenced by different sources. Therefore, their work is very different, but you can't say objectively that Picasso is better than van Gogh or vice versa.

I know your life will be incredible, and it will feed into your work. This trip was only the beginning of your travels, I'm sure. As you see more of the world and more art and life, your work will grow and develop, the same as you will.

You are a talented, beautiful person and I'm glad that our paths have crossed. But even if I felt the same as you did in the gallery, you know that as your teacher I could never follow through on those feelings.

D

Dear D

How do you know my life will be incredible? I can only imagine that being the case if you share it with me. I understand it's difficult now, but you won't always be my teacher. And what about you? Don't you deserve an incredible life? Shouldn't you be painting? And travelling? Your life should have been the one that you imagine for me. She derailed it. Get it back on track. I can help you. And you can help me. I'm not sure I can, or want to, do all this on my own. You have been there to help me with my painting. Come with me and help me with the rest of my life.

We can travel and paint the world together. Imagine how super incredible BOTH our lives would be! That's synergy, isn't it? Our two lives, better than each on its own.

Until then, if all I can have is this correspondence, I'll take it.

M

Dear M

It's a lovely idea, but I know I'd hold you back rather than pushing you forward. College will change you and give you the confidence to strike out on your own. You'll be fine.

D

Dear D

I'm not letting this go. You have to come with me. Even if I have to wait. A future with you would be worth waiting for.

M

CHAPTER EIGHTEEN

The end of school bell rang on Friday and everyone dashed for the gates. Everyone but Martha, who made a detour to check the Post. She bent to check for a note and felt a rush of adrenaline when she found one. And another when she heard Amy behind her calling, "Martha! Martha!"

Martha stood up, shoved the note behind her into her knickers and smoothed down her skirt.

Amy arrived, panting. "I wanted to catch you before you got on the bus." She stopped to get her breath back. "What were you looking for?"

"Nothing. I thought I saw something shiny, but there wasn't anything. Walk with me to the bus, otherwise I'll miss it."

"Martha, we haven't been out to the pub together in ages – "

"Yeah, sorry. It's just that I've got tons of work to catch up on..." began Martha.

"No, that's cool. I've still been going out with, um, well... things have got a little more serious with Brian."

"Oh, really?"

"Yes, but I don't want things to be awkward, what with Toph and all that…"

"Don't worry about me. I'm behind on my coursework anyway, so I shouldn't be going out so much. Plus, I need to save up for college. It's only a year away and even with the scholarship, I'll have bugger all money; my parents can't afford to pay the rent and stuff."

"So you don't mind me going out with Brian?"

"No way. You guys are an awesome match."

"Thanks. He's really sweet when it's just the two of us. He makes me feel special, you know?"

"Absolutely. That's terrific, Amy. I'm thrilled for you." The bus driver beeped the horn. "Oops. I'd better go. Have a fun weekend!"

"You too!" Amy beamed and waved Martha off as she hopped on the bus.

Martha took the last seat on the bottom deck, dropped her backpack to the floor, and slouched down in the seat, relieved. She hadn't been out with Amy in ages and had no desire to. It wasn't only because of Toph. Going out to the pubs to jostle with boys was pointless. Faking an interest in teenage relationships again was a waste of time and money. It wasn't a lie to say she had lots of work to do. Dean was interested in every piece of art she worked on, which encouraged her to produce more. She spent all her free time drawing and writing and thinking about Dean. His notes were more guarded, but she understood that. He couldn't put things in writing that he was feeling. It was disappointing that he only wrote about art or the upcoming student art exhibition in his notes, but it was better than nothing. She collected the envelopes from the Post and saved them until she got home. When she opened them, she breathed in the burst of his soapy smell. Closing her eyes, she imagined he was in her room with her.

Dear M

Your parents told Miss Staverly that you stopped drawing after Joan died. Is that true? Sometimes things happen in your life that make you withdraw. They may stop you from going out, seeing friends, taking part in activities that you would usually enjoy. But art can continue, can be an escape, a release. I see that now in your work. There is a maturity there that wasn't there before. You'll have noticed that in your coursework grades, and I'm sure people will appreciate it when they look at the paintings you'll be exhibiting.

Talking (writing?) of which, I took your suggestion of providing wine at the exhibition to Miss Staverly. She won't allow it. Something about licensing rules and not being able to oversee students etc etc.

D

Dear D

Yes, I stopped drawing then. Now I see how important it is for me. It's like therapy, right? I suppose that's why basket weaving is a thing for people whose brains don't work right.

Certainly, creating something for you got ME back on track. I'll never stop painting again. It's a primal need, like eating or breathing. Which is why I can't understand why you stopped. Or at least I can't understand why you never started again.

Please ignore Miss Staverly, for once. If we don't provide alcohol, how are we going to sell any art? You've seen the work – most of it is terrible!

M

Dear M

I'm glad to hear you'll keep painting. The painting you did of me buoyed my spirits. Each painting you do reminds me of the potential art has to move people. It's impossible now, but the time for me to paint again is coming soon.

D

P.S. I figured out a way to get the alcohol past Miss Staverly. I'll put bottles of sparkling apple juice on the table and make sure we only give her that. Everyone else can have sparkling wine if they want it! Not students, of course...

Dean smiled to himself as he buried his note in the grass and looped back to the path. He'd seen most of his students drinking in the pubs around town, and many of them were sure to drink a glass or two if their parents weren't watching. A glass or two would be fine.

He carried on home, opened the door, and his good cheer evaporated. Kristina was home.

He forced a smile. "No book group tonight?"

"We've pushed it back to Friday." The tone of her voice was colder than normal – which was like sleet in February. "I found this in your shed." Kristina was holding out Martha's painting of him as if it were something she had found in a drain.

A punch to the gut, but not fatal. "What were you doing there?"

"Is it by one of your students?" she sneered.

"Yes, it is." Dean kicked himself for not being fastidious about locking his shed. Kristina had never shown an interest in it before.

Kristina turned the canvas around, took a big gulp of wine, and looked down her nose at the painting. "Is this what you teach your students to do?"

"In a manner of speaking, yes. Techniques, composition, how to see and interpret a subject."

"This student must be blind then. I mean, you can see it's you, but she hasn't captured your essence, has she? It doesn't have the negativity, the failure, that desperate look you have."

"I guess people who live together reflect each other over time, don't they?"

Kristina let the painting flutter to the table, picked up her glass of wine and slammed it onto the canvas, twisting the glass as she stared at Dean. "Maybe you're right."

Dean snatched the painting away, letting the glass fall back into Kristina's fingers and wine splash onto her silk blouse. She shrieked, cursing him as he turned around, walking out of the door before he could do anything he might truly regret. He had to keep his distance, bide his time until the year was out.

Dean finished another glass of the alcoholic bubbles and surveyed the work in the hall. The sculptures were terrible, but most of the drawings and paintings weren't bad. Some of them were actually quite good. Half the work on the walls had red stickers beside it. And they hadn't all been bought by the parents of the artists who'd made them. Every one of Martha's paintings was sold, though her mum and dad were nowhere to be seen.

"Martha, where are your parents?"

"I have to talk to you about that. Can we step outside?"

Dean looked around the room. The students, teachers and parents were busy looking at the art, drinking the free drinks and generally having a good time. He scanned the room for the headteacher. About an hour earlier, Dean had left Amy to fill in on the bar, forgetting to tell her not to serve Miss Staverly the sparkling wine. She was leaning on a sculpture and laughing like a backfiring car at one of Julia's dad's blue jokes.

"Okay, you go out and I'll follow you."

Martha slipped out of the room and stood out in the playground, looking up at the moon. It was nearly full and cast a beautiful light over the ugly surroundings. She waited for what seemed like an eternity. Just as she was about to give up and go back inside, the door opened and Dean came out.

"What happened to your parents?"

"I didn't invite them."

"Why? They would've been so proud to see your work."

"They can see my work any time. But I wanted to have this time with you. Alone." Martha moved closer to Dean, so that she had to look up to maintain eye contact. She caught her boot on a drain cover, wobbling forward. He instinctively put his arm around her to catch her and she leaned in, going up on tiptoes to kiss him.

A switch was thrown. He kissed her back. He knew it was wrong.

CHAPTER NINETEEN

It was reckless to kiss him, but she had to know how he felt. Whether what she had been reading between the lines was true or not. At the moment she kissed him, he stood still and her heart dropped like a cold stone, but then it changed. She was right. They were right together. His kiss was gentle, but there was an intensity behind it. Like being too close to the edge of a cliff in high winds. It was like nothing before, nothing like Toph. She tasted cheap wine, but smelled earth and forest beneath the soap. A place she wanted to explore further, but Dean had pulled back and gently pushed her away.

"Martha, I'm sorry. I can't."

"I know." He looked pained, and Martha touched his arm. "I won't be a student forever, you know."

He reached for her hand and squeezed it, before letting go to walk back through the door. She watched him return to reality alone.

She crossed the playground to her bike, unlocked it and cycled the ten miles home in the moonlight. She felt she was flying.

***

Martha checked the Post when she got off the bus the next day and was excited to find a note already. She couldn't wait and opened it, slumping to the ground as she read:

***

Dear M

I'm so sorry about what happened last night. It's inexcusable and there are no circumstances where a teacher can lead a student on. I've let my personal situation at home encroach on my relationship with you, which should always have been professional. My concern for your artistic future blurred into our personal lives, and that was wrong.

You have your whole life before you, not just your artistic career. I'm getting in the way of that. I see it now. Obviously, I shouldn't have let things go on like this. I was being selfish and it was unfair to you.

Please don't be upset, but we can't write to each other anymore. After stopping our correspondence, I should never have started again, but I wanted to encourage the work you had returned to after Joan's death. My mistake, not yours. You must see that I don't want you to be hurt. It's got out of hand because I've let it go on too long. The temptation to transgress is there because you are special, but there are no extenuating circumstances: I am your teacher. You deserve more than what I can give you.

I hope you will understand that it is better this way.

D

Dear D. D! D!!!

How can you think that breaking what we have is the right thing to do? I'm not an infant. I can handle how I feel about you. Why can't you? Is it because of your wife? If I knew that she loved you, I'd walk away. You've never said she doesn't, but it's clear to me from how she treats you that she doesn't.

Maybe she's afraid of being alone, but why is that your problem now? Why can't you be with anyone else?

Why can't we be together?

M

But when Martha checked the Post the next few days, there was nothing. She wrote again:

Dear D

Okay, I was rushing things. We can back this up to where it was before the exhibition. We can continue to write. I love your letters. They brighten my life. Please write.

M

But he didn't write back. Every day she left the same note:

Dear D

Please write.

M

Each day she checked the Post the note was gone but there was no reply. She wrote one last letter, left it at the Post and didn't go back.

CHAPTER TWENTY

Dean picked up the letter on his way back home. It was one of her bigger ones and he struggled to fold it, to stuff it in his back pocket. He would read it when he got home, as his wife had her creative writing class that evening, or maybe it was her book club. She was out a lot of evenings now, which was better for them both. But then he felt a tightness in his chest, thinking about Martha. Not writing to her as he kept reading her letters was dishonest. It was stringing her along, even if she couldn't be sure he was reading them. He shouldn't be reading them; they only massaged his ego while she pined for something he couldn't give her. He might be stuck in this god-awful situation, but he didn't have to hold her back too. She should be free to enjoy the world. Even if it meant going out with boys who she wasn't madly in love with. Wasn't that how you grew up? He didn't want to think of Martha with boys who weren't a good match, but it was wrong of him to interfere and not let her relationship with Toph run its course as teenage romances do.

He walked through the cul-de-sac to his house. Then he remembered it was bin day and retraced his steps to drag the empty bin to its spot by the shed. The shed door was open, so he closed it, then went to the front door, turned his key in the lock, and found that it was already unlocked. His heart sank. She must be home. He pushed open the door.

"Hello, I'm home." There was no answer, but a chill ran over his back as he entered the kitchen diner. His wife was sitting at the counter.

There was an empty wine glass and piles of letters. Martha's letters.

"I decided not to go to book club."

"Why?" said Dean, knowing the answer.

"Why? Why? Why do you think? Do you seriously imagine I want to carry on as normal, when I've just found out my husband has been having an affair? You must be stupider than I thought."

"It's not an affair."

"What's all this, then?" she said, brushing the letters off the bench top.

Dean wanted to run over and pick them up, but kept close to the door, breathed in deeply and said, "It's not what you think, Kristina. Nothing's happened. Nothing for you to be concerned about."

Kristina snorted. "I'll decide what concerns me. What concerns me is that everybody thinks that you're a man of high morals, a loyal husband, a trustworthy teacher. What bollocks! It's a sham. You're nothing but a weaselly fake. I can't believe I was taken in by it for all these years. And when I found these letters – "

The calm Dean had mustered was gone, and anger bubbled up in its place. "How did you find them?" he said, scooping them up and stuffing them into his bag.

"I was looking for something in the shed."

"Looking in a locked box? My locked box? In my shed? It's the only part of this house that is mine!"

"You're still my husband. You've been acting all weird, and I had to find out what was going on. I needed to see what you had to hide. Because I knew something was going on, you see. You seemed too... happy." Kristina gave Dean a sardonic smile that warned him of what was to come.

"What are you going to do?" he asked.

"You mean, what have I done?"

"Oh, Kristina. Kristina, what *have* you done?"

"You'll find out soon enough. You'll get what you deserve, and it isn't a seventeen-year-old schoolgirl!" She threw the wine glass at him before running upstairs.

Dean flinched as it grazed his ear before shattering against the wall. There was nothing more he could say. He left the house, slamming the door behind him.

CHAPTER TWENTY-ONE

Dean walked out to the forest. He dropped his bag under a beech tree, sat down, and fished out the unopened letter in his pocket.

Dearest Dean

Okay, I get it. I know you are receiving my letters because they're being taken from the Post and if it wasn't you taking them, all hell would break loose (maybe we should have been writing to each other with codenames, but I guess it's too late for that!). So yes, you wrote we shouldn't be writing to each other, but where does that leave me? Don't I get a say in this? Because it's bullshit. You are trying to pretend that if you don't write, our feelings will go away. But I can tell you, mine won't. Ever.

I am more certain about this than I've been about anything in my life (and don't tell me how short a period that is. Just don't). Yes, you're thirteen years older and that seems like a lot. But when I'm 40, you'll be 53. That doesn't seem so different. We'll both be middle-aged and we can grow old together.

Even now, we have so much in common. We think the same way, appreciate the same things. I like the art and books and music you like. I can't imagine listening to that music with any boys my age. Toph was nice to be with, to do active things with, but we didn't have a connection, not like how I felt when we were in the gallery, or when I catch a glance from you in class, or any time we are close together. I can't say that I understand it all. There is a chemistry; is it hormones, the way you smell, or the effect of the sound of your voice? There is that attraction, for sure, but it's more than that: you reach the depths of me with your words. No one else comes close or could do. I know it deep down and it's only our circumstances that keep us apart. We can change that, if you give me time.

I'll study at St Hibbert's like you want and I'll become a better artist. And older, of course. Then we'll move away from this town and out into the countryside we love. And we'll be near the sea, which we love. And we'll both earn money by painting, which we'll love. I'll garden and you'll cook and we won't care what anyone thinks because we won't have to see anyone we don't have to.

And we can travel! If we went to Spain together, we would be completely free. No one would know us. I want to see the beaches Sorolla painted. To experience that light.

Don't you want to do that? Sometimes England feels so grey. Not that I don't want to live here. I love my family. And it's good to be able to visit them, I know. But we could spend a few months in Spain and really experience things. I think it's quite cheap to live there. We would find a run-down place that cost practically nothing and maybe stay a while, sell our paintings to the tourists, learn the language.

It would be better than staying here with people who have nothing better to do than gossip.

A Spanish adventure – it would be brilliant!

I don't know what to write that will convince you. I know that you're pushing me away. You think you're doing the right thing, but you're not. How can it be right if it leaves all of us – you, me and even your wife – unhappy? Our relationship has grown through these letters. They've shown that we're kindred spirits who are meant to be together.

Joan used to say that people don't change as they age, they just become more so. I know who I am and who you are, and that we're both meant to be together. I know you could see that too, if you stopped worrying about what other people might think.

You said before that you were stubborn and determined, but so am I. You have spent most of your life doing the right thing. How has that worked out? Is your wife happy? Are you happy? You said my letters make you happy, but you want me to stop writing them. That doesn't make sense. But I will stop, because I don't want to risk ruining our relationship because of some accidental discovery. That is the only thing I worry about. I don't worry about being in too deep because I enjoy swimming out of my depth. You should come in with me, the water's lovely!

I will keep checking the Post and you can change your mind about this if you want to be happy. Don't you deserve some happiness? What happened to your brother happened a long time ago. I know little about him, but if he was a decent guy, he wouldn't have wanted you to give up your life because his life ended, I'm sure of it. Life is short. We don't believe in the afterlife; we don't believe we get to have another crack at it. So what are you waiting for? You've persuaded me to change the course of my life and paint, and I'm going to try. Can't you try too? Can't you give us a chance?

You've been doing the right thing by your wife, but what has it got you? Nothing but misery. It's a commitment to misery! Your wife broke her vows to you already by not loving and caring for you. If you can accept that and leave, I'll be here for you. I'll always be here for you. I'll wait as long as it takes. Some people wait a lifetime for true love and never have it. Now that I've found it, don't make me let it go.

Maybe I was born at the wrong time, but I ended up in the right place. Over-thinking what we know is right in our hearts is only going to break them.

Yours, forever

Martha xxx

Dean folded the letter and put it in his bag with all the others. Then he had a terrible thought. He tipped out the letters and sorted them from beginning to end. As he read them again, his heart swelled with tenderness towards Martha. A girl who had given new meaning to his life and hope for the future. But he couldn't think about that now and swallowed his feelings. He sorted through the letters again. There was definitely one letter missing. It was the one

Martha had written after their visit to the gallery. The one in which she had declared her love to him. Dean didn't have to wonder where that letter was. He knew where Kristina would have sent it. He packed his bag, went back into town, and found a phone box.

"Robert, it's Dean."

"Hello, mate. What's wrong? There must be something wrong; I haven't even had a haircut since I last saw you."

Dean paused. "Are you free?"

"Sure."

"Can you meet me at the Cross Keys?"

"The Cross Keys is even more of a dive than the last pub we met at. You must really be in trouble."

"Yeah. Half an hour?"

"I'll be there."

Robert arrived an hour later. "Sorry, mate – traffic was a nightmare."

"You drove from home? We're a twenty-minute walk from your place if you take the footpath."

"You would know that – I didn't. Anyway, I've got to see some art at eight. Someone tipped me off about a young guy in Padstow who does interesting things with collage and gouache. So what's this all about?"

Dean told Robert about Martha and the afternoon confrontation with his wife.

"Blimey, you're a dark horse, Dean. I never would've thought you, of all people, would have an affair with a student."

"It's not like that. I didn't sleep with her, Robert."

"Well, that was a mistake." Robert laughed and ordered another round.

Dean glared at him.

"No, seriously, your real mistake was keeping those letters. Your wife is a piece of work, but you can see why she was upset."

"But she wasn't upset. Yes, she threw a glass at me, but there were no tears. And she cries over the slightest thing. The weird thing was, she seemed to enjoy having caught me out. Like she had been waiting for me to slip up."

"In that case, she must've been waiting a long time. I'm going to sound like a broken record, but you have a nasty habit of always doing the right thing."

"That's what Martha says too. She also noted that it hasn't worked out for me all these years."

"She's a smart cookie, isn't she? As for me, it's reassuring that you're fallible after all."

Dean raised his glass to Robert and looked at his watch. "Don't you have a boy genius to see?"

"He can wait. We'll see how keen he is to have an agent when I rock up a little late. So what are you going to do?"

"If she sent that letter to the school, I'll be out of there pronto, even if it doesn't end my career necessarily. It's an all-girls' school – the headmistress won't want the scandal. I'm going to save her the trouble and drop off my resignation in the morning."

"Won't that look like you're guilty of more than Martha's letter suggests?"

"People will assume that, anyway. Besides, I'm done with teaching and I don't want to risk the girl's future. It's not just her talent for painting – she's a sensitive soul, without a huge group of friends. Any hint of gossip around her could knock her back. It's imperative that she gets through the sixth form and moves on to St Hibbert's. That's where she'll be safe to spread her wings without the danger of having them clipped. I'm certain she has an amazing future ahead of her, if I don't mess it up." Dean looked away and stared out of the window, which had a less than scenic view of the car park.

"Oh boy. You've got it bad, haven't you?" said Robert.

Dean looked down and hoped Robert didn't see a tear drop into his beer.

Robert coughed. "She sounds intriguing. And if you think she's a talented painter, she must be good. Maybe I could see some of her work."

"Hah! No way. Anyway, you've got that kid's collage stuff to occupy you – be off with you!"

"Good point." Robert got up and slapped a twenty quid note on the table, his serious face warning Dean not to argue.

"Grab yourself a meal before you head home, okay? And call me if you need anything."

Dean asked for a pasty to take away, left the change from the tab on the counter, and walked home. He was relieved to find his wife wasn't there.

CHAPTER TWENTY-TWO

The following day, Dean let himself into the school an hour before registration was due to start. He slid his letter under the headteacher's door and put his keys in his desk drawer, where he told her she'd be able to find them. Then he gathered a few things, made his way to the exit, and walked back to the house.

He was having a cup of tea, mulling over what to do next, when he heard keys in the lock. His wife walked in briskly, closely followed by a man who looked familiar. She pulled up short when she saw him. "You should be at work."

"I'm not going in."

"Did the headmistress call you?" said Kristina, a smile creeping up her face.

"No." Dean was glad not to give her the satisfaction she'd expected. "Hello," he said, directing his gaze towards the man. "I'm sorry, I think we've met, but I don't remember your name..."

"Martin." Martin had the decency to flush red with embarrassment. "I'm in Kristina's book club."

"Right. Book club. Yes." He turned to look back at Kristina, who was watching him with narrowed eyes.

"Martin is here to help me pick up a few things. I've called the estate agents. They're coming round to look at the place tomorrow. I think it's best if we put it on the market, don't you?"

He saw the complete picture now. This was what she wanted. To be the injured party. Finding the letters had been a gift. But Dean wasn't upset. He was relieved. At least he wouldn't have to worry about Kristina any more.

Shortly after that, the letter arrived from 'Whitmore & Perkins, Solicitors', petitioning for divorce on the grounds of adultery, and demanding half of everything. Dean wrote to them and said that was fine, but that she could have everything but his car, what was in the shed, and the clothes he could fit into an old backpack.

When he met his friend again, Robert told him he was a nutter. "You're playing right into her hands, you know that? She's probably been having an affair long before you started up with your student girl. Don't you see what she's doing? She's taking advantage of you to take everything."

"That's not true; she would've taken half, but I didn't want it. I never wanted any of it in the first place. She's doing me a favour, really. Now I have no excuse not to paint. And I won't be making a mess of the bloody awful carpets."

"That's good news, at least. I know I can sell your paintings."

"It's too early for that, Robert,"

"Okay, fine, but what are you going to do for money?"

"I've cashed in some old premium bonds and sold my bike."

Robert knew that wouldn't amount to much. "Then what?"

"I'll find something. Something a long way from here. At the end of the Earth, preferably."

"Well, I might be able to help you there. I've been asking around; a friend of a friend has some space in her old barn. I saw the place a while back; it was a wreck then, so god knows what it's like now. Anyway, she needs someone to clear it out and tidy up the garden, so that people staying in her cottage don't have to look out onto a wasteland. You could probably live there until the cold weather comes. It's on the other side of Truro, which might as well be the end of the Earth as far as people around here are concerned. How does that sound?"

"Tell me more."

Before Dean left, he made Robert swear not to tell anybody anything about where he was. Robert did so on the condition that Dean promise he would let him sell his paintings when he was ready.

By the end of the week, Dean had packed his backpack and the contents of the shed into his car and was ready to drive west. He knew it was a risk, but he had to write one last letter to Martha. He left it at the Post and hoped she was still checking it.

CHAPTER TWENTY-THREE

When Martha went to her art lesson, she was surprised to find Miss Staverly beside the teacher's desk.

"Hello, girls. Mr Finlay is off sick. I'm sure you all have coursework to be getting on with, so please do so. I'll be in the next classroom and I don't expect you to have any problems, but if you do, come in and interrupt me."

No way would they do that, thought Martha as she got out her paints. She wondered what was wrong with Dean.

The following Tuesday, a substitute teacher was at the front of the room. Now Martha was worried. When the bell rang, she went to the Post and felt for a letter. Nothing.

That afternoon, she was called into Miss Staverly's office.

"Come in, Martha. Take a seat."

Martha sat down in front of the headteacher.

"I see from your reports that you are doing well in your subjects."

Martha said nothing. It was better to say nothing and find out what she was here for.

Miss Staverly continued. "Art appears to be a particular talent of yours."

"Yes, Miss."

"I hope the disruption caused by Mr Finlay's leaving won't affect your performance in the upcoming exams."

"No, Miss." Martha waited, but Miss Staverly didn't volunteer more information. She was desperate to know and had to ask. "Why has Mr Finlay left?"

"I think you know why," said Miss Staverly, looking at Martha over her reading glasses.

A wave of sickness washed over Martha, but she tried not to give anything away and kept her silence this time. She stared back, willing Miss Staverly to tell her more, but she was clearly finished with the business.

"So, can I have your assurance you'll focus on your school-work, Martha?"

"Yes, Miss."

"Good. Leave the door open on your way out."

There was half an hour left of her last class, but Martha couldn't go back there, not yet. She slipped out of the back door, across the playing field and out to the next field over. Far enough away to think. Dropping her backpack, she slumped to the ground and thought about what had happened. Her first thought was to contact Dean, but he had been careful never to tell her where he lived, or what his phone number was, "In case they torture you when you're captured," he had joked. Well, they had caught them both now, and she was being tortured. If he wasn't at school, his wife must know what was happening. But it appeared no one else knew. Miss Staverly would be sure to keep it that way, not wanting to mar the reputation of the school.

So where did that leave Martha? Dumped by a married man whose wife had found out? How stupid she had been to think that this could go on forever. Martha brushed away the tears and picked up her bag to head into town to get an early bus home.

Despite her anger, Martha kept checking the Post every day. Partly it was habit, but mostly it was because she clung on to a sliver of hope. Hope that was rewarded at the end of the week. There was a tightly taped plastic bag there. Ripping it open, she found the letter she yearned for.

Dear Martha

It's hard to write, but I owe you an explanation for what is happening. I have to leave my position because I became closer to you than a teacher should. None of that was your fault. You have a bright future ahead of you and my moving on is for the best. Apart from my wife stumbling upon the letters (with a crowbar), no one knows anything. I assume she forwarded one of them to Miss Staverly, but I have the rest. I have a feeling that we can count on Miss Staverly's confidence.

Kristina shouldn't bother you either. She didn't lose any time moving in with a friend of hers and I have taken what I needed and left her the house and everything in it. I'll be living in a quiet place where I can find my old self and hopefully return to painting, something you have inspired me to do.

Now that I have left the school, you can work without my interference. Please see this as an opportunity to focus on your last school year. Your techniques are at a point where there is little more I could have taught you, but you will need to follow through to pass the exams that will get you into St Hibbert's. You will flourish there, as anyone with talent does. You know how much I think of you and your art. I hope you pursue whatever course you take with the passion I have seen in you. You are one of the special ones whose soul shines brightly. Like foolish Icarus, it dazzled me in a way that could only do harm.

I'm sorry to have let my attraction to you disrupt your life. Every teacher wants the best for their students, but that intention led me to cross the line. I am the one to blame. You are talented, beautiful and empathetic. A combination that may be hard to resist, but I should have. There is no excuse and I'm sorry for the mess I'm leaving behind. It's not too late to make good, though. You have a brilliant future as an artist and an individual and my only regret is not being able to witness more of it.

Take care.

Dean

CHAPTER TWENTY-FOUR

Martha folded the letter and stuffed it deep down in her backpack. That was it? He was going to step away from her life, just like that? Martha felt blindsided. What was done was done, but the outcome had been decided by his wife and the headmistress. He was her world, not theirs. They didn't care about him. His wife had never cared about him, and all Miss Staverly cared about was the school. It was so unfair.

As for Dean, she couldn't believe he had agreed to all of this without talking to her. That he hadn't told her about the discovery immediately. They could've made a plan together, worked out their future. This was bigger than school. This was their life and he wouldn't have had to wait long. She would be moving out in just over a year. She would be an adult in every sense.

Dean, his wife and Miss Staverly were treating her like a little child.

A child to be punished and not consulted. There was no comeback. No argument. She had no choice but to let him go. He wasn't doing the right thing; he was falling into step with them. Well, sod them. She wasn't going to play by their rules any more. Martha turned and walked away from school and headed towards home.

The route was one she had cycled many times in the past. At first she walked fast with her anger, oblivious to the houses she passed. The smell of the brewery that hung over the town on a Friday faded as her legs drove her forwards, her way-finding automatic. Pollen from the avenue of plane trees that led out of town tickled her nose. She so wanted to talk to him. If they talked, they could sort it all out. With their minds on the same wavelength, they would find a way to sail out the storm into calm water. They could be so happy together. He just needed to come to her. The answer was being together, not apart.

The roadside banks were bursting with the flowers of late spring. Hoverflies zipped between landing pads of cow pars-ley. A cuckoo sang in the wood ahead, and she slowed to her normal pace, breathing in the perfume of the wild honey-suckle that threaded through the hedgerow.

Why had he left? And what remained for her now he was gone? She couldn't go on without him. He was the reason for everything. He was her everything. She was nothing without him.

She peeled off the back road, opened a gate and stepped into the wood, feeling utterly alone. She collapsed to the ground and let out big, heaving sobs. When she had cried herself out, she pushed herself to her feet and continued along the muddy path. The last of the bluebells were fading, as the leaves filled in the gaps of sky. She hopped puddles, and climbed the gate to leave the forest and meet her long shadow across the field of grass. The bridle path joined a farm track, and she was nearly home.

When she let herself into the house, it was over three hours since she had left the school. Having two parents who worked late was an advantage.

She made herself a cup of tea and looked out at the little garden. She knew Dean was hard-wired to do what he thought was right. Until discovery, he had clearly fought against that because of the way he cared about her, but now she could see that he felt he had no choice. But damn it, she would have liked to have at least tried to change his mind about that.

She had walked away from the school thinking that she would never go back, but for what? To prove a point? Who would care? Not Miss Staverly. She probably wanted her gone to save her the worry. Dean wouldn't know, because he had left. Her worst fears had been realised, but trashing her life would be another trophy for his wife to take. She'd taken so much from Dean; Martha would not give her anything more.

Martha wasn't sure what she was going to do next in her life, but she wanted choices, and if she quit studying and flunked out of school, she'd be stacking shelves, drinking her wages away at the pub every weekend and living at home like the rest of the deadbeats. One thing she knew was that she wanted to get as far away from Stoneview School as possible. St Hibbert's College was as good a place to go as anywhere. She wasn't going to give up on Dean, but she certainly wouldn't find him by moping around. If he moved school, he probably wouldn't start until the next school year, in September. She might be able to find him then, to write to him once the dust had settled. In the meantime, she would keep busy, quieten the agony of thought, just bloody carry on.

She worked harder than she ever had in her life. She stopped her doodling and paid attention in her Spanish and biology classes and even listened attentively to Miss Saunders, who was filling in for Dean. The geography teacher was out of her depth and barely took her eyes from the textbook as she plodded through the remainder of their Art History syllabus. Martha used her lunch breaks in the library to read every book on her biology reading list, and her time on the bus to listen to Spanish tapes on her Walkman. She was off the bus and in the door before 4.30 most afternoons, did her homework, fixed herself some dinner and left a note for her parents before heading to the allotment. It was only a matter of time before the annual fee became due and wouldn't be paid. Then it would go to the next person on the waiting list, but for now it was where she could ground herself, stop herself from spiralling downwards. Without Joan there to talk to, Martha filled the space, listening to Radio 4 or audiobooks as she planted, weeded, and watered until the light faded, working late into the evening. It was only in the few minutes it took before she dropped off to sleep that she let herself think of her lost love, crying soundlessly as Joni Mitchell sang to her, then sleeping into silence at the tape's end.

Summer was starting, and it was busy enough in the garden centre to make working another day there welcome. With school, the allotment and work, every waking minute was filled and stoppered up tight, so that she could endure the rest of the term, sitting her mock exams and passing all with straight As.

As Miss Saunders handed the results out in Art class, Amy teased Martha. "Are you trying to become head girl or something?"

"No," said Martha, "I'm just trying to get through to the summer holidays."

"And some. Have you had a brain implant, or been taken over by aliens? Who stole my friend? Why are you so serious all of a sudden?"

Martha didn't want to talk about how she felt to anyone, even Amy. "You're just taking an interest in me now because you broke up with Brian." Brian had been seen out with big-boobs Tracy more than once and everyone in school knew about it. Amy was tolerant and forgiving, but not a doormat. When she saw him kissing Tracy in the Cellar Bar, she picked up the pint on the table beside him and slowly tipped it over his head and down his precious brown suede jacket. It was one of the few evenings Martha had been out with Amy recently and she was happy to witness the cheer that erupted in the bar as she followed her friend, who marched up the steps to the street, head held high until she was out of sight of the crowd and free to burst into tears.

Amy stopped asking questions. Martha knew she had played a trump card at the wrong time. "I'm sorry, Amy. That was low. I know you cared about Brian. He was a bastard and I've been a crap friend. But I'm going to be better."

"I hope so. I passed my driving test, you know. This means we could have the best summer ever."

"Great. I need that. I need to have a good summer more than anything."

Amy didn't ask her what she meant. Everyone was sick of school and looking forward to six weeks without it. Her face brightened at the thought and she said, "I'll get a job to pay for petrol and we'll go to the beach whenever we can. We'll be bronzed bombshells by the end of the summer. Boys won't be able to get enough of us!"

CHAPTER TWENTY-FIVE

During the summer holidays, Martha needed distraction. She occupied herself physically by working, gardening or going out with Amy, but now that school work was on hold, her mind was back to obsessing over Dean, where he might be and how she might find him. She missed him – missed him so much.

Amy got a job in a clothes shop in town. That meant a hefty discount, and she insisted Martha update her wardrobe. She bought a bikini, a skirt and a couple of fitted tops. Unlike Amy, Martha didn't care about what clothes were fashionable or flattering. She didn't care that the boys in town were paying her more attention than when she wore jeans and T-shirts. She bought them because she didn't have the energy to argue with Amy. Going out with her meant less time at home, thinking of Dean. Boys looked her up and down, tried to buy her drinks and came over to talk to them. Amy was friendly, but it was Martha they were interested in, and she brushed them all off.

"Come on, Martha. Aren't you interested in any of them? What about Zach? He's a little short, I know, but he's cute and he's funny and he really likes you."

"I'm not interested in boys, Amy," said Martha, thinking of the man she had lost.

"Oh, oh really? I had no idea... when did you start fancying girls?" Amy said, making a smooching sound as she bumped hips and sidled up to Martha at the bar.

Martha laughed. "Don't be daft, Amy; I'm not a lesbian, but these boys are all so immature."

"Yeah, too true. But what can we do about that? Wait for them to grow up, I guess. Unless you want to go down to the Cross Keys and find yourself an old man," said Amy, laughing as she knocked back the last of her lager top.

Martha wasn't laughing. She turned away as she drank her cider.

Amy grabbed her shoulder. "Martha?" Then she put an arm around her. "Martha, what's wrong?"

Martha was so close to telling her everything to relieve herself of the burden of her loss. Amy would be shocked, of course. Then sympathetic. She might even stop trying to set Martha up with any boys. For a while, maybe. But would she really understand? And would it help her find Dean?

It wouldn't.

Plus she wasn't sure she wanted Amy to know, with a whole year of school still ahead of them. Perhaps one day she would tell her. Or maybe Amy would find out, when Martha and Dean got together.

If everything worked out, she and Dean could tell her together.

That would be something.

Something worth waiting for.

Martha wiped her eyes, forced a smile and said, "Nothing. I think I'm just a bit tired. Do you mind if we go home?"

The next time that Martha and Amy were out at the pub and Martha had turned down a couple more boys, Amy asked, "Why don't you go out with any of these guys?"

Martha had prepared a new tactic, something Amy wouldn't argue with. "Those guys? After what happened with Brian? No way! This is the summer of fun, remember? Girls together. No boys allowed."

Amy smiled at her friend. "You don't have to do that, Martha."

"Amy, seriously, I want to." Martha meant it. It was a good excuse to not engage with any of the boys, but it was also good to spend time with her friend. Martha enjoyed her company. When the weather was doing the typical English summer thing, they stayed in town and trawled through charity shops to find old vinyl records (Martha's idea), or to the record store to listen to new ones (Amy's). And Amy and her parents taught Martha to play mah-jong, which was a fun way to fill a long summer evening.

When shifts and pleasant weather aligned, Martha and Amy took off to the beach. If a cold easterly was blowing,

Martha persuaded Amy to help her out with the heavy work in the sheltered allotment. They put up a fruit cage to protect against birds, and Martha picked strawberries and raspberries to take for their beach picnics, in return for Amy's help. They exchanged trashy novels, swam, sunbathed and talked about their plans for the future. Or at least Amy did. Martha couldn't think beyond the end of the summer, but she was happy to listen to Amy tell tales of the job that she was going to get, working on super-yachts and sailing around the world. That was after she aced her degree in English literature at Manchester University, where she was going to meet so many more sexy boys than Cornwall had to offer.

Halfway through the school holidays, a new manager took over the garden centre. Headquarters had sent him down to improve sales, but he knew more about balance sheets and bottom lines than broad beans and begonias. He hid away in his office, leaving customers roaming the aisles to find someone who could help them. They besieged Martha with questions: where to find the advertised specials, when plants were coming in, how to grow things better or kill things better. Most people were polite, and even when they weren't, Martha let it wash over her, smiled, and carried on. But it wore her down shift after shift.

She volunteered for the dirty jobs instead, sweeping up and tossing mulch and compost into piles, or dragging the hose out to water the big trees that were potted up behind the garden centre. It was when she was turning on the tap to one of those hoses that one of the regulars, Lady Roseham, collared her.

"Oh good, you can help me. It's bedlam here today and I can't find anyone – "

Martha put on her brightest smile. "How can I help?"

"I want some cyclamen."

"We don't have any, I'm afraid."

"Nonsense! You grow them here, don't you? I've seen them before."

"Yes, but they don't go out on display until the autumn. They're winter flowering."

"I know that, girl, but I want to put them in the ground now."

"I'll go and find the manager."

"Don't bother, he's busy, apparently. Which is why I'm talking to you. You've worked here long enough to recognise a cyclamen, I take it?"

"Yes."

"Good. Get me five plants. It doesn't matter what colour."

"I can't do that."

"Yes, you can. I'm telling you to. I'm giving you permission."

"But you're not my manager. I need to talk to him."

"No, you don't. Now stop being so rude and do as you're told."

Martha took off her garden gloves and her Heath Valley Garden Centre apron.

"What are you doing? Do you know who I am?"

"Yes. You're a snooty old fart, who thinks they can boss people around just because they have a bigger house. But you can't. I'm not your bloody servant. No one is the boss of me. Not now, anyway."

Lady Roseham stepped back, her body ramrod straight, her face pinched as if she had chewed through a lemon. Martha brushed past her, past the lines at the tills, and opened the door to the office, where the manager was snogging the new girl beside the filing cabinet.

She slapped her apron and gloves on the desk and said, "I quit," before turning on her heels, slamming the door behind her, a smile growing on her face as she walked to the glass doors. By the time she was on her bike, she was laughing.

"But aren't you going to miss the money?" said Amy, as they looked in the shop windows on Church Street.

"Yes, but I won't miss the customers. I enjoyed working with the plants, but ever since the manager changed, I've been out in the shop more and I hate that. Anyway, I'm ready to do something different."

"I know what you mean. Working in a clothes shop is great for the money and the discount, but some customers are real dickheads. Especially the grockles that come down from London... Hey, look at this: they want a dishwasher." Amy was reading the note on the Blue Ram Café.

"That I can do," said Martha. "I don't mind washing dishes."

"And you wouldn't have to deal with customers – only their dirty dishes."

Martha read the notice. "I'm going in."

"Shit," said Amy, "I've gone over on my break. I'd better go back to the shop. Let me know how it goes!" she shouted as she hurried off.

The café was busy, and dirty crockery and cutlery had piled up on the tables. Martha couldn't see anyone who looked like a manager. She collected up some dishes and pushed through the swing doors to the kitchen. She put the plates by the sink, where a woman was up to her elbows in suds.

"Hi, do you know where the manager is? I'm here about the dishwasher job."

"I'm the manager and you're hired. Can you start now?"

"Um, sure."

"Great. Here are the rubber gloves – I can't wear them – I'm allergic."

Martha put on the gloves, got stuck in and walked out two hours later with £12 and a £20 bonus.

One late August day, it was blisteringly hot. After running down the burning sand, the girls dived into the sea and the beautiful cool enveloped them. Amy never ventured much out of her depth, but Martha swam as she always did, ducking under the waves and breast-stroking underwater until her oxygen ran out and she had to surface to breathe, then float in the deep water. She usually felt calm and happy at this point, but the new school year was about to start and it hit her. With no way to look for Dean, she had been treading water all summer and now she risked going under. Nothing was certain, and she was afraid she wouldn't find him. Instead of turning and swimming back towards Amy, Martha continued, swimming a slow, strong crawl directly out to sea. The rhythm of the waves comforted her. As the swell moved beneath and lifted her, she felt as though she was moving further away from the depths and not towards them. But after twenty minutes, the cold snapped her back to reality, and she looked back at the shore, which was a long way away. She bobbed a moment, not thinking about anything at all, just letting her worries drop down into the dark blue below her. Then she swam back to the beach, where Amy was wrapped in a towel, arms folded and shoulders boxing her ears. She was shouting. Martha couldn't hear, but could see she was mad.

Amy retreated to where their things were and Martha shivered her way up the beach to join her.

"What the hell were you doing? You had me worried. I couldn't see you for ages."

"I was just going for a swim."

"Why didn't you tell me?"

"I just decided. I'm not sure why. I'm sorry."

"Okay, I'm just glad I didn't have to call the Coast Guard."

"Me too. I'm sorry. I'm sorry I worried you, Amy."

CHAPTER TWENTY-SIX

September brought change, as always. After doing her best to shunt him to the back of her brain for the summer, Dean was now foremost in Martha's head. She had to find him. There were two entries for D. Finlay in their area's phone book, issued when he was still living with his wife. She didn't call those numbers. When a new edition was released, she looked again. The number for one of the D. Finlays had changed. A new number. Barely containing her excitement, she scribbled it down and dashed out of the house, running to the phone box at the end of the street. A heavy-set woman was in there finishing a call. Martha hopped from foot to foot as she waited for her to put down the receiver, allow the unused coins to drop before taking them one by one and putting them in her purse, double checking that none were left behind. Eventually, she leaned against the door, opening it with a grunt and stepping out onto the footpath. Not a second passed before Martha was inside and putting her phone card in the slot. She held the receiver to her shoulder as she punched in the numbers in her notebook.

Three rings and then an answer. "Hello, David here."

"Sorry, wrong number." She fumbled to replace the handset and fell against the heavy metal door to escape. She called the other D. Finlay just in case, and gently put the receiver down when she heard an old man answer.

The new year at school introduced a new Art teacher. Mr Sangbourne, a tweedy elbow-padded sixty-something with a nicotine-stained beard and foul breath, had taken Dean's place in the classroom. He was everything Dean wasn't, and Martha was out of each class before the bell stopped ringing.

In her school lunch hour, she widened her search at the town library. She transcribed the numbers of all the D. Finlays in the phone books of neighbouring areas. Then she went to the phone box outside the library entrance and called each number in turn, simply disconnecting every time someone answered who wasn't Dean. After a couple of days and phone cards, she had exhausted all the numbers. If Dean was living nearby, there was no number listed for him. She needed to find him some other way.

On Saturdays, Martha had an hour after her café shift ended before she went to meet Amy at the clothes shop. She went back into the library to trawl through the reference section. One librarian had noticed her regular visits and came over. She stood by Martha as she flipped through directories.

After coughing softly, she asked, "Can I help you?"

"Erm, no, it's all right." Martha kept on searching through book after book.

The librarian didn't leave. "I can help you, if you're looking for something in particular."

Martha's shoulders dropped as she turned around. "I'm looking for a directory of teachers. Is there something like that?"

"Oh yes, it's over here." The librarian took her to another shelf and pulled out a thick paperback volume. She looked over Martha's shoulder as she scanned the entries. "They are listed by school at the front, but the back lists them alphabetically by surname."

"Thanks," said Martha, skipping to the back. A stab of recognition in her heart as she saw his name, still listed with her school.

"Did you find it?" said the librarian, clutching her lanyard with expectation.

"No, it's not up to date. Does it come out every year?"

"Oh yes. Actually, we should have a new one now. Hang on a mo." The librarian unlocked the door behind them and Martha heard her opening packages. She came back, holding a new directory aloft as if it were a championship trophy. "It must've come in this morning. Hot off the press. Brand-spanking-new. Here you go."

Martha's hands were sweaty as she flipped through to the back. There was no entry for him. "Dean Finlay BA (Hons) PGCE" had vanished.

Martha ran out of the library, ran up to Long Castle, ran until daggers in her legs made her stop. She slumped on the verge, breathing hard. Insects buzzed around her and she smelled wildflowers and crushed grass. Barely a breeze blew at ground level, but clouds raced across the blue sky above her. Life went on, despite it all. She looked at her watch and jumped up to jog back down the hill and then to the café, minutes after her shift had started.

"Sorry I'm late," she said to the kitchen staff, who clattered around her. She attacked the stack of coffee cups and plates and worked furiously, silently, until all was quiet and clean and her boss came in to tell her she was locking up.

Martha waited for Amy to finish work, leaning against the shop wall like a half-quit smoker. At 5:05, Amy busted out, unpinning her name badge before she slung her bag over her shoulder. "Boy, that was a drag. How was your day?"

"Okay," said Martha, looking down as she scuffed her heels along the pavement.

"That bad, huh? Don't worry, we'll have an excellent night out tonight to make up for it." Amy waved her pay packet in front of Martha's nose.

Martha stopped walking, looked up and said, "Hell, yeah. I'm sick of it all. I need some serious fun."

"That's the spirit. Let's go out and paint the town the brightest red you can imagine."

The girls walked back to Amy's, made small talk with her parents, and then dashed up to her room to listen to records until dinner. Martha loved Mrs Chen's cooking. Her stir-fries were the best – fresh greens with chicken or pork, flash-fried in a wok, and served with spicy noodles. Good food to eat before a big night out.

Then they got ready. Martha had brought a plain black scoop neck T-shirt to pair with jeans, but let Amy transform her face with lipstick, liquid eyeliner, mascara and a sweep of shimmering eyeshadow.

"You are so pretty, Martha. You should show it off more. We're young, free and single, right?"

"Right. Yes. Amy, you're right. I've been stupid, stupid, stupid," said Martha, looking at the bottom of her glass.

Amy refilled it. "What do you mean?"

Martha thought briefly about telling Amy everything then, but it was too painful to start. She winced and said, "Nothing, really. I've just been so boring, haven't I?"

"No." Amy laughed. "Well, maybe you've been a little on the square side."

"A little? Like a rhomboid?"

"I have no idea what that is, but probably, yeah," said Amy as she filled Martha's glass again. They giggled and gossiped and finished the wine. Martha felt better than she had in months.

Martha switched to pints of cider at the pub and Amy groaned as she came back to the table with another round and two shots of Sambuca.

"Steady on, Martha. That's the third round you've bought and I haven't even finished my second white wine spritzer."

"It's okay. I saved masses over summer and I owe you for putting up with my miserable self for so long."

"It's not the money."

"Then what? You used to say I was the lightweight," said Martha, as she slammed down both shots in front of her friend.

"I was kidding around. And no more shots, okay?"

Martha drank her pint and then burped. "Okay."

"Martha!"

Half an hour later, Amy was holding Martha's hair back in the loo. Afterwards, Martha washed her face and Amy looked at her in the mirror. "You okay, mate?"

"Not really."

"What are you trying to do to yourself?"

"I want to make up for lost time."

"Well, don't do it all at once or you'll end up in hospital, all right?"

Martha nodded.

"Come on; you'll feel better after we've walked home."

Martha woke on Sunday with a cracking headache. Amy came into her room with a glass of water containing two fizzing tablets.

"What time is it?" asked Martha.

"10 o'clock."

"Blimey. I got up earlier, but must've fallen back to sleep."

"Yes, I heard you spend ages in the toilet…"

"Yeah. I don't think I have anything left to throw up now."

Amy handed her the glass.

"Thanks," said Martha, drinking it as fast as the fizz allowed.

"Mum and Dad have gone out; I think we should too."

"Where to? And can I have a shower first?"

One shower and a short walk later, the girls were in the railway café with two full Englishes and fat mugs of tea.

"I feel so much better," Martha said, her hands wrapped around her mug.

"Good. But what got into you? You're supposed to be the sensible one!"

"I know. I guess I'm tired of it."

"Are you going to be like that every time we go out now?"

Martha grimaced. "No way. Hey, thank you for looking after me."

"No drama. It was kind of nice to be needed by you for once."

Martha reined in her drinking and found a new way to let loose. After a couple of glasses of wine, wearing make-up and figure-hugging clothes approved by Amy, Martha was all set to flirt. The boys came flocking, and this time Martha didn't turn them away. Before each evening was out, Martha was kissing someone. Tall or short, stocky or slim, with dark hair, ginger, brown or blond, she had no preference. She wasn't picky about how they looked, because when she closed her eyes, she was thinking of Dean. But none of them kissed the way he did, with that mixture of softness and strength, with the feel of a beard pushing through a close shave. None of them smelled quite the way he did. None of them were a match for Dean, and she would pull away, apologise and say she had to go.

Amy went from glad to impressed to horrified. It was now the run up to Christmas, with tons of parties and opportunities to let their hair down, out of the gaze of parents and bar managers.

"I've been looking forward to Carlie's party for weeks," said Martha, putting on another layer of mascara and adjusting her top to make sure it showed off her assets.

"Me too, but take it easy, eh?"

"What do you mean?" Martha smoothed down her skirt.

"You're getting a reputation."

"What kind of reputation?"

"Every week you snog a new guy, sometimes two."

"What's wrong with that?"

"Not all the guys are nice, Martha. And when they are, you leave them hanging anyway. You must have a fist full of phone numbers and you never give out your own."

"You're just jealous because you and Marcus are going out and you're missing the single life."

"Maybe. But don't go crazy, okay?"

"Okay, Mum."

Like so many Saturday nights before that, Martha stood at the side of the room, more observer than participant. She felt broken and alone despite the crowd. A guy she had never seen before was making his way towards her, carrying two plastic cups. He was short but pushy and got through the crowd quickly. With a theatrical exhalation of breath, he slammed back against the wall next to Martha, spilling some of the liquid on her sleeve.

"Hey!" she said.

"Sorry, I thought you might like some of this punch," he said, as he passed her one of the cups. "It's packed in here, isn't it?" He ran his free hand back through his long fringe and gave her a look she imagined he had practised many times in front of the mirror. When she didn't look away, he tipped the contents of his cup down his throat and coughed. "Not bad. Try it."

Martha took a sip from the cup and looked down at it with disgust. It tasted like someone had been emptying random bottles from the drinks cabinet into the punchbowl. "This is the last party before Christmas. It looks like everyone came. And a bunch of gate-crashers," she said as she looked him straight in the eye.

The boy threw his cup across the room. "I'm not a gate-crasher. Didn't you see me talking to those guys?" He nodded to the boys in the corner of the room who were looking over at them, nudging each other and laughing. "They know you. Said that you were someone I would like."

"Why is that?" said Martha, drinking more of the punch, despite herself.

"They said you're a good kisser. Is it true?" The boy moved in to kiss Martha.

Martha pushed him away. "Hey! I don't even know you. What do you think you're doing?"

"My name's Andy. Is that good enough?" He moved in again to kiss her, this time also pushing his hand up her top to grab her breast.

"Get off me, you bastard," said Martha.

The guy pulled at her top, ripping it towards him. "Come on, you tart. Everyone says you're a prick-teaser. It's time to give us the goods."

But before he could lay hands on her again, someone grabbed him by the collar and spun him around.

Andy was clearly used to confrontations. "Yeah, mate? D'you want some?"

Amy's boyfriend Marcus replied, "Yes, I do. Outside. Now."

The boys headed towards the door and Amy put her arm around Martha. "Where's your jacket?"

Martha nodded towards a chair. They went over and Amy threw the jacket around Martha, picked her own off the floor beside the door and then they left the party, buttoning up against the cold.

Marcus was outside, but on his own. "Who was that guy?" he asked.

"I don't know," said Martha, shivering.

"He ran off as soon as we got out of the house. Good thing too," said Marcus.

"Thanks, Marcus," said Martha.

"Don't mention it." He looked towards Amy.

Amy said, "Can I see you later, Marcus? We'd better get going."

"Sure. I'll catch up with my mates inside. I'll call you tomorrow."

Amy and Martha began walking home. Martha was crying, silently at first but more and more, until she was wracked with guttural sobs by the time they got to Amy's room.

"Martha, come on. The guy was a random. A jerk."

Martha slumped down on the bed beside Amy. "Yes, but he was right. I'm no good, Amy. I messed everything up and I can never make it right."

"What? What are you saying?"

Martha blew her nose and looked up at her friend. "I have to tell you something, Amy. But you can't tell anyone else, okay?"

"Of course, Martha. What is it? Why are you so upset?"

CHAPTER TWENTY-SEVEN

Martha took a deep breath and confessed to her friend. "I'm the reason Mr Finlay left the school."

"What? What are you saying?" Amy stood up and put her hands to her mouth. "Oh my god... Did you have an affair with Mr Finlay?"

"No. Well, yes. Kind of. We didn't sleep with each other or anything."

"But you kissed him?"

"Yes."

"No bloody way!" Amy sat back down. "What was that like? Was he a good kisser?"

"Amy!" Martha laughed.

"Come on – half the bloomin' art class has imagined kissing him. I bet it was dreamy," she said, clasping her hands together.

"It was – but we only kissed once. I kind of ambushed him."

"Where?"

"At our art exhibition." Martha could see Amy replaying the evening in her head.

"Right... Yes. I wondered where you were. But hey, one kiss is hardly an affair. He shouldn't have been fired."

"I know. The kiss wasn't the problem." Martha told Amy about the letters.

"So his wife found out about your letters, probably assumed that more was going on and then told Miss Staverly, but went on to shack up with her lover, and Mr Finlay moved out?"

"That about sums it up, yes."

"He didn't tell you where he went? Not even a clue?"

"No. He doesn't want me to find him."

"Maybe he'll come back once the dust has settled."

"His listing has gone from the phone book and they've sold the house that was listed. It's in the window of the estate agents on Church Street."

"Wow. You've done your homework."

"I'm good at doing homework," said Martha, laughing. And then crying, as Amy put her arm around her.

She squeezed Martha hard. "You poor, poor thing. No wonder you've been so... weird."

"I'm sorry."

"Don't be daft. And cheer up; there's still a chance he'll come back."

"I don't think so. He didn't like his life here, anyway. What's he got to come back to?"

"You?"

"He was conflicted about me. He thought it wasn't the right thing to do."

"You can see his point. If this got out around the school, the place would go bonkers."

Martha looked startled.

"Don't worry, your secret's safe with me."

"Promise you won't tell anyone, not even Marcus?"

"I promise. It's our secret. Well, ours and Miss Staverly's. I never thought I'd have anything in common with that old bat."

Martha laughed. It felt good to unburden herself.

The rest of the school year was fairly uneventful. If Martha went out on a Friday or Saturday night, she would play gooseberry with Marcus and Amy, or join them and Marcus's friends who were also coupled up. Often she worked extra shifts at the café, which had a late licence for the weekend. It kept her out of trouble and trickled money into her depleted savings account. London was going to be expensive, and Martha's parents were worrying about it. They sat down with her one evening to talk about exactly how much they could pay. The scholarship she'd won (one of the last things Dean had done for her was to apply for that) covered her tuition, and her folks could pay for the accommodation in halls. She would have to fork out for her food, textbooks and materials. Going out would be a luxury if she didn't get herself a part-time job. She said she'd figure it out, telling them she'd be fine, but she kicked herself for spending so much money on clothes and going out before coming to her senses.

"You should come to Manchester," said Amy. "It'll be half the price of living in London."

"You'll spend all the money you save on heating," said Martha.

"Don't be daft. I'll wear this all the time." Amy pushed up the collar of her Afghan coat, her latest acquisition from a vintage clothing shop that had opened up in the arcade. The two friends were walking around Long Castle. It was a clear April day and the sun was warm on their backs, but an easterly blew the cold through Martha's sweater.

"Will you wear that in bed? Woo, what a turn on! Marcus will love that..."

"Marcus won't be there."

"What? Have you two split up?"

"No, but we might as well. He got into Exeter through Clearing."

"That's brilliant for him. And why can't you stay together? There are trains, you know."

"Right. There's a train down to London, a Tube across and then another train to get to Devon. It literally takes all day. I'd get there and then have to get on the next train home."

"Bugger. I like Marcus."

"I know. Hey, maybe you can go out with him. He likes you too."

"Ha ha – not like that. He's not my type. Anyway, it would be weird."

"True. But you should go out with someone, Martha. It's been ages…"

"It feels like it was yesterday. It's like there's a hole in my chest where part of my heart was, and I can't find a way to fill it."

Amy wrapped Martha in her coat as they walked down the track to the car. The wind whipped away her tears and Amy squeezed her tight, leaning into her to say, "You're going to be okay, mate. You're going to be okay."

CHAPTER TWENTY-EIGHT

Dean sat in traffic on the dual carriageway. The cars were filled with people fleeing from city life, desperate for West Country calm. It was a chance to think over his life before and his life to come. He didn't have a plan, didn't know what he was going to do exactly, but he knew what he didn't want to do. He didn't want a normal life, or a normal job, or to live in a two-up, two-down perfectly nice house in a perfectly nice estate in a perfectly nice town. It was clear to him now that he had wasted the last decade doing the right thing wrongly, letting his wife decide how he should live, as a penance for the mistake he had made so many years before. Now he was free to make his own decisions and live a life he'd chosen, though that freedom came at a cost. He had to fill his new life so that the thought of what had happened with Martha didn't consume him. But it was hard. He blinked back the sadness as the traffic picked up speed, and nearly missed the exit he needed to take. Robert's scribbled directions were now more detailed. Roads became windier and narrower until hedges scraped the car on both sides and a line of grass ran down the middle. He shot past a couple of turnings and got himself back on track with his road atlas and the help of fingerpost signs. Just as he thought he was lost again, he saw the marker of his destination – a large granite boulder and an ash tree at the entrance to a rutted dirt track.

This was where the Land Rover felt at home, bumping along the track at ten miles an hour. It was overgrown, and he had to get out of the Landy to bend back branches that tussled with his wing mirrors. Disturbed pigeons whoop-whooped away as he drove into the clearing in front of the house and barn. He parked up and found the keys to the cottage under the old milk churn by the door. A random selection of lights came on when he turned on the power. Dean went around the cottage, checked everything looked undisturbed, switched off the lights and found the kitchen to put on the kettle after he'd scraped hardened instant coffee into a mug. There were unopened bags of real beans, but he couldn't be bothered with that. The refrigerator door was ajar, and he opened it, knowing it would be empty. It would be easier to begin to have his coffee black. His spirits lifted when he found an unopened packet of digestive biscuits in the pantry. They would keep him going for the time being.

The sun shone through the trees and lit up the long grasses and umbelliferous flowers. Insects flitted from one to another and he watched a sparrow deftly dart in to snag a fluttering whitefly. Dean sat on a wobbly wooden bench, drank the coffee and ate half the packet of biscuits as he observed the wayward garden returning to its normal activity. A chatter of starlings and sparrows peppered the shrubs, and green and gold finches cracked open seed heads. Blackbirds and a robin were rifling through the leaves strewn about vegetable beds gone to seed. He could hear the churring of blue tits and the knocking of a woodpecker in the forest beyond. It was good to be a bystander in a world others liked to conquer. Part of the deal of living at the barn was to tidy up the garden, but he would make sure he left the edges for wildlife.

When he finished his coffee, Dean investigated the barn. The heavy door hung badly on its hinges, opening reluctantly as he pushed and lifted it. Sunlight forced its way through the grimy windows, illuminating dust that danced in its warmth. There were crates, rusted old tools and hessian bags everywhere. But the wooden floor looked sound and he couldn't see daylight through the tiled roof. Dean propped open the door with a seized-up push mower and tidied up a corner, stacking tools into crates, and sweeping out dirt and windblown chaff. He unloaded the Landy and unpacked his camping roll and sleeping bag. The proper work could wait until the morning. He went to bed with Hardy's *Tess of the D'Urbervilles* and was asleep before Tess made her appearance.

As soon as he was up, Dean cleared out the barn, dragging out anything he couldn't lift and sorting it all into piles. Rotten timber and logs to stack at the edge of the garden to return to the ground. Good wood to be repurposed. Holey oil drums, corrugated iron riddled with rust and cans of chemicals, labels long gone, would have to go to the dump. Tools were old, but well-made and could be cleaned, sharpened and oiled to bring them back into service. Lunch was what he could find in the pantry: a tin of chickpeas and pasta well past their best-before dates tasted fine with a little salt, pepper, and parsley from the garden. When the edges of the barn were empty, Dean cleaned the windows with newspaper and vinegar and swept the floor before turning in for the night.

The light woke him at dawn the next morning. He had coffee and the last of the biscuits, then mopped the barn floor with hot soapy water, leaving it to dry as he went out for supplies.

The nearest village was four miles away, an easy bike ride once he fixed up the old Raleigh five-speed he had found in the barn. It had a couple of flat tyres and a rusty chain, but it was from the 1970s, made in England with pride, and would come right. For now, he walked, enjoying the solitude and the birdsong. Mevacombe was small – a pub and a church with a post office/general store on the other side of the green. Dean ambled across the grass to the shop and found the door still closed. The shop opened at 8 a.m. It was ten to eight. He read through the notices in the window – babysitters, dog walkers, logs on offer. And casual workers needed for cleaning, gardening and working in the pub. The door opened with the sound of a little bell as Dean went in, surprising himself when his voice cracked as he sang out, "Good morning!" It was the first time he had spoken to anyone in days.

"Morning," said a woman, as a statement of fact. Her back was turned to him, hands deftly sorting through newspapers. "Let me know if there's anything I can help you with."

Dean grabbed a basket and filled it with food, bike bits, candles, matches, an extension cord, and other things he could find that he would need in the next few days. He picked up a bottle of wine and put it back on the shelf as he thought about the £80 he had left in his bank account. The woman behind the counter had a face that had laughed a lot in plenty of weather. Softly curled, faded ginger hair reminded Dean of his late mother and he smiled kindly at her.

She smiled back and looked at the basket. "Are you planning on staying a while? I shouldn't say this, but you know there's a supermarket five miles up the road, just out of Truro?"

"I expect there is. I'll go there if I have to."

The woman waited for him to answer the other question.

"I'll be here a little while, yes."

"Good. My name's Demelza," said the woman, automatically pulling out a plastic bag.

"I'm Dean," he said. "It's okay, I have this." Dean packed everything into a haversack. He paid and looked at his scant change before asking, "When does the pub open?"

"It's a bit early for that, don't you think?"

Dean laughed. "I was after the job. Dishwasher."

"Oh." The woman looked at him anew. "Are you okay?"

"I'm fine."

"It's just that teenagers usually do those kinds of jobs. The money's not great – "

"I don't need much money. Just enough to get by."

"Right. Well, Stan rarely arrives until ten, but if you're serious…"

"I am."

"Turn up at 5:30 this evening and he'll take you on. Assuming you can wash dishes, of course."

"I can. Thank you." He picked up his haversack and cheery bells farewelled him from the shop.

Dean cycled to the pub just after it opened, was given a trial shift and worked fairly constantly until closing. Running plates, cutlery and glasses through the dishwasher, scrubbing pots and pans, rinsing and repeating, was a moving meditation that calmed his mind. When dinner service was in full flow, no one had time to talk, leaving Dean's hands to the dishes and his mind on the barn, working out how to fix, make, or arrange things into a liveable space. But thoughts of what he had done to Martha rose to the surface, like the fatty scum left in the sink. He couldn't kid himself that he had acted only in her best interests, or that he hadn't become overly involved. He should have stopped her before she fell. As he had fallen, too. It was unforgivable.

Dean wasn't unaware of the effect he had on teenage girls. Schoolgirls have crushes. That hadn't been far from his mind when he was reading her letters at first, replying to them with caution, not wanting to encourage anything but an application to her art. However, the letters drew him in, made him forget about the hard line between teacher and student that was his responsibility to maintain. He enjoyed their platonic connection, but he knew the risk and it was no surprise when she tried to take it further. He had not resisted enough. Like so many schoolgirls before, she had flattered him with her attention, but this time he had let it grow like a pretty weed that should have been cut down before it flowered. It would have been easier if she had been like all the other students that had come on to him before, students who had nothing but the attraction of youth and beauty. If he hadn't felt that connection beyond the physical. If she hadn't been so much easier to communicate with than his wife. His bloody wife. She had dirtied Martha's name and his, after running their world through the rough filter of hers.

He scrubbed harder.

At the end of the evening, Stan called time. The last lone man was gently pushed out of the door, clutching a bottle of Diamond White to his chest. The female bartender, who looked barely old enough to be in the pub, dashed off home to leave the three men around the bar to drink one for the road. Stan had grey pepper hair and a white beard that belied the fact he was only in his late 40s, all muscle and sinew and able to break up a fight or take away keys from a man who didn't want to pay the eye-watering cost of a taxi home. Gavin, the cook, made the bar stool creak as he shifted from one bum cheek to the other. He enjoyed eating his food more than the customers did, and could drink anyone under the table. Stan cut him off at two pints. Dean was happy with one, but it went down fast after a hot evening in the kitchen.

"Can I get you another?" said Stan.

"I'd better not. I'm not sure I'll find my way home after one, and two would make that a certainty."

"Where are you staying?" asked Stan, as he upended the glass on the dishwasher rack.

"I don't know the address. It's about five miles from here, down an overgrown track. There's a barn and a – "

"Sheila's cottage," said Gavin.

Stan laughed. "So she finally found some mug to take that on, eh? That place is a mess. It'll take years to sort that out."

"I've got time." Dean put on his jacket and tucked the stool under the bar.

"Well, good. Because Gavin says he can see his face in pans that used to be black. Welcome aboard. Have you got lights on that bike, or do you want a lift?"

"The bike's got lights, but dead batteries. I'll pick up some more later in the week. I'll be okay though – it's a full moon." Dean headed towards the door.

"Suit yourself. See you tomorrow."

Dean gave a mock salute, turned the lock, and was out in the crisp air. Despite the staff meal of egg and chips he had wolfed down in a lull, the pint had gone to his head somewhat. He felt he was flying on the moonlit road, and his heart soared as a barn owl guided him down the track home.

It took a couple more days in the barn to finish sorting out the stuff, mending anything he could, then taking the few things beyond rescuing to the local dump, where he picked up a log burner with plenty of life left in it. One of the pub's regulars was a gas-fitter and did the metal work Dean needed, cash-in-hand, so Dean could install it at the barn without the risk of burning it down when he lit it. When he had resurrected the neglected garden tools, he put them to use in the overgrown wilderness outside the barn. An old scythe that felt unwieldy when he lifted it out of a rusted-out oil drum came to life under his care. It was light in both hands, weighted just right to cut through the long grass with ease. He cleared around the cottage and barn and down the track. After that, he repaired and oiled the shutters, opening them up completely to let in the morning light through two massive windows that faced out over the cut grass.

His new routine was working inside in the morning, when the light was best, before moving out to the garden. There, he cut and hacked his way through to reach the entrance to the overgrown orchard.

As he brought order to the inside of the barn, he was able to rig up a hammock. It kept him off the cold floor and would do until he worked out where he was going. He slept better than he had done on the sofa bed in the 'cul-de-sad-sack', as Martha had put it. So many things – the garden, music on the radio, passages in books – made him think of her, and each thought cast light and shadow: chiaroscuro in his mind. The hard physical work was the only way he could sleep at night.

CHAPTER TWENTY-NINE

Dishwashing didn't pay well, but it was enough. Dean worked five nights a week, which meant five big staff meals. That wasn't the only food he ate from the pub. When customers sent back an overcooked steak, or they left a sausage or a chop uneaten, he put them in a bag to take home instead of putting them in the pig bin. The first time Gavin saw him, Dean said it was for the dog. An almost truth. If he had a dog, he'd feed it nothing but the scraps from the kitchen; there was so much wasted. Gavin nodded and Dean smiled to himself; one day he'd get a dog.

With no rent to pay and expensive food covered, the wage packet went a long way. He bought staples from the Meva-combe shop – porridge oats for breakfast, bread, and a few vegetables to have with any meat he had for lunch. Perhaps a hunk of cheddar and crackers with some fruit. He looked at a rack of seed packets and realised it would be cheaper to grow his own fruit and vegetables. They would be fresher, too. It was satisfying work to pull the weeds from the garden beds, plant rows of lettuce, beetroot and carrot seeds, and water them in, keeping them weeded – and thrilling to the small success as they germinated.

The birds uprooted what the slugs didn't eat. He tried again, this time starting the seeds in potting mix stuffed into the piles of cardboard toilet roll tubes he'd found in the outhouse. Then he rescued plastic bottles from the pub's overflowing bins and cut them to make mini cloches to protect the young seedlings.

It was impossible not to think about Martha as he was gardening. He had steered her away from horticulture to study art. Now here he was, fingers in the dirt, his art teacher career forgotten. Would she laugh to see him becoming excited watching plants grow from tiny little seeds? He hoped she would; he remembered how she laughed, throwing her head back and unselfconsciously snorting when she found something particularly funny. He smiled as he transplanted seedlings to the prepared ground, hoping she would laugh a lot in college, that she would find a group of friends like he'd had. And that most of them wouldn't drift away when times were hard.

It was full summer by the time he ate his first homegrown salad, and it tasted significantly better than the limp offerings that came out of the pub kitchen. When he wasn't working at the pub, he spent all afternoon and much of the evening gardening before he downed tools, made himself mint tea to pour over ice, and fixed a salad to have with leftover food from the pub. Now that the garden was presentable, Dean used the phone at the pub to call Robert, who contacted Sheila, who advertised the cottage for holiday lets. Visitors could call Demelza at the shop to arrange to stay, but they rarely did. Most holidaymakers didn't want to holiday somewhere so far from the coast or from local amenities. Those who wanted to come weren't the types to pester a caretaker. Dean did any maintenance that was needed during their stay: fixing leaky taps, replacing burnt-out light bulbs, sanding down windows that refused to close. Then he cleaned the cottage after the guests left and freshened it up before new ones arrived, opening windows, making up the beds with fresh linen, and sweeping the flagstone and wooden floors. He gave everything a wipe down with vinegar and lemon juice and started up the fridge. He didn't use it for himself, preferring to take ice from the chest freezer in the back room. There wasn't much in there apart from some questionable old meat, but he pushed it to the side and used the rest of the space for whatever he needed frozen, which was mostly trays and bottles of ice. It was easy to use these bottles in a cooler he'd found in the barn as his own little fridge.

The presence of a young, good-looking man on his own didn't go unnoticed in the village. Women lingered in the shop when Dean bought his groceries, or popped back for things they had 'forgotten'. Demelza had filled them in on what he was doing here as she packed their bags, and Stan told their brothers and husbands what he knew when he pulled their pints. Which was not much. The mystery only made the men speculate more and heightened the women's desire.

The shopkeeper handed Dean an unwanted receipt as he packed his bicycle panniers. "I'm getting a lot of questions about you."

Dean raised an eyebrow. "About whether I'm a murderer or on the run for some other heinous crime?"

Demelza chuckled. "Yes, and whether you're married. Or looking for an accomplice, perhaps?"

Dean clipped the panniers shut. "Ah. No, and no."

Demelza opened her mouth to ask another question, but Dean was out of the door and on his bike before she could.

Fine weather made it a pleasure to garden, driving his way through the towering weeds of the orchard with broad strokes of the scythe, back to the blackberry bushes that formed a circle within its walls. He attacked the long arches of thorns with loppers and secateurs, protecting himself with a denim jacket and thick leather gloves. The cooler evenings were perfect for turning the old, dry brambles into ash in the log burner. Ash he could use to sweeten the soil. Once he had made compost bays from discarded wooden pallets wired together, the green and woody garden waste went into those. Gradually he cut through the orchard, liberating apple and pear trees from bindweed and strangling vines of old man's beard. The trees looked weedy and bedraggled, even more so when he sawed off the dead branches, but within weeks they sent out fresh growth to capture the light.

On rainy days, Dean turned his attention back to the barn. He was working his way through the sound timber. If he suspected the wood was treated, he cut it to make steps in the slopes of the garden. He could repair and build benches, shelves and seating by grabbing bits and pieces from around the barn and cobbling them together. But he was running out of fasteners, and he had limited tools and big ambitions. When enough cash filled the cigar box he kept behind a tea chest of tools, he went into town.

After two months of the pub and the village shop, Truro unsettled him with its traffic and crowds of people pushing their way through the narrow streets. He ducked into the library and felt calmer as he wandered the aisles, browsing the shelves to see familiar authors and much-needed reference books. The librarian at the front desk tempered his excitement: she wanted something with his address on it before he could register. It was only then he realised he didn't even know his address. 'The old barn, four miles southeast of Mevacombe' wasn't going to cut it.

Dean put his hand on the door to leave, hesitated, and turned back to the woman. He looked at her lanyard, back up at her face and said, "Sue, I'm going to be here for some time. I need books. I need to learn from them. I need the company. Do you understand what I mean?" He stared at her, and she blinked rapidly, flushing red.

Sue was a good librarian and wanted to help, but needed to follow the rules somehow. "Do you have any ID, any proof of employment perhaps?"

Dean unfolded the pink paper of his driving licence and piled up the pay packets from the pub. Sue opened a little brown envelope and carefully extracted the paper enclosed with the cash. "The Badger, Mevacombe, Cornwall".

She looked at him and he smiled. "We'll just put that as your address. Is that okay?"

Dean's smile broadened to a wide grin. "That's just fine, Sue. Thank you."

Sue reddened again. "You're welcome. You can take out eight books at a time. Do you want to find some books whilst I sort you out a library card?"

He did. Dean left the library half an hour later with books on carpentry, self-sufficiency, and gardening, plus a couple of novels. He also left with a map of the town that Sue had annotated with the best place for coffee, the hardware store, and her favourite charity shops for secondhand bargains. After a decent espresso and an enormous pasty, Dean was ready to shop. He bought hand tools, nails, screws, nuts and bolts, and other paraphernalia he thought he might need. Sue's tips also led him to find a great secondhand waxed jacket and some Wellington boots to help him endure the worst of the weather. His book stash grew by a few more novels and the giant *Reader's Digest* DIY manual that could fill in the gaps in his handyman knowledge.

At the end of the afternoon, he loaded the Land Rover, dashed around the supermarket, then drove home, glad that he didn't work on Tuesday nights, luxuriating in reading a book by the fire with a tumbler of wine at his feet.

The summer passed quickly, with work that changed with the light. He harvested courgettes, beans and tomatoes to add to his salad greens. A thick mulch suppressed the weeds, courtesy of a trailer load of woodchip dropped off by a local arborist. Pleasant weather aided the mending of stone walls and terraces and the rehanging of the barn door and property gates. He stacked the cut wood from the orchard outside the barn, making a lean-to shelter for it so that it would dry, arranging it in order of burn from long-dead to green, this winter to next. He knew then that he was planning to stay a while.

Winter was still some way off, and autumn was a season he had always loved, despite the end of the school holidays and the return to work. He sat out in the last warmth of middays, eating his lunch at a bench he had made of roughhewn timber, looking out over the garden and thinking of Martha. He trusted she was at St Hibbert's, showing them what she could do and finding out how much more she was capable of.

CHAPTER THIRTY

Martha packed her books, tapes and toiletries in a cardboard suitcase she had got free with a shopping catalogue. Her clothes and the rest of her belongings fitted in a large red rucksack which was a going-away present from her parents. Her dad had nervously offered to drive her to London, but Martha was keen to start her independent life as soon as possible. So they drove her to the station and their faces remained bright as they waved her off from the platform, wavering only when the train moved away and she saw her dad crying and her mum turning away to wipe her eyes.

The pang of loss Martha felt was at once familiar, but different. This time, it was the bittersweet transition from the cocoon of family and friends in a small town to the unknown of the big city. There was a hard feeling in her stomach, a knot of anxiety. She did not know the city well, but she knew there were no beaches, green hills, or crystal-clear streams there.

She'd be back at Christmas, but Martha had never been away from home for more than a couple of weeks. She listened to James and Joni singing from the 70s of fire and rain and California calling. The green hills and blue sky gave way to a jumble of roads and jammed-in buildings. When she disembarked at Paddington, the noise slammed into her. Then everyone in a hurry, squeezing through gates, tumbling down steps to be swallowed by the gaping hole of the Underground. Standing near the doors of the carriage, she checked off the stations to change lines at South Kensington, then on to Leicester Square, where she was carried by the crowd through tunnels and up steps and out of an exit to the confusion of the street above. Her newly minted A to Z couldn't tell her which exit she was at, or even which way was north or south. Though the afternoon sun was out, it was hidden behind the tall buildings. Martha walked with false confidence until she found a named street that told her she needed to turn around and make her way, finally, to Soho.

It was 5 o'clock by the time Martha found the college, the admissions, and the room in halls that would be her home in term time. There were two single beds, with a couple of small drawer units in between. A wardrobe was set into one wall and there were two desks opposite. The window looked out to the building across the courtyard. She opened it to look down on the birch trees below, which had been planted optimistically then left to struggle and wither.

Martha slumped on the bed, tears bubbling from beneath. She blew her nose. The tissue was black with soot from the

Underground, diesel fumes, the filth of the city. Why had she come? She should have picked a course in a smaller town. It was Dean, of course, Dean had led her here and left her stranded. Before she could give in further to homesickness and heartbreak, the door burst open.

"Oh, hi, you've arrived. I thought I might have the room to myself." A tall, slim girl dressed all in black, with short spiky jet-black hair, gave a thin laugh and looked at Martha with disappointment.

Martha forced a smile. "Yeah, sorry, I'm not used to sharing either. I'm Martha, by the way."

"Beatrice. Or Trix. But not Trixie. No one calls me Trixie. That's like a dog's name."

"Right." Martha noted Trix was wearing a studded dog collar, but chose not to mention it.

Trix went over to the wardrobe and shoved her hangers across, rearranging her shoes below. "There, that should be enough space for you." She looked Martha up and down. "I take it you aren't doing fashion?"

"No. Art."

"Good. I mean, it's good we're doing different things, right?"

Martha didn't know what she meant by that, but she knew she wouldn't be happy doing fashion. And that she certainly wouldn't have as many clothes, judging by what was hanging in the wardrobe. She noticed Trix had only left her two hangers.

"Do you know where the canteen is, Trix? I haven't eaten since breakfast."

"Haven't a clue. We're going out to find some good ethnic food."

Martha could see 'we' would not include her.

Trix grabbed a long red plastic mac from the wardrobe. She hesitated at the door for a moment. "But hey, there's one of those induction folders on your desk. You might find a map in there." A swish of her mac and she was gone.

There was a map in the folder. Martha took the folder to the canteen and read it through as she ate a tuna melt and drank a glass of chocolate flavoured milk. As well as the map and lists of amenities and rules, there were three pages detailing the freshers' week activities designed to help her fit in. Only she didn't fit. She wasn't a team player keen on hockey, rowing, lacrosse or athletics. She didn't want to be stuck indoors playing squash or badminton or chess. It looked as if she would be keeping her own company, unlike everyone else she could see in the canteen who had already organised into twos, threes and more, who were already chatting and getting stuck into their college life.

She went along to the freshers' fair in case there was something for her that hadn't been described in the folder. With no luck. There were no gardening groups. No singer-song-writers-of-the-1970s appreciation groups. And country pursuits like hill walking or swimming in the sea were nowhere to be found inside the dingy hall on Charing Cross Road.

The rest of the campus was showing its age. A smell of mould lingered throughout, though the rooms were cleaned daily. Martha would keep fit taking the stairs, as the lift never seemed to work. The freshers quickly discovered that the studios were bitingly cold most of the year; one of the biggest sellers in the college shop were fingerless gloves. The lighting was terrible, and Martha began the first term by working near the windows. She retreated to the interior gloom after a window fell out of its frame and left a gash in the shoulder of a fellow student.

At least the first term's timetable had gifted Martha free Friday afternoons and Monday mornings. She used the long weekends to explore all the green spaces in the A to Z. It was cheap and easy to take the Tube out to Zone Two and walk back, trying to connect parks as she went. Her favourite was from Holland Park, through Kensington Gardens and on to Hyde, Green and Saint James's Parks. The route surprised her with the casual majesty of Buckingham Palace, the mundanity of Downing Street, or secret gardens that popped out when you least expected them. The river calmed her too. Slow in its meanderings, the eel-like Thames cut away the buildings and the traffic to open up the air above. Its underbelly was all murk: grey, muddy stones, rubbish and carcasses of countless shopping trolleys on the low tide. It was cleaner than it had been in centuries, but still filthy. A kayaker told her that falling in left your clothes with a stink that wasn't removed for several washes. It certainly wasn't a swimming river, with its mysterious submerged cargoes in the powerful tides and currents. Too cold, as they edged towards winter, in any case.

Martha visited Amy once that term. She liked the train journey best. Watching the countryside scroll by was soothing. Manchester was not. Amy introduced Martha to all her friends, and they went out to cheap student bars and an Indian restaurant. Amy kept checking on her, smiling across the table, squeezing her hand, asking her if she was having fun. She nodded her head. She wasn't.

Amy promised to come down and visit Martha in London, but weekends were often busy with gigs she was going to with her friends. In the run-up to Christmas she pleaded poverty, and they both looked forward to the holidays and meeting up again on familiar turf.

When Martha stepped off the train in December, it was as though she had been holding her breath for months. She couldn't get enough of the clean country air, and fought back tears when her dad dashed from the car to hug her, apologising for being held up by an escaped herd of cows.

The tatty paper chains and tinsel that festooned her parents' house filled her heart with joy in a way that the lights on Oxford Street never could. The rest of the seasonal traditions rolled into place. Her dad had waited for her return to drag down the tree from the attic so they could dress it together and argue about which decorations would make the cut. They all did, like every year she could remember. She helped her mum cook mince pies, sausage rolls and an oversized Christmas dinner. Her dad's mum took the train down from Leicester and ate like a bird at every meal, but demolished all the After Eights as always.

Martha took long walks in the short days, brushing off the cold by striding through the woods and up the hills to look out over the hills dotted with the ruins of fortifications from centuries past and the shadows of ancient burial mounds. Going to the beach was always either drama or serenity at this time of year, with few tourists to mar the walks by wild dunes or along coarse sand with its flinty, salt tang smell. But no matter how much she loved being in the countryside, she couldn't shake the hollowness. Snatches of Dean's letters came back to her with the scenery and gave her the sense of him being there, only to remind her he wasn't.

As the crowd shouted out the last seconds of the old year, Amy hugged Martha and they raised their glasses of vodka and orange to toast the new year: 1992.

"I'm sorry I've been a crap friend, Martha," slurred Amy.

"You haven't. You've got to make your new friends, haven't you?"

"Yeah, but I don't have to get rid of the old ones. And besides, they aren't like you. We'll always be friends, Martha, won't we?"

"Of course."

"Anyway, what about you? Have you found your people yet?"

"At St Hibbert's? Are you kidding? They're total weirdos. At least all the ones I've met."

"Have you met many? Maybe you should join some clubs – find some like-minded people."

"People who don't like fashion, or modern music, or shopping? I'm in the wrong place for that. I don't fit in, Amy. It's a completely different world and way of thinking. I can't imagine that anyone there would like long country walks, biking to the beach, and just hanging out in nature. It would probably terrify them. All the bugs!"

"You're being a reverse snob. And ridiculous. You'd find friends if you were a bit more open-minded. Tourists come from all over the world to visit London, and they aren't all crazy. You need to chill out and enjoy the best bits of the city. Otherwise, what's the point? You might as well quit and grow pots of petunias for stuck-up cows like Lady Pruneface for the rest of your life."

Martha gave Amy a shove, but knew she was right.

CHAPTER THIRTY-ONE

A week later Martha sat on the train, pressed her nose to the window, and made a new year's resolution to change. Wild green gave way to grey; Martha was left behind in the countryside. Now Marty looked out over the city, excited about throwing herself at all that London had to offer.

Marty took the Tube around to second hand market stalls in Paddington and Camden, and the galleries and food vendors of the East End. She went alone to late night dance parties on campus and lost herself in music Martha had no taste for, only wanting to dance the pain away., She rugged up, packed her lunch, and found a bench in Regent's Park to sketch or read a book, when the city was too much for her. Which happened less and less.

The tennis, swimming, and Spanish conversation groups gained a new member, who introduced herself as Marty. In her head she had a mantra: "I'm Marty. Marty likes to party" to remind herself to stay in character. She figured out the rules no one had told her before – being popular was a confidence game. She wasn't alone anymore when she went to the student bars or joined the crush at the Marquee stage, pogo-ing to music that thudded through her chest, obliterating all else.

One of her new friends was Camille, whose Spanish was worse but who faked it better. "The key to conversation is talking, Marty. You should try it."

Martha let go, and Marty enjoyed making mistakes. Making mistakes was a way to progress and also to have fun, she realised. Camille talked her into going to France, even though they spoke less French than Spanish. They made several day trips to Calais. Each one started with clambering onto a minibus before dawn. It then became a mess of cafés, bitter coffee and croissants, being hassled by guys on the street, and buying more than they could carry at the hypermarket. Then it ended with drunken singsongs on the bus home, stopping every half hour for people like them to throw up.

Marty stretched a student budget beyond the bars by developing a taste for eating out at places that catered to others with constrained budgets. They came with a force of flavour: Thai, Indian, and Vietnamese were her new favourites.

Now, like the rest of the first-year students, Martha was rarely in her room except to sleep. When she had an overdue assignment that she needed to get done, she worked at the library and hush-chattered with the increasing number of students who knew Marty and wanted to be with her. The inner Martha couldn't help but marvel at the change.

Initially, Martha had been dismissive about the course. Dean had said that she would learn a lot, but it wasn't from instruction; she learned little from the tutors. Instead, observation, encouragement, and freedom to experiment took art to another level. Everything was used to create the new. Rubbish from the streets, balls of hair, bodily fluids: all was fair game as a medium. Tutors suggested subjects and guided students, but they spurred you on to go off on a tangent. Sometimes way off: there was no censorship. Would Miss Staverly have written Martha's letter of recommendation if she had seen the roadkill collage that hung in the student bar? Not that Martha's work was in that vein. St Hibbert's ate the ordinary. Martha was challenged, survived and then grew outside her old boundaries, the way that ivy left unchecked grows up and around an old shed before pulling it apart. She didn't concern herself with grades and qualifications anymore – only with being different, apart from the mainstream, better.

Martha let herself go so that Marty exerted her influence when painting, preferring grey and brown over blue and green. She leaned into her painting, applying layers of oil paints with a palette knife to build works with the depths of despair that countered her outward emotions. It confused her tutors, challenged interpretation and got her the marks she needed but didn't seek.

Marty was happy and busy, which kept Martha from thinking too much about times past and what the future might hold. When she went home for Easter, Amy wasn't there. Her mum said, "Didn't she tell you? She's working through the holidays at the Mexican restaurant. Gets extra pay and more tips, she said, but I think it's the boyfriend she's staying for."

"I bet you're right. What's his name again?"

"Tony. He sounds lovely on the phone, but that Italian accent works on everyone, doesn't it?"

Martha laughed, thanked Mrs Chen and hung up. She didn't know what Tony sounded like because until that point she hadn't even heard of him. She hadn't talked to Amy all term. And now she wouldn't even see her at home. It wasn't entirely Amy's fault. Martha hadn't called or written either. It would've broken the guise of Marty and left her in limbo again.

The Easter holiday dragged on. There was no reason to be home without Amy. There was nothing to do except walk and bike around the reminders of before. Joan's allotment had been taken over, she noticed, as she watched a young couple pulling the weeds that had already swarmed over the previously neat beds.

Her parents asked questions about her social life and she described what she knew they would like to know about her nights out and weekends away. It only took a day for her dad to ask if there was 'anyone special' in her life.

"Just a lot of friends, Dad. I don't want to be all coupled up and miss out on all the fun."

Because there was no one special in London – not unless that was where Dean was hiding.

CHAPTER THIRTY-TWO

The highlight of the summer term was when the swimming club had an excursion to the ponds at Hampstead Heath and Marty discovered the delights of wild swimming in the city. From there, she explored further with Camille and another keen swimmer, Frankie. Frankie was better than an urban fox at getting into places she shouldn't. She scaled fences and picked padlocks to open up dawn swims in reservoirs and old gravel pits at the limits of their travelcards. Swimming in the locks at Teddington after a night out in Richmond left them on the street at midnight, with the Tube closed and no night bus to get home. After that night-time escapade, Marty, Camille and Frankie became inseparable.

As the term came to an end, Frankie told the others about a crazy cheap flat her mate Garth had found by the railway arches near Brick Lane. It was miles away from the college, a half-hour on the Tube, but an amazing, part subterranean place whose catacombs of rooms popped out at several locations, all of them by run-down industrial buildings. Dives which were divided into squats and studios, filled with artists and musicians grinding their way into discovery or obscurity. Marty and Camille jumped at the chance to move in. Garth was rake-thin and immaculately dressed when he wasn't screen-printing. His work got them into gigs for free because of the T-shirts he made for the bands. He was tipped off about the flat by a previous occupant: a drummer in a band who split because of musical differences brought on by too many drugs.

They had to take over the lease immediately and pay rent through the summer. Frankie's parents wanted her home, but Camille was staying and urged Marty to stay too. It was a straightforward decision for Martha. Paying for a flat she didn't live in would be tough, especially if she took menial work at home. Amy was still loved up and living with Tony in Manchester. Dean was still lost to her. The west country could wait.

Marty spent the clear, warm days reading and picnicking in the nearby Allen Gardens, or swimming with Camille. It was their mission to tick off all the old lidos in London. Garth often went with them, as he was keen to get an all-over tan to show off at the baths he went to near Oxford Street. Marty and Camille didn't join him there, but went along to the occasional club night in Clapham or Brixton, on the proviso that Garth would pay his third of the taxi fare home if he scored with a guy and left them to it. Or they took the busy night buses back, revelling in the after-dark company of other clubbers. Garth didn't drink, preferring party pills and powders. Camille often joined in, either with them or with whoever she had picked up on the dance floor. Martha was afraid to lose the last shred of self that remained. She stuck to vodka and tonics, switching to tonic alone after four and always sleeping at home, despite all the offers. Camille was ruthless at night, often disappearing with her latest conquest, sometimes winking at Marty if she saw her leave. Garth looked straight enough to keep sober men away from Marty early in the evening, but later on, when inhibitions were lowered and Garth drifted away, Martha was often approached. They were never her type. Good-looking guys were the worst. She looked in their eyes for depth, and stood up in the shallows. They had no soul.

There was an exception at a gig in a basement bar in Camden. A guy at the bar with blond hair that kept falling over his face was looking at her all evening. He didn't walk over until she stared back at him. Then he ordered another beer and sauntered over.

"Hi." He waited.

"Hi." Two could play at that game.

"Are you having a good time?"

"I wasn't. This band is terrible. You?"

"Me neither. But I think the evening's going to get better."

Marty caught the eye of Garth, who was chatting to the keyboard player smoking offstage. He held up his right hand – all right? Marty held up her right hand. Left meant "rescue me".

"Friend of yours?"

"Yes, my flatmate."

"Good. I'm glad someone is looking out for you. But can we go upstairs? The smoke is doing my head in."

Martha laughed. "Sure. Yes. Mine too."

He was Adam, a trainee lawyer, but he was going to be the good kind and help people. They went out into the street that was empty but for shift workers and a couple of groups of friendly drunks.

"Where do you live?" asked Adam. "I'll walk you home."

"I don't think you want to do that. I live in Whitechapel."

"It's a lovely night and I can't think of anything I want to do more than to walk with you for as long as you'll let me."

Martha agreed, and Adam led the way. "Do you know where you're going?" she asked.

"I've got a good sense of direction. We're heading pretty much southeast and there are a lot of landmarks around here to get my bearings."

"Okay. I guess I've got my A to Z if you get lost."

"It's good to meet a woman who keeps something useful in her bag. Let's head to our first landmark: Mornington Crescent."

They walked around the beautiful curved terraced street, and Adam pointed out where two painters had lived.

"Spencer Frederick Gore and Walter Sickert were two members of the Camden Town group of post-impressionist artists and they met in Walter's place. A bit fancier than most of the places my artist friends live in."

"How do you know all this stuff? I'm studying art and I've never heard of them."

"I paid my way through university by working for the company that makes London's blue plaques."

"Really?"

"No – I happen to like those artists, being a Camden boy. But I do love buildings. I even began a degree in architecture, but it was stultifyingly boring. I blame reading *The Fountainhead* as an impressionable teen. Howard Roark ruined my life."

"Who?"

"Never mind. It's a terrible book, and I'd have made a terrible architect. I'm not sure I'll make a good lawyer, but at least the degree doesn't take seven years to get. Anyway, let's crack on, otherwise you'll never get home and I'll be in trouble with your friends."

They chatted like old friends about their favourite artists, and Martha began to think that she liked Adam, liked him a lot. If he kissed her, she'd kiss him back.

Then Adam pulled her to a stop by some wrought-iron gates. "Do you mind going into a churchyard at night? This is one of my favourite places of all."

Martha saw the sign and her stomach lurched with recognition: Saint Pancras Old Church. This was the place. She had forgotten about it until now. Maybe her recollection was wrong, she thought, as Adam took her hand and walked her into the churchyard, to the left of the church and around to where there was a majestic ash. Then there was no mistaking it, because the tree had grown into the gravestones circled around it. Gravestones that had been disin-terred by Thomas Hardy. The place Dean had told her about in letters burned, but half remembered.

Martha panicked, let go of Adam's hand, and ran.

He called out to her. "I'm sorry! I'm sorry, Martha! Please don't go!"

But Martha ran and ran until she was lost in the back streets and struggling to breathe. The feelings she had pushed under the surface had broken back and been magnified by the shock of his written word brought to life. She regained her breath, then walked a while until she reached a main road, flagging down a taxi to go home, descending the stairs with relief to find that Camille and Garth's bedroom doors were open and she was alone.

It took days for her to think things through. Who had been falling for Adam back there? Marty? Maybe. But seeing Hardy's tree had killed Marty stone dead for a moment. Martha was resurrected to the horror of her loss once again. She was careful to conceal her emotions from Marty's friends, but she used the excuse of poverty to withdraw from their social life as much as she could, and they didn't seem to notice. She picked up a job at a local framer's, and bar work to fill evenings and weekends. No one asked why her shifts always coincided with their nights to go out. When the second year of college started, she threw herself back into her work.

One year bled into the next as she studied, worked her jobs and went out with her flatmates now and then, each time careful not to get too close to anyone again. Her art was inconsistent as she flipped between Martha and Marty, but the one thing that never changed was Dean in her mind. She couldn't stop thinking about him and his life in parallel, wondering where he was. She went to the big city libraries, made a note of all the D. Finlays in every British phone book, and called them again. Still nothing. Still vanished. She couldn't think how to find him, if he didn't want to be found. But she didn't give up, and she kept a list up to date, cross-checking it whenever the new books came out. Every new entry was hope, every phone call disappointment.

She stayed on through the Easter and summer holidays to work. The city sucked at her soul; she missed the country-side almost as much as she missed Dean, but when she went back to Cornwall, it undid her. Everywhere she went reminded her of him, but he couldn't be found. He had been erased from the area, the way that the new, fast bypass had obliterated fields, hedgerows and water meadows. Grief was easier to bear when the ashes of memory weren't being raked over. What should have been a joyful time of discovery at college was tinged with sadness that caught her throat and pricked her eyes any time Martha allowed her true self to emerge. Each time she returned to London, she had to punch through the sadness in her shift from Martha to Marty. She was a shell of a person, without substance or meaning.

Her parents drew her back for Christmases, but New Year's Eves were unspeakably sad, as all parties and celebrations careered towards coupling. Though Amy had split up with Tony by the end of the first year, in the second one she quickly found herself another steady boyfriend, Brendan. Despite repeated invitations up to Manchester, Marty found reasons to decline. Instead, Amy invited herself down for a long weekend and Martha blew it.

It started well as they tiptoed around each other, trying to find the friendship they had both neglected. On the Saturday, they looked for bargains in Spitalfields Market, ate bagels in Brick Lane, and laughed at the exhibition of silkscreened phalluses in Whitechapel Gallery. Then they went back to Martha's flat to get ready for a night out. But their guards came down with a shared bottle of rosé.

Martha told Amy about her encounter with Adam, the lovely lawyer.

Amy couldn't believe it. "So he was a nice-looking guy, who was sweet to you and interesting and smart, and you didn't go any further because of Mr Finlay?"

"Yes. I suppose you can boil it down to that."

"Martha, you're ruining your life for a flight of fancy."

"That's not what it was. It was real. He felt something for me, he really did."

"There may have been flirtation there, but that's all it was."

"That's not true. You never read his letters. We were soulmates."

"Okay, I'm sorry. But it's been years now. He's moved on and so should you."

"You don't know that. I do. I know it in my heart. He only left me to protect me, and I need to find him."

"Martha, what you need to do is grow up. There's more to life than Mr Finlay. He's not the only man out there who can make you happy. You have to be open to other relationships."

"I went out with Toph."

"Poor Christopher didn't stand a chance. You were loved up on Mr Finlay even then, weren't you? I know it breaks your heart, Martha, but it was just a crush, a schoolgirl crush. You need to get over it."

Martha drained her wineglass, refilled it and looked out of the window at the streetlight that flicked on and off, unable to decide whether the evening had begun. Amy really didn't understand. She was too immersed in her own life to connect with Martha's now.

Amy topped up her own glass and asked, "Why don't you visit me anymore? It's been too long since we've seen each other. And when did you become Marty?"

"It was a way to reinvent myself, to become more popular. Martha wouldn't have made these friends."

"You don't need to reinvent yourself. You just need to find your people. Are these really your people? When we came in, they looked me up and down like I was something the cat had dragged in. And they've ignored me ever since. What have you said to them about me?"

"Nothing. I haven't said anything about you. I guess you're just part of my old life that isn't relevant here." Martha saw Amy wince, but continued. "They're okay, Amy. They may not be the type to have the conversations we have, but they are a good way to keep me out of my head. I needed people to help me survive college. It's not like Cornwall here."

"Of course not, but you can still find your kind of people. Friends shouldn't just be something that collects around you the way dust balls up in a corner. Why do you need to be out of your head? You're going to go insane if you keep pretending to be something you're not. You need friends who aren't so..." Amy struggled to find the right word, but gave in. "Superficial."

Martha folded her arms. They weren't friends like Amy, but they were her adopted tribe to protect her from the worst of London and college life. She needed them and defended them. "At least they've been here for me. At least they haven't disappeared every time they've got a steady boyfriend."

Martha immediately regretted what she said. "I'm sorry, Amy. I didn't mean that."

"Yes, you did. Maybe you're right. Maybe you're better off here with these people, without me." Amy glanced at her watch, grabbed her bag and headed towards the door.

"Amy, stop! Don't leave. Where are you going to go?"

"I can make the last train if I leave now. Goodbye, Martha. I mean 'Marty'." Amy slammed the door and was gone.

CHAPTER THIRTY-THREE

The work in the barn and garden gave Dean purpose and a satisfaction that he hadn't had from most of his teaching. Until he had met Martha. He was glad that the tasks he had now were physically tougher. He was paying for his mistakes again, though this time there was always a reward.

Dean made his way up the slope, cutting out dense thickets of thorny brambles and sawing old trees that had fallen over the hillside. When the second summer showed its warmth, he saw the bones of the orchard emerge. The remaining fruit and nut trees fanned out along stone terraces that captured the rain that fell, and powered up in the midday sun. With the blackberry gone, he saw shoots of raspberry, red and black currant, and gooseberry emerge. There had been a gardener before him who had grown a forest of food. He had uncovered the foundation that would make it easy to build again.

The design showed him where it was best to plant as he followed the contours back to the main garden, ripping out the elder and hawthorn bushes seeded by birds to find the raised beds that would grow his vegetables. He saw the structure, what had fallen into disrepair, what needed rebuilding and where the beds were missing, with no time left to be made. It was a labour of love interrupted, then neglected.

The gardener must have been sad to leave. Perhaps their life had finished before the work was done. Dean was a willing apprentice, learning from the structure of the garden, his books, and the lessons of failure. He was deciphering the garden's past and working towards the garden to be, as it was intended. It would provide an abundance for him, whoever followed, and the surrounding wildlife. He felt a pang as he realised that when he finished, the garden would be enough to provide for two, more than two. A family.

A now-dark corner had been a hazel coppice, providing shafts to make the hurdles that had protected the growing garden from the wind, before rotting beneath the over-growth. Now each stand had grown thick and tall. Dean cut the hazel for firewood, being careful to saw the trunks as low to the ground as possible. The stools would reshoot and provide useful poles again.

The garden awoke from its years of slumber, shaken by the apprentice who became a master with the passing of the seasons. Where Dean had grubbed out the elder, hawthorn, and blackberries from the raised beds, flower seeds saw sunlight and burst forth – poppy and yarrow and flowers he didn't know the names of but would later learn. Yellow daffodils and buttercups pushed their way through the early spring green. Then the blues of phacelia and borage gave way to the pinks of godetia and red campion. Hoverflies and bumblebees zigzagged from bloom to bloom. The garden exploded with life.

It was an experience Dean was desperate to share with someone. Someone who would understand how wonderful it was. Another gardener. Thoughts of her pushed themselves to front of mind, inspiring him to create something she would be proud of. The way she had created paintings that made him proud as a teacher. As the garden became more vibrant, he ached with loneliness, wishing he could show the woman who had opened his eyes to it all. Because she would have left her girlhood behind by now. Once more he wondered how she was doing and chastised himself for the thought, knowing it was better for her that he wasn't there to derail her again. He hoped she had forgiven him, or better still, forgotten him. Forgetting him would have put her back on track.

CHAPTER THIRTY-FOUR

Martha graduated with a BA degree that made her parents proud. But she wasn't. A lower second-class degree reflected how she had let Marty take the reins, cruising through the last couple of years of college and doing just enough to not be completely average. What had she gained by going to St Hibbert's? Confidence in sculpting, print-making and throwing anything at a canvas. And a so-so set of friends she had little in common with. The Marty facade was crumbling, leaving Martha feeling more alone than before, yearning for someone to pull out the remains and breathe life back into them. She dreamed of Dean and his kiss, a kiss that could resurrect it. It was a fairy tale that she couldn't stop playing in her head.

The scaffold of school and college was now gone and Martha felt unsteady, unsure of what direction to go in. She was in a strange limbo, not able to go back along the clear path she had followed, with the paths forward so faint they were impossible to find.

Instead, she was frozen in the moment, painting her flatmates, local scenes, dogs and parks and buildings. All of it perfectly executed, but flat. She was observing and creating without engaging. Dean would've been disappointed in her. Though she didn't know what grade he had got at St Hibbert's, it was irrelevant. She knew he would have wanted her to realise her potential, and she hadn't. Sometimes she talked about it with Frankie, who had channelled a nasty break-up with her first true love into a blistering series of collages and screen prints that secured admiration from the faculty. All of her work sold at their final show. Martha sold nothing.

Frankie consoled her. "I only did it as a way not to go crazy," she said. "I'll probably never be able to do it again."

"Nonsense. You will. And it's amazing work. The best in our class. You deserve your first."

"It doesn't matter out there, Marty. You're only as good as your last sale, isn't that right? No one will care what our degree was in a year or two."

Frankie was right, but Martha had to start somewhere, and she was nowhere still. She had lost the self-belief and confidence she had started with.

After graduation, she continued to paint, but her work didn't excite her and she wasn't surprised when it didn't excite gallery owners either. Instead, she persuaded a local café to display them for sale or return.

A couple sold, one was stolen, another damaged, and the rest she had to pick up after a couple of months before storing them in her tiny room. She had barely covered her expenses. And it certainly would not pay the rent. She continued working at the framing shop, where at least she got a discount for her own frames. Time marched on, and she was left standing in place as her flatmates moved with it.

Garth met Samuel, a charming man from New York, who stayed over at the flat for an entire weekend. They only emerged from Garth's bedroom to raid the fridge, order takeaways, or use the bathroom. Samuel had to fly back crazily early on Monday to his design job on Madison Avenue and his flat on the Lower East Side. He invited Garth to come with him and he jumped at the chance, buying a cheap last-minute ticket to fly Virgin the next day.

Martha confronted him as he was packing anything that mattered into one large suitcase. "What if it doesn't work out with Samuel?"

"There are plenty of gay men in Manhattan, Marty. Plenty! Of course I want it to work out, but it's not my biggest worry."

"I hope you're worrying about the other stuff then. Be careful, won't you?"

"I'm careful enough," said Garth, giving Martha a squeeze, "but being careful is your problem, Marty. Maybe you should come to New York too. I think you've had enough of London, haven't you?"

Garth was right. Martha couldn't argue. Instead, she changed the subject back to him. "Okay, have fun, for you and me both. New York won't know what's hit it!"

Garth's leaving was a catalyst for change. Within three months, Camille and Frankie had moved out to pursue a new job and a girlfriend, respectively. Martha was left with the lease, the shabby furniture and three young student flat-mates who paid the bills but kept themselves to themselves. It was time to let go of Marty and find herself again.

CHAPTER THIRTY-FIVE

Dean wanted Martha to forget him, but he would never forget her. He couldn't fill the void in his paradise with plants. The joy of the garden was countered by sadness that wouldn't give way. He needed catharsis. It was years since he had painted outside the classroom. He had no canvas, no paper, but the walls of the wooden barn were bare.

He dragged out his old wooden box, flipped the catches and unfurled the leather roll of paintbrushes. Then he tipped out the tubes of paint and knew instantly by the way they fell that too much time had passed. They bounced sharply off the floor, dried solid. He checked his watch – he just had time to drive to Truro before the shops closed.

After restocking at the hardware store, Dean asked the guy at the counter for directions and made his way to the only art supplies shop in town. It was ten minutes before closing when he walked in; he saw the proprietor's face fall. Half an hour later and the man was beaming and affable, as Dean left with canvases, paper, oils, and a new line in acrylics the owner insisted he should try.

Dean put the art materials in the cab of his Land Rover and paused before locking it back up. He hadn't eaten since breakfast and wasn't working that night. With a couple of unopened pay packets in his pocket, he felt an urge to eat in company. There was a Badger and Barrel pub in the High Street, part of a chain that Dean would normally steer clear of. But it did food all day and had guest beers on tap. He went in past the signs saying no to bare feet and chests, smoking, and other evidence of poor patronage that he failed to acknowledge before seating himself at the bar. A surplus of meat-heavy leftovers at home made him crave something different. He ordered a plate of vegetarian nachos and a pint of bitter to wash it down. The serving size was enormous, but so was his appetite.

"You must've been hungry," said a woman beside him.

Dean hadn't noticed the bar fill up around him. "Yes. Very."

The woman was a few years older than him, he guessed by the lines around her eyes and the puffiness around her jaw. Not unattractive, though she had stuffed herself into a top a couple of sizes too small. He tried not to look at the plunging neckline.

"Buy me a drink?" She tapped her empty glass on the bar.

Dean nodded at the bartender, who topped it up. "That one's on me, but I have to be going."

"Keep me company, won't you? I hate to drink alone."

The bartender hadn't moved, clearly used to the routine.

"Okay. One more." He smiled wanly at the bartender, who poured Dean another pint and turned to serve his other customers.

The woman whooped as she spun around on her barstool. "My name's Linda. What's yours?"

Dean didn't know why, but he kept his name to himself. "Robert," he said. "Nice to meet you, Linda."

And Linda was away. She told him stories of Truro types and tourists that made him laugh. Tractor joyrides into sewage ponds and couples caught out when the cathedral floodlights turned on. It had been some time since Dean had relaxed in a stranger's company and Linda made it easier with each passing drink she ordered on his tab. She stopped him leaving with a pool game started, then grabbed him when he let her win by potting the black.

"You like to make a girl happy, don't you?" she said as she pulled down on his collar. Then her mouth was on his, tasting of Jack Daniel's, cigarettes and too much time alone.

He didn't want her, but biology betrayed him.

She drew back, smiled and said, "Walk me home." Instructing more than questioning.

He nodded, gave the barman the last of his money and put the few coins he got back in the tip jar.

The cool night air was the slap in the face he needed. Mercifully, Linda only lived a couple of streets away. Dean waited as she got her keys out of her bag. Once the door opened, he was down the path, out of the gate and walking fast.

"Hey! Where you going? Charming you are, just charming! Aren't you even going to take my number? Come on, Bobby boy! Come back!"

Dean's heart was beating fast. It wasn't from the walking, but from a memory of over a decade past, when he had been invited in and gone. And gone the ten years after. He wouldn't spend another second in regret. He walked, knowing he was too drunk to drive, and it paid him to walk it off. The alcohol and the feeling of being with the wrong woman. He was better off without company than with the wrong company.

As he left the brick and the concrete, he slowed his walking and looked up from the road ahead. The street lights gave way to stars and moonlight as he kept going, hugging hedges when headlights approached, getting to Mevacombe by midnight and the barn an hour or so later.

He drank down his thirst, fell into his hammock and slept through to a hangover with the relief of nothing worse.

CHAPTER THIRTY-SIX

It was the morning after 1997's general election and, after eighteen years of Conservative government, New Labour had got into power. There was a sense of optimism everywhere, as Martha picked up the paper from the cheery newsagent, nodded to her smiling neighbour by the mailboxes, and returned to the flat. But she didn't feel optimistic. The more time she spent in London, the more she missed the countryside. She was still in touch with her art school friends, but didn't see them much. Camille was working and partying hard in Manchester, Frankie was loved up with a girlfriend and two pugs in Brighton, and Garth had fallen on his feet in the fashion world in New York; he was having too much fun with his work and a succession of boyfriends to consider coming back to England.

The last vestiges of Marty had withered away to leave Martha feeling like a hamster on a treadmill in a cage in a travelling circus. Everything changed around her, but she was running in place, getting nowhere and wondering what the hell she was doing there. She was in the same flat, subletting it to a succession of students and young profes-sionals. None of them were like Camille, Frankie and Garth, let alone how she used to be with Amy. To fill the void, she had made friends of necessity. There were work friends to have a drink with early on a Friday before heading home, and activity friends to play tennis with at the community courts. But she didn't know anyone she could have a real heart-to-heart with. If she left the city, the friendships would fade like writing on a morning misted window. They weren't her kind of people; they weren't even Marty's kind of people. With each passing year, she went out less, preferring to stay at home and work in her cramped room. Now and then, her flatmates persuaded her to go out with them. That was when she missed Dean the most and needed to obliterate the pain. She drank too much and went off with unsuitable men. But it was better for her and them. She didn't want to risk broken hearts again. It was more than she thought she could bear.

Martha needed a change, but didn't know where to start. She hung up her coat and went to make tea to have with a sharing-sized bar of chocolate that she would relish eating alone. The kettle boiled, she poured the water over a second-use tea bag and mashed the last of the flavour out with a teaspoon, cursing when she heard the entrance intercom buzz. The intercom that the landlord hadn't fixed, and that Martha hadn't mentioned again, since it was years since he'd last put the rent up. It was probably someone calling on one of her flatmates. She padded down to the entrance, hoping she could usher them away in a hurry. She certainly didn't expect to see Amy when she opened the door.

"Hello, Martha."

"Amy! What are you doing here?"

"Is it a bad time?"

"No, no, it's not. Come in."

Amy took off her coat and closed the door behind her as she followed Martha into the kitchen.

Martha clicked on the kettle. "I didn't realise you were in London."

"I've been here a while. Brendan and I split up a couple of years ago."

"I'm sorry."

"I'm not. Things were never really the same after we graduated and our crowd broke up. Living together was the last straw. It wasn't ever going to work. I kept dropping hints of getting married and having children someday, but that's not what he wanted and it took me too many years to see that."

"So what are you doing here?"

"When we broke up, I needed a change. There was a business development job in Highgate with an engineering company. I applied on the off chance and got it. I've been here ever since. Sorry."

"Don't be. I was a complete arse. I should've apologised before. Though I sent you a card actually, but..."

"It's okay. I forgot to redirect my post when I left everything in a hurry. You wouldn't know."

"I would if I'd been keeping in touch with you. Sorry."

"No more apologies! I'm here now, and thankfully so are you." Amy gave Martha a big hug and then stepped back to look at her. "You're still in your pyjamas at 1 p.m. Have I disturbed something?"

"Don't be daft. Nothing like that happens to me these days."

"Well, I'm here to change that. We need to change everything."

Amy and Martha made more tea and shared the chocolate before moving on to corner shop rosé and olives as they caught up with each other's lives. As always, Amy hadn't been single for long, and had met Mike, an Australian, in a bar in Shepherd's Bush.

"Kind of appropriate really," said Amy, "as he really is a shepherd."

"What was he doing in a bar in London?"

"The same thing as most of the Aussies and Kiwis – working on his OE, overseas experience. He had a visa for two years. A visa that runs out at the end of the year."

"Oh dear. What are you going to do?"

"Well... he's invited me back with him."

"To Australia?"

"Yes. He's going back to the farm he grew up on in New South Wales. He's invited me to work with him on his farm."

Martha gave Amy a quizzical stare.

"I really like him, Martha. I think this is the one."

"That's great, but what do you know about sheep?" asked Martha.

"Absolutely nothing. But it's got to be better than the boring job I'm working in now. And besides, I'm sick of this grey English weather. Australia has better weather than this."

"It'll be a shame to see you go. I've missed you, Amy."

"I've missed you too. Which is why I think you should come with me."

"To farm sheep in Australia? Er... no."

"No, not to the farm. I was thinking I would travel for a few months before I settle down there. You know, do my own OE. And I think it would be great fun if you came with me."

"I don't have any money, Amy."

"You could get a working holiday visa and earn some money while you're there. And we could save up. My parents would kill me if I left before Christmas, anyway. So we could work our arses off until the end of the year, go down to Cornwall to catch up with the olds and then get on a flight in the New Year to set off on an adventure."

"That does sound good. I'd have to find another job and save up some money though. It's not like the old days; my parents said you used to be able to emigrate to Australia for ten quid."

"A visa will cost a bit more than that, worst luck. But we could definitely help each other save. You can come round to my place for big nights in. I've got a DVD player and make a mean curry. We'll be the most boring women in London, but we'll have one hell of a time Down Under."

"How can I resist? You're on."

CHAPTER THIRTY-SEVEN

The Truro encounter had shaken Dean. The art materials were a reminder and made him hide them away, like the things he found hard to think about. Instead, he relished his time alone, accountable to no one, thinking for one. There was nobody to tell him to come in for his dinner when he worked late in the garden. He didn't have to put his tools away each night when he was building in the barn. And no one was there to criticise how he worked, which was often for hours on end, sometimes without eating for a day or two. Everything around him took the shapes he saw in his mind.

The garden was transformed. Dean learned more about how to grow things by reading books he borrowed from the library or picked up at secondhand shops, but mostly he learned by trial and error, finding out the peculiarities of his own particular microclimate. Seeds he saved gave him plants that were adapted to his garden. Each year, an expanding range of fruits and vegetables grew better. He had excess to trade with Demelza for things from the shop. He scoured builder skips for offcuts of wood from renovations and old timber from demolitions. The hammock was fraying, so he constructed a proper bed with a workbench underneath that pulled out to give him plenty of space for his bigger projects. On one of his rarer trips to Truro, he bought well-made dovetail-jointed oak drawers from a charity shop and built shelving around them to store all the tools he was accumulating for his carpentry and gardening.

Dean was working on a mezzanine level, where he could keep his clothes and books, and dry some of his excess produce, when disaster struck. He had propped the bottom of the ladder against a big box of tools as he had done countless times before when he was putting in the boards and rails of the mezzanine. All that was left was cutting out the area where the proper steps would go. The ladder was just short of the rafters and Dean was careful as he made his way up it, holding his toolkit in one hand with his other on the rungs. Spring sunshine lit up the roof, and it felt pleasantly warm as he reached the boards. The top of the ladder nudged against something round and brittle, lodged in behind a rafter. His stomach lurched as there was a slight jolt, but the ladder was firmly in its place and he felt secure.

Until the wasps took him by surprise.

He knew the error as soon as he made it, letting go of the ladder to swing with his free arm as the weight of the toolbox pulled him sidewards, letting the ladder be pushed away in an equal, opposite and terrifying motion.

The two-storey drop onto floorboards might have been okay if he hadn't hit the big box of tools with his thigh first. The sickening crack told him what the pain then confirmed.

He had broken his leg. This was going to be tough.

Dean heard a small car driving too fast down the track. Then a slammed door and the rapid crunching of gravel before Demelza's voice called out, "Dean? Dean? Where the bloody hell are you?"

"In here. The barn!" Dean yelled.

Demelza blazed through the door, ducked under the fallen ladder, and winced as she saw Dean sitting against the wall, one leg not as straight out as the other, an empty bottle of wine beside him.

"Did you drink that before or after you busted your leg?"

"After."

"Good. Sorry no one came looking for you sooner – Stan didn't think to mention your absence last night until he came in for the papers today."

"I've never missed a shift. I was hoping he'd notice."

"And you usually pick up the local newspaper on a Thursday – I noticed that too. Now let me help you up and get you to hospital; it'll be quicker than fetching an ambulance, since we can't call one from here." Demelza gave Dean a stern look. One that reminded him of all the times she had told him he should reconnect the phone.

"Sorry," said Dean, as Demelza helped him shuffle to the car.

"You will be – it's a hell of a bumpy ride out of here in an ancient Honda Civic."

Demelza took him to Truro hospital and waited the five hours it took for the staff to admit him, examine his leg and set it in plaster. He didn't complain, and neither did she.

She then helped him fold himself back into the Honda. "Right. You'd better come back with me then."

"I can't do that."

"The doctor said you need support, and you've got none at the barn – you'd be stranded with no means of contacting anyone. Don't be bloody stupid."

"I'll get the phone connected."

"Good. Until then, you're staying with me."

It took nearly two weeks before Dean could stand long enough on his crutches to wash dishes. He insisted on sorting the papers each morning and writing out invoices each afternoon. In between these chores, Demelza ushered him out of the shop and back into the lounge, where she had set up the sofa bed for his convalescence. The lounge door opened to the back porch, and Demelza maintained she had lost the key to it years before. There was no escape for Dean from the female well-wishers who inundated the front room with hand-picked flowers and home-cooked meals.

Joanne 'recently divorced, but it was over a long time ago' Sawyer was making her third visit and had stayed beyond the time needed to ask how he was doing and discuss the weather. Silence hung in the air like damp laundry on a windless day, but Joanne was oblivious to it. Dean limped to his feet, and was thanking her, wishing he could free a hand to guide her towards the door, when Demelza came in, nodding to Joanne as she squeezed past her to leave. She looked at the casserole dish and back at Dean. "I reckon neither of us will need to cook till that cast comes off."

"Can't you make them stop coming?"

"Why? They're all attractive single women. And some of them can cook. You could do with someone in your life, love."

"I've got you, Demelza."

"Don't get cute with me, Sunny Jim. You know what I mean. You could do with a partner, someone to share your life with."

"I'm not too good at that."

"Were you married then?"

"Yes. But I never should have got married."

Dean told Demelza about how he had come to marry Kristina and spent too many years regretting it. "With hindsight, I can see how crazy it was to be with her for so long. But it started out as a means to survive, to keep her well from day to day, then week to week. Then the years slipped away... There was no point at which I could decide enough was enough, until she did. The veil over my eyes came away with the burden lifted, and I saw what a massive mistake I'd made. I hope she'll be much happier with her new partner."

"What about you? Don't you deserve to be happy with someone?"

"I was happy for a while, but it was complicated."

Demelza waited for Dean to explain, but no explanation was forthcoming. "So she broke up with you, did she? Which is why you came down here?"

"No, I broke up with her."

"What was wrong with her?"

"Nothing. The situation was wrong."

"Then change the situation."

"I couldn't."

"Or you didn't want to."

"I did. Believe me, I did."

"Yes, well, where there's a will, there's a way. Never mind. Perhaps she wasn't the one. Perhaps she wasn't right for you, either. It's hard to find someone who you click with enough to spend a lifetime with."

"That's not it. We clicked all right, it was just the situation. She was young, that's the problem."

Demelza kept quiet.

"But she had an old soul and wanted what I want in life. We both love nature and would like to leave the world better than we found it. She didn't care about money, or the stuff that money can buy, unless it would help her grow a better world. She made me feel connected to that again, reminded me of my dreams as a young man."

"You're still young, Dean."

"I'm 40 next year."

"Ha – when you're my age, 63, you'll know 39 is young. How much younger was she? The One. Because she sounds like The One."

"The One? You could call her that. I've never connected with anyone else that way, so she's unique in my life. But she was too young. I was 30, and she was 17."

"Yes, I see. That would have been a problem. But not now she's 26."

"And has her own life. And is probably married. With kids, even."

"You're reading too much into something you know nothing about. It sounds as if you need to find her and finish that chapter, or close the book."

"I can't do that. I can't go back. She's better off without me at this point."

"Have you asked her that? It wouldn't be hard to find her these days."

"No, I haven't asked her. It's not that simple."

"It is that simple, if she's worth it. Otherwise, you have to move on. If you don't get her out of your head, how can anyone else take her place?"

"I don't want anyone to take her place. Which is why you have to stop these women from visiting me."

"Okay, I'll put the word out that you're not to be disturbed here. The freezer's full, anyway."

CHAPTER THIRTY-EIGHT

Amy and Martha left London on a suitably grim January morning and backpacked around Asia until the thrill of sunny beaches and cheap, delicious street food was tempered by a series of stomach upsets and cockroach-ridden hostels.

"We've been here too many times before," said Amy as she held Martha's hair back in the bathroom, whilst another sickly backpacker banged on the door. "It's time to go to Australia."

Martha washed her face and dried it on the towel Amy offered. "The next stop on our ticket is New Zealand. We're supposed to be working there. I'm nearly out of money and Camille has an uncle in Mount Maunganui who can employ us straight away. That was the plan, Amy."

Amy made a face and looked away. "I'm tired, Martha. And I miss Mike. I really miss him. He'll look after us. You can come with me."

Martha didn't want to be a gooseberry on a sheep station in the middle of nowhere. They went to the airport together, and she waved Amy off, promising to see her in a couple of months, knowing that she wouldn't.

The months of running up and down ladders to pick avocados gave Martha muscles, money and a reason to move on. She got on a tourist bus and saw the bubbling hot mud of Rotorua, swam with dolphins in the Bay of Plenty, learned to surf, skydived over volcanoes, floated through caves starlit by glow worms and ate 35 flavours of ice cream. The bus route went in a big loop around the country and she fell in with backpackers who bought into the same experiences, leaving them behind when they stayed places to bungee jump, jet boat, or take helicopter rides. She ventured off the beaten track to tramp between old deer huts in the wilderness. Her luck with the weather ended when May brought gale force winds and sleet to Queenstown, a reminder that it was time to move on before her money ran out. She went into a bar, where a blond guy nudging the end of his twenties was leaning against the coffee machine, reading a Graham Greene novel.

"Hi."

The bartender smiled and put down his book. "Kia ora! What can I get you?"

"Internet. If you have it."

"There's a machine in the corner. Two dollars gets you fifteen minutes. Is that enough?"

"To book a flight to Australia? I hope so."

"Why are you going there? It's full of Aussies!"

"And Brits. I'll be on one of those buses going up the east coast with all the other backpackers."

"You don't want to do that."

"Why not?"

"Because you don't look like the type of girl who wants to drink and shag her way to the Top End, that's why."

"Ha! What do I look like?"

"A woman who prefers good food, art and literature to drinking herself senseless. Am I right?"

"Maybe. What about you? Do you like all that?"

"Yep."

"Then why are you in a bar in the most touristy town in New Zealand?"

"I'm filling in for my brother. It's his bar, and he's taking me to the airport tomorrow. I've got a job in London. Come with me."

Martha laughed. "I can't. I've got a round the world ticket and I've only reached here. There's so much I haven't seen. I want to go to Australia, the Americas, and... Spain. I've never been to Spain and I've wanted to ever since..."

"Spain is a stone's throw from London. I'll take you to Spain. Come with me."

"You're joking – we've only just met!"

"I'm deadly serious. I know things about people. I know enough about you to want to get to know you better." He jabbed his hand across the bar. "I'm Carl."

Martha felt the strength of his grip and his intention as she shook his hand and held the gaze of his grey-green eyes. "I bet this routine works on a lot of girls, eh, Carl?"

"I'm hoping this will be the first and only time," he said as he drew back his hand and rubbed his close-cropped hair.

"Worth a try, but I'll get that Internet time and sort out my flight, thanks."

Carl took her money and wrote on the back of the ticket. "Put this code in the machine for your time – I've given you half an hour. And then look me up when you get to London. If you don't, we'll both regret it."

Martha looked at the slip of paper when she logged in to the computer terminal. Carl had written his email on the back. She folded it away in her purse and booked her flight to Melbourne.

Martha took temping jobs, each one more boring than the last – filing, stocktaking, data entry. It paid for a room in Saint Kilda and the chance to explore the city and every-where she could get to in a weekend by train. The money was good, but three months of office work, collecting complicated coffee orders and putting up with the unwanted advances of grey men in suits whose dreams had gone bad, felt like a lifetime. She took the bus up the coast and it was everything Carl had said. She shared dorms with teenagers who were either humping each other or throwing up in their sleeping bags. The scenery was spectacular. Intense white sandy beaches echoed the sunlit paintings of Joaquín Sorolla and made her feel more alone. Dean was looking over her shoulder, calling her home. By the time she got to Darwin, she was done. Even the natural beauty of the beaches and rainforest couldn't tempt her to stay. It was hot and humid, but she couldn't swim anywhere for the crocodiles, jellyfish and sharks.

Amy emailed her, full of joy and wonder at her new life, imploring Martha to visit. It only made her more homesick.

She flew back to London, got her old jobs back, a bedsit in Hackney and a niggling feeling that she was making a big mistake. One rainy Thursday in an Internet café, she dug out the slip of paper from her purse, typed a greeting with her number and name, and hit 'send' before she could change her mind.

CHAPTER THIRTY-NINE

Martha emailed Amy to tell her about Carl. She must have been online, because a chat box immediately opened up in AOL messenger.

A: You met a guy in New Zealand and didn't tell me about him?!

M: There was nothing to tell. We had our first date last night.

M: He's been in London for ages.

A: What's he doing in London?

M: He has a job in sales, which he's super good at. Gift of the gab and all that.

A: What's he like?

A: How was the date???

M: He's good-looking if you go for the Robert Redford type. The date was nice.

A: So he's short?

M: Yes. But he makes up for it in other departments!

A: He's a good kisser?

M: No.

A: Give him a chance.

M: It seems like a deal-breaker to me.

A: Maybe he just needs some coaching…

M: Don't worry, I've agreed to another date. We're going to see The Truman Show on Friday.

A: Great! Whatever that is.

M: Have you been hiding under a rock?

M: It's a movie.

M: It's been out for ages. You must be busy.

M: How are you?

A: Sorry. I wasn't ignoring you. Our connection is bad.

A: I'm good. I'm getting great at sorting sheep out, checking their feet, drenching them, that sort of thing… But I'd better go because I need to get dinner on the table before we both crash out on the couch.

M: Sounds like domestic rural bliss!

A: No, it doesn't. It reads terribly, doesn't it? But it's not like that.

A: The truth is my feelings for Mike differ from anything I've had before. It wouldn't matter where we lived because we make our own universe. I don't need other distractions, because everything I've been looking for is within us. We have a connection, but I can't explain. Do you know what I mean? I'm not able to articulate it.

M: I know exactly what you mean. Exactly.

A: And how's London?

A: I have to say there's nothing I miss about the city. I'm not sure I could go back, even if I had to.

M: I can't stand it. I don't know why I came back here. I'm not sure what I'm doing with any of my life.

A: Hey, it's sounding like fun. Not as much fun as you had in New Zealand, but you have to settle down sometime, right?

M: Do I?

A: Maybe Carl's the one to settle with.

A: Maybe he will want to move to the country with you.

M: You're getting ahead of yourself now – better get that dinner going!

A: Okay. Talk soon. Miss you. xox

M: Miss you too XXX.

Martha went on more dates and the kissing didn't improve, which made his performance in the bedroom no surprise. However, Carl made her laugh, his friends were good fun, and she started enjoying the city again as they trawled markets for secondhand bargains, ticked off every museum in his battered guidebook, and ate their way around the world on a budget. It was better being with him than being alone. She was surprised at how quickly the time passed, that she had been with him for nearly two years. When his company sponsored his residency and gave him a major pay rise, he suggested they get a flat together.

"Maybe next year, if I sell a few more paintings." Martha didn't want to be dependent on him.

"You don't need to sell any paintings. I can pay for it. The agent has been showing me places and there's a great two bedroom one in Shoreditch. It even has a balcony. You could grow some things in pots, right? And I can cover the mortgage myself. You don't need to pay anything."

"I want to pay for things, but it sounds like you've already decided."

"I've not decided, but it doesn't make sense for us both to be throwing away money in rent, and I'm sick of sharing with flatmates when I could be sharing with you. Will you come and see the place and we'll decide then? You can pay some of the bills. We'll sort it out so it's fair, I promise. And you can continue painting. You can give up your odd jobs and paint more."

"They're not odd jobs; they've supported me for years. Besides, it's inspiring to see the work coming in to be framed now. It's my primary contact with the art world at large."

"I've made another contact for you, look." Carl gave her a card. "She's a gallery owner in Shoreditch. She'd love help from someone who knows art like you do."

Martha didn't know how to feel. She was touched that Carl had looked for work for her, but bristled at his stepping into her world unbidden.

He did his puppy dog look and hugged her and kissed her all over her face. "Please come and look at it with me. Please, please, please."

She looked at the flat, which was just as he had described and more so. Light streamed through windows that looked out over rooftops. She could see herself painting there, and there would be no neighbours to look in on her doing it. Then Carl dragged her into the old warehouse gallery, where she met Rosie, who looked to be barely out of school and was dwarfed by the huge empty space around her. She was pretty and bubbly and completely clueless about art, but she was in awe of Martha's qualifications and had a father who was prepared to back her dream to the hilt. Martha agreed to a partnership after Carl suggested a fifty percent share of net revenue instead of any salary. She raised her eyebrows, but knew she could make the gallery a success with the contacts she had. Rosie looked up at Carl as though he was some sort of saviour.

Martha quit the bar work, gave notice at the framer (promising to work until the new year), and shifted her world more into Carl's. They moved into the Shoreditch flat on Christmas Eve of 1999 and had a housewarming party on New Year's Eve. The expensive champagne corks popped, salmon and caviar blinis were eaten or half-eaten, and people danced to the DJ's iPod mixes or rubbed their noses and giggled after trips to the bathroom.

Carl and his friends were having the time of their lives and she didn't know why she wasn't.

255

CHAPTER FORTY

Once the cast was removed and Demelza had given permission for him to leave her care, Dean returned to the barn, to gardening and to painting again.

The first few canvases were terrible. The paintings all looked like things that had gone before, but he knew he had to keep working through, to keep painting until he found himself in the present.

Demelza called him daily and their conversations were brief, being mainly about the weather.

After a week, Dean answered the phone with, "You don't need to check on me, Demelza."

"How did you know it was me?"

"I haven't given anyone else my number. And you call at 9 o'clock every day. Have you set an alarm for me?"

"Maybe..."

"I'm fine, Demelza, really. You can stop worrying about me."

"What about me, Dean? I live alone too. I'm not getting any younger and I could slip in the shower or something."

"You only take baths."

"Well, you know what I mean."

"I do. But can I call you instead? Sometimes I'm out in the garden and have to run for the phone."

"Certainly, but if you don't call, I'll call you. And I'm still waiting for an invitation to dinner..."

From then on, Dean called her every day before he walked out into the garden. Every Tuesday night, Demelza came to dinner, meaning Dean had to make another chair and buy another set of crockery and cutlery.

Dean needed the hard work in the garden and barn to help him to sleep, but it didn't erase his waking thoughts when Martha was back in his mind. Shutting the thoughts away hadn't lessened the missing of her, and since talking to Demelza he had given up hope of ever being able to. As the seasons came around again and again, the memory of her didn't wane; it entrenched itself in his soul the way a brand from a hot iron cools but never fades.

One day, as he was looking out of the window, he thought about Martha and how she would love the garden if only she could see it. It was a feeling of pleasure that overrode the underlying pain. He needed to express the feeling in the only way he could, through paint. He painted the garden as if it was their garden, not his. It wasn't a representation of what was there, rather the idea of what he wanted to be there, what she would like and how he could bring it into being in time. The colours and form and feel were a plan for how the garden was going to grow over the years and how it would feel to them both if they were there together.

When he finished the painting, he put it aside, turning the canvas to face the wall. It was the first painting he'd been happy with in a very long time. Maybe ever. Wanting to recapture the feeling, Dean kept going, though he painted nothing else that was as satisfying as that first painting of the garden. But it was enough: he could continue from where he'd left off as a young man, before his marriage had derailed him. That he loved his painting was no surprise; however the time spent in the garden was becoming magical. He spent evenings looking through catalogues and ordering seeds and bulbs to paint the landscape in his mind. As he improved the soil with piles of manure from local stables, the garden responded and grew. Most of the old trees that he'd pruned in the orchard began to bear fruit, and he replaced the ones that didn't with a variety of pears, apples and plum trees.

One beautiful day in late spring, there was a knock on the door. Dean went to it, expecting to have to show someone around the cottage.

But it wasn't a tourist, it was Robert. He was standing with a bottle of wine and asked, "Any chance of a spot of lunch?"

Dean found a couple of glass tumblers and put together a plate of cheese and crackers with some cut vegetables from the garden, whilst Robert opened the wine. He poured it, after giving the glasses a clean with his handkerchief.

"I like what you've done with the place," said Robert. "I only came here once, a long time ago, but it was a dump. To be honest, when I suggested you stay here, you were desperate, and I didn't think you'd be here that long. But now I can see that it suits you. And I see you've got back into your painting too," he said, as he surveyed the canvases around the barn. He stood up and walked over to look at them more closely. "These are fantastic. Let me sell them."

"I'm not sure about that, Robert."

"Mate, you don't want to be washing dishes all your life. It's not what you should do with your time. I can sell these paintings to all the depressed Londoners who work twelve-hour days, dreaming of living somewhere like this. We'll earn a fortune."

Dean laughed. "Well, if it makes those poor buggers happy, I guess I'll let you do that."

"Whoa... and this, this is even better," said Robert as he picked up a canvas and turned it around to reveal the painting of the garden.

"No, that's not to go to London. I want to sell it locally, to support a gallery that has art I admire."

"Okay," said Robert, as he thought things through. "Let me photograph it with the others and I'll get some cards printed, too. I'll contact a local distributor who can sell the ones of the coast to all the tourists."

"Fine. But I don't want my name on them, or on any of the paintings."

"Well, there has to be somebody's name on them. How about mine?" said Robert, smiling.

"That'll only go to your head," said Dean. "You can call me 'Barn Owl' if it makes your life easier. But I don't want to be known to anyone, anyone at all, you understand?"

"No problem. The idea of a talented recluse will add to your allure."

Robert went to the car and came back to wrap the paintings in heavy brown paper. His phone beeped.

"What do you know? I must've had reception for a second," he said, looking at the screen. "I'd better go – the city is missing me."

As Dean helped him load the paintings into his car, Robert added, "It's missing you too, buddy. Come up and have a night on the town with me, eh?"

Dean nodded, knowing full well he wouldn't. Robert slapped him on the back, got into his shiny new BMW, and drove off.

Like a substitute mother, Demelza pestered him over their Tuesday meal. "Why didn't you go to the city with your friend? He might have had more luck setting you up with a nice lady friend?"

"We've been through this a million times, Demelza. I'm happy on my own, thank you."

Demelza persisted. "Why don't you go out with anyone, Dean? It's such a waste! You're a fabulous cook and a gardener, not to mention those dreamboat looks of yours."

Dean frowned at her as he ate.

"Well, when you aren't giving me one of your withering looks."

"I have a good life, Demelza. The barn is now comfortable, and the garden is rewarding me double for any effort I put into it. It feeds me, you, guests that stay, and I still have left-over fruit and veg for the shop."

"It sells well, Dean – it's making me more money than news-papers these days. I guess fresh organic produce is some-thing you can't get on the bloody Internet. Stan is worried you'll sell so many vegetables, you'll give up the dish-washing job. Especially since you must be selling your paintings, too." Demelza nodded towards the one remaining canvas leaning against the wall.

Dean was glad Demelza had veered away from the topic of his non-existent love life. "Yes, Robert is delighted I've pulled my finger out finally."

"It's dreadful that he has to drive all the way here and back to collect them. Why don't you take them up next time? The change would do you good. Maybe you could go on some of those Internet dates."

Dean laughed. "Demelza, are you trying to drive me insane? I love my life here, love being in nature and living a simple life. Do you think I would find a woman like that in London, via the Internet?"

"I don't know. I don't really know how the Internet works. My niece tried to show me, but I'm too old to be getting into that nonsense."

"Me too."

"You're twenty years younger than me!"

"I'm old enough to know what I like."

"And you don't like any of the single women around here?"

"Remember when you set me up on that date with Carly?"

"My other niece – she's a looker."

"Possibly. But it's hard to know, with all the make-up she was wearing. It's a good job she never came here – she'd break an ankle walking up to the barn in the heels she wears."

"She likes to look her best."

"And she was horrified to eat in the pub. She barely touched her meal."

"She's watching her weight."

"Never mind. I'm sure there are dozens of men who would love to have Carly on their arm, but she's not the type of woman I'm looking for."

"Oh! So you are looking..."

"No. No, I'm not."

"You know why that is, Dean? It's because you already found her, didn't you?"

"I did." Dean said this to stop the conversation, but it was true. Every woman he'd come across since had confirmed it.

There was always something missing in them. No spark of connection. Nothing in their eyes that told him of more there if he wanted to reach for it.

Demelza continued. "Why don't you try this Internet thing, Dean? You could find her again. Make amends for whatever you did that was so wrong."

Dean sighed. She wouldn't stop unless he told her. "I was her teacher, Demelza. She was seventeen."

That cut Demelza short.

For a moment.

"Well, she's not seventeen now! What's she doing now? Have you looked?"

Dean had thought about this many times over the years. Hoping Martha had enjoyed college as much as he had, but that she'd gone on to travel and do so much more with her life. He knew he had to give a Demelza a plausible reason to stop asking more questions. "She's smart, attractive and talented. Someone like that doesn't remain single. She's probably married with kids. Hopefully painting. She's a better painter than me, Demelza."

"Are you good?"

Dean went over to the canvas and took off the dust sheet.

"Oh my," said Demelza, walking towards it to take a closer look. "She must be very good."

Demelza stopped asking questions about Dean's love life, but their routine of phone calls and dinners continued. It felt as if nothing would ever change. Before everything did.

The last time Dean saw Demelza, she brought bad news. "Sheila called."

"Cottage guests in winter? They're brave."

"She didn't call about tourists, Dean. She's selling the cottage."

"Damn. Well, at least I'll have some time to sort something out – no one will buy it in winter."

"They did, Dean. The sale will go through after the survey. It's a formality, apparently, and then Sheila promises you thirty days' notice after that. Unless you find something sooner, of course. Like being my live-in cook."

Dean gave Demelza a wry smile, but felt a rug being pulled out from under him. "Bloody hell. Who's buying it?"

"A middle-aged couple from the city. The wife loved the place when they stayed in September. She said her husband can work from here using the Internet. I don't know if he knows it's not that broad bean one."

"Broadband. No, he won't like the dial-up Internet. I remember them. She was a sweetheart, loved the garden and the wildlife. He did nothing but complain about the track, how long it took to run hot water, the lack of Sky TV... Shit. What a nightmare."

"You'll find something. You can stay with me until you do."

"Thanks, but I'm not worrying about me. It's the garden, the barn. This is the only place that has ever felt like home in my adult life. I put all my love into it and they'll not be able to. It will fall apart."

"Can you counter offer? Do you have any savings?"

"Not enough. And the bank wouldn't give me a mortgage, as a middle-aged painter and dishwasher. I'm stuffed and so is the barn. The guy will probably turn it into a garage for his Porsche."

"Nothing lasts forever, Dean. I'm sorry."

"Don't be. I'm sorry you had to be the bearer of bad tidings. I should've told Sheila I had a landline, so she didn't have to call you. Never mind – we can't worry about what we can't do anything about. Let's eat – I made venison stew."

"Are you sure you can't afford this place – if you can buy venison?"

"Buy it? Some drunk wrote his car off and took a young stag with it last week. I've filled Sheila's freezer with it, so eat up!"

Demelza and Dean enjoyed a last supper of venison stew and a decent Aussie Shiraz. When he called her the next day, Demelza never answered.

CHAPTER FORTY-ONE

Rosie and Martha refitted the gallery and had one opening before the end of the millennium to showcase the work of three local artists who Martha knew well. Despite selling half of the paintings on the night and most of the rest in the run-up to Christmas, the gallery made a loss.

The new partnership learned from it. Rose had a flair for connecting with people online and Martha designed flyers that circulated widely in the real world. They pared back costs to the essentials to break even, then profit. Each opening was more successful than the previous one, with better artists and higher prices, as word spread of the new place to buy the art of young talent.

Rosie insisted Martha put up her own paintings in the gallery. She relented by hanging them in a back room they used for packing materials. The paintings sold. She told Rosie it was because they were cheaper than anything they hung out the front, but they appealed to locals who wanted mementoes of the area, or to give to those who had moved away. Many of the artists Martha was now working with encouraged her to take her work further, but Martha was reluctant, knowing she didn't even deserve to be in the gallery now she and Rose had transformed it.

One artist, Reuben Erickson, was insistent. "Martha, I wouldn't be where I am now without your encouragement, your drive to put me centre stage, and your advice on which of my pieces would work, how to frame them – everything you've done for me."

"Thank you."

"Now it's your turn. You're wasting your talents in the back room."

"My painting's not good enough."

"It could be. Take time off. Take that trip to Spain you've always talked about. Get out of your head."

"What do you mean?"

"I've been into your gallery dozens of times. I see you thinking. You're somewhere else, and I bet it's not in the paintings you do, either. But when it is, when you put your true self in your work, contact this guy."

Martha took the card Reuben gave her.

"My agent – he's the one to talk to you when you're ready to do the real work."

A week later, Carl spent two nights away from her, with the excuse of a client conference. It was another one he had insisted he told her about, but that she couldn't remember.

She felt aggrieved, and not for the first time. If only she could switch her life in an instant. She called the number on the card Reuben had given her.

The agent came to the gallery the next day, but confirmed what she already knew. There was no passion in the paintings. He admired her technical ability and said that her work had potential and to keep in touch. She kept his card as a promise to herself to be better. And life went on as it had before.

As the gallery proved itself, Rosie bloomed into a confident businesswoman, adept at promoting the gallery and its artists by blogging and using the tools of social media that were coming online. She was good at talking to potential customers as well, leaving Martha to talk more to the artists. Carl was proud of them both and celebrated their success by flexing his new platinum credit card at the trendy restaurants that mushroomed around the formerly decayed areas of London's East End. He had moved on to a web marketing company, where the money was flowing in faster than they could recruit people to spend it. Carl had the golden ticket, and he wanted to share his winnings. Marty would've adored him.

When Garth, Camille or Frankie visited London, they revelled in Carl's company. Everybody loved him. Everybody except Martha. She wanted to love him, knew that she should. He was up for doing anything that the city could offer and charmed everyone he met. She found him easy to live with, once he started paying for a cleaner. They never argued about politics, religion, or what to watch on the TV.

But he made jokes when she steered the conversation to serious subjects, and they didn't have the depth of connection that she thought might grow, given time. And time moved on relentlessly, leaving her trapped in a gilded cage.

As for Carl – well, Carl loved everybody. That was the problem. As the years passed, his work trips became more frequent, and he spent more evenings out entertaining clients. He often came back the next day, because he said he didn't want to wake her when the company had a flat in the West End he could crash at. But she knew what was happening. She confronted him about it one evening when he had come in late, smelling strongly of perfume.

"Are you having an affair?"

"Don't be silly. It's been a long day and I need to have a shower."

"You have a lot of long days and a lot of showers."

"What do you mean?"

"I'm not stupid. I don't understand why you're still with me, that's all."

"Martha. You're the one, Martha. You're the one I want as the mother of my children. How often do I have to tell you that? Marry me."

"I'm not sure I want children. I haven't achieved what I want in my own life yet."

"You'd better work on it now. We're not getting any younger. Now let me have that shower and I'll come to bed and show you how much I love you."

Martha pretended to be asleep when he came to bed, and resolved to reduce the hours she was putting in at the gallery and work harder on her paintings.

The next day, Carl told her to book a week off work. "We're going on holiday. And no more cheap packages to Greece. I've booked us a fancy hotel."

"In Spain? I've always wanted to go to Spain."

"I know, but I went off Spain that time in Pamplona that I nearly died."

"Because you ran with the bulls like all the other crazy Aussie tourists."

"Martha, you don't understand. You were in Australia at the time, remember? You didn't see me until months later, but it was very traumatic."

"We can go to another part of Spain. It's a diverse country. Let's go to Andalusia, or Valencia, or – "

"Maybe another time."

"You always say that."

"Look, I'm trying to do something nice for you. For us. I've booked a lovely hotel."

"Where?"

"Cornwall."

"We aren't even leaving the country?"

"I need to be on call. There's a big contract coming in, and I'll have to drive back if we need to close the deal. But you don't need to. The place is in Truro and if you have to, you can get the train back. Plus we can call in on your parents on the way there and back. Get your mum to make that coffee cake, will you?"

Martha resolved to book herself a week in Spain when she got back. Solo. However, she enjoyed being back in Cornwall more than expected. It was like settling back into a shabby but comfortable chair. Diabolical late spring weather that made Carl shrink into his coat energised Martha as she breathed in big lungfuls of clean air. When Carl needed to go back to the office for a forgotten Friday meeting, she breathed even more deeply. There would be no more nights of driving him back to the hotel drunk from each country pub he had to tick off in his Good Pub Guide.

She rented a bicycle, packed her lunch and a thermos of tea, and cycled out to the north coast each day. In between bracing dips in the sea and dodging rain showers in cafés, she soaked up the landscape, filling sketchbooks with pencil drawings and colour notes, and taking photographs to jog her memory later.

When she let herself into the London flat after a long train trip, she was relieved to find herself alone and started to paint, stopping only when the dawn light came through the east window. She was channelling something, not working, feeling as she hadn't felt since she was a kid, needing to get it down before the inspiration died. But it remained alive, and she kept painting, calling in sick to the gallery and stopping only to grab food from the fridge, or greet Carl on the days he came home. Late nights and early mornings let Martha wring out all her visions for a fortnight, after which she had created four finished paintings. She gave a month's notice at the gallery. Rosie only agreed to accept it if she could hang the new paintings out front, and host a proper opening. Martha said no to the opening, but she let Rosie price her paintings higher than she wanted to. They all sold by the time she had worked out her notice.

Carl was happy for Martha to go to Cornwall every couple of months, and she began a new routine of country life and city painting that would last for years, but take their toll. Every trip to the country made London more oppressive. Carl wouldn't move. He couldn't move. He was an urban man. The city had made him a success and changed him in a way he liked.

On a grey December day, Martha whiled away the time before the train back to London by wandering through the old streets of Truro. She glanced in a gallery that she'd been in many times and her heart stopped. There was a painting there like nothing she had seen before. She went in and walked over to the back wall to look at it more closely. It was a beautiful piece, abstract but clearly a garden full of living green and light and splashes of colour. She stared at it, trying to fathom why it was giving her goosebumps. She must have been standing there for longer than she thought because the gallery owner came and tapped her on the shoulder.

"I'm sorry, miss, but I'm closing up."

A small red sticker beside the painting declared it sold, but there was nothing to say who the painting was by or even what it was called.

"Who painted this?" asked Martha.

"Well, that's the funny thing. I don't know. The artist calls himself 'Barn Owl'. Actually, I'm not even sure the artist is a him. It was a condition of sale that we don't know his or her real name, or the name of the agent. There isn't even a signature on it, but it's lovely, isn't it? I could've sold it five times over."

Martha glanced at her watch, thanked the gallery owner, and ran for the train. She'd never seen Dean's completed paintings, but the line and colour of the painting was distinctive. It reminded her of the work he had done in class when demonstrating techniques and media. She sat on the train and the feelings she had tried to suppress came back to her as if the decades had never happened. A love lost. A love never realised, but real. These were feelings she had never had for Carl, no matter how hard she had tried. She had to do everything in her power to find Dean now.

She returned to the Truro gallery the following weekend with her camera at hand, but the painting was gone, leaving only an after-image in her brain like sun spots in her eyes. She went back to London to search again, scouring the libraries and spending time online on Friends Reunited, art discussion boards and anywhere she thought she might find a trace of Dean. It was hard to ask people to look for someone who had been so careful to cover his tracks. She had no photos of him and no one recognised him from drawings she had done twenty-something years before. She quizzed the gallery owner, but the person who bought the painting had paid in cash when they picked it up and there were no prints or cards for Martha to show anyone.

She kept going back to Truro, hoping that one day she might see him, but years passed and she didn't. Each time she returned to London, she felt more alone. It wasn't because Carl was always away for conferences and client dinners. Life was turning to make each of them face their own futures instead of their shared past. One ordinary day it was done. He came home at lunchtime and she knew from his face that everything was going to change.

"What's happened?" she asked.

"It's over."

Martha didn't know what to say. She felt nothing, but she knew she should say something, so she asked, "Why?"

"It's just not working, is it?"

"No, it never really has." Curiosity got the better of her. "So what's happened now? Why now? Why not ten years ago?"

"I thought you'd come around, Martha. I thought we would have kids."

"Kids don't fix anything. Do you think kids would have improved our relationship? Would they have connected us, or just separated us further?"

"I don't know. I do know that I wanted to be a dad and I made that clear to you early on. There was always hope that you'd sort out whatever it is you want from life and put some of the rest aside for what I wanted. I thought you'd be the best mother to my children."

"It never felt like the right time. It probably never would. I'm sorry, Carl."

"No, I should be. I haven't been honest. But I am going to be now because everything is different. I'm going to be a father, Martha."

"I see." Even though Martha knew they were not meant to be together, she felt the blow. She spat out the question, "Who is she?"

"Martha, calm down. I don't think we should drag her into this."

"It's too late for that. And you owe me her name, at least. Otherwise I'm going to find out sometime, aren't I?"

"Yes, but I don't want you to take it out on her."

Then Martha twigged. "I know her, don't I? It's one of our friends."

"No. Not exactly."

"Oh, of course." Martha thought back to the many times she had walked in on Carl at the gallery, when she hadn't expected him to be there. "Rosie, from the gallery. Where I've worked for so many years. The job you arranged for me. Has it been going on all this time?"

"Martha, don't be upset. It was an ideal arrangement. You and Rosie have worked so well together to make the gallery what it is. She would never want you to be unhappy."

"Right. What about you? Have you ever really cared about my happiness, or is it just about how my life fits into yours?"

"Don't be like that, Martha. Things haven't been easy."

Martha laughed. "Oh, I think they've been very easy for you. You've been able to have your cake and eat it. What I don't understand is why you didn't leave me earlier."

"I love you, Martha. I do. I guess I'm driven by different things to you."

"Too right. You've always been driven by what's between your legs."

"That's not fair. I've tried. And it's not just that. I've always wanted children, you know that. And Rosie really wants this baby."

"Well, that's convenient. I'm sure you're thrilled. You've now got everything you wanted in life."

"Martha, you know I'll look after you."

"No, you won't. I'll look after myself now. I haven't been doing that for years and it's time to start."

CHAPTER FORTY-TWO

It didn't take long for Martha and Carl to sell the flat in Shoreditch, an area that had skyrocketed in value as artists and students had made way for website companies, coffee shops, and marketing consultants. Carl offered her half of the profit that he'd made and she negotiated him down to a quarter, since she'd never paid the hefty mortgage, only the bills. It was still more money than she had ever had in her life and more than enough to start a new one. She rented a tiny storage unit to pack away a few boxes of things that she could collect once she had found somewhere to rent.

When Martha checked into her favourite Cornish bed-and-breakfast, she felt more at home than she had ever felt in London. The frenetic pace and fashion dictators were gone, replaced by people who had the time to nod in greeting, or even stop to chat. The low-level anxiety that had come from not fitting in fizzled out. It felt as though a vice in her mind was being unwound, releasing an urge to create that was impossible to suppress.

In her old life, she had forced herself to record the world around her in a sketchbook. Now it became as essential to her as breathing. A physical looseness mirrored her mental clarity. Her shoulders dropped and the aches and pains she had attributed to middle-age fell away. She walked the streets feeling giddy with the possibilities of the day.

Truro had the same chain stores as in every town's high street, but there were sweet little side streets where local shopkeepers began to recognise her from her repeated visits. As she was passing her favourite newsagent, she stopped as always to look at the noticeboard, perusing the adverts for dog walkers and gardeners and odd-job men. There were TVs, bikes and beaten-up lounge suites for sale. She skipped past the rooms to rent that dredged up bad memories of flat- and fridge-sharing. But then another card caught her eye.

It read, "Secluded barn to rent. Would suit artist/quiet person with a love of gardening. £250 pcm."

It was as if someone had written the advert for her. She called the number on the card.

It took a while for someone to pick up and a flustered woman answered. "Hello, Helen here."

"Hi, I'm calling about the barn."

"You are? Great, er, that's great!"

"I'm staying in Truro. When would be a good time for me to see it?"

"How about today? I can give you directions if you can drive over this afternoon."

"I'm afraid I don't have a car. Is it walking distance from here?"

"Not unless you want to be walking until tomorrow! But if you catch the number 29 bus, I'll pick you up at the bus stop. There should be one leaving from outside the library in about half an hour. Get off after Mevacombe, at the stop just beyond the humpback bridge. I'll park in front of the white cottage there."

Martha got on the bus and it snaked its way through the countryside. After about fifteen minutes of waiting by the white cottage, she was beginning to think she was at the wrong one, when a battered blue Citroen 2CV came haring around the bend.

Helen opened the door and apologised. "Sorry I'm late. I had to stop for some sheep. Hop in."

Martha moved a bag of jumper cables into the footwell, sat down and belted up as Helen took off at speed. Hedges scraped down both sides of the car, and Martha gripped the seat as she was thrown around the corners. Her breathing slowed when Helen turned off and drove more cautiously up the gravel track to an old farmhouse.

"This is it. This was our country dream."

"Was?"

"Yep. My ex-husband and I spent years and years talking about moving to the country. Within a couple of years of finding this place, he decided he liked the city's comforts better. He detested the mud, and the winters here can be muddy. Very muddy. Do you have a pair of Wellington boots?"

"Yes, with my stuff in London."

"It's dry enough now," said Helen as she got out of the car, slammed the door shut and gave it a shove with her rear end to make it click. "It's funny, we'd never owned welly boots until we moved here, and then we practically lived in them eight months of the year. That was just one adjustment he struggled to make. It was water off a duck's back to me."

They walked to the cottage and Helen removed the key from under an old milk urn to unlock the front door. An enthusiastic chocolate Labrador bounded out.

"I hope you don't mind dogs. Sorry, but I don't understand people who don't like them. It's just bizarre. I mean, unless you're allergic, of course. Are you allergic?"

"No, I'm not allergic, and I love dogs," said Martha, as she gently pushed down the dog, who had gone from sniffing her pockets to jumping up and trying to lick her.

"I got Monty as soon as I moved here, which was another thing that annoyed my ex, as he insisted it wasn't fair to take him back to our small apartment when we went back to London. But dogs adapt to wherever you live, don't they? They don't care about where they are as long as you're with them. They are completely different to cats. Now I do like cats, but I like birds too and there are a lot of birds around here, so I didn't think it was a good idea. Do you have any pets?"

Martha shook her head.

"Yes, Monty and I have found our true home, which is what made going to London so hard. I spent less and less time going up there, until I didn't go back at all. My husband came down for long weekends when he had to, but he preferred his bachelor pad and the life that went with it."

Martha shivered.

"Are you cold? I can find a coat if you like."

"No, I'm fine. You've just reminded me why I'm here."

Helen continued. "I told him he couldn't have his cake and eat it, so he chose the city and I chose the country. You'd think he'd be happy, but he's been a shit about the divorce. Even though it was him who found the dolly bird. It has dragged on and on and probably cost more than if he'd just let me have this place. The lawyers have settled it now, taking a chunk of our savings with them. The only way I can afford to stay here is by renting out the barn. But it seems most people don't want to live in a barn like this."

"Like what?"

"You'll see. Let's show you around!"

They crossed a gravel courtyard past old barrels full of geraniums. Helen opened up the large barn door and Martha took a big breath.

"Wow."

"It's odd, isn't it? Whoever lived here had a very, let's say, *different* life."

"It's amazing," said Martha, looking at the little wood-burning stove and the built-in bed, shelving and cupboards. There was a large table and a couple of chairs, and everything had been made from recycled wood. But it was built with care. All was in proportion; nothing seemed out of place. The shutters opened to reveal large windows that filled the barn with light.

Martha stood silently in the barn, taking it all in. It was as if it had been designed for her. It was the ideal space to live a simple life and work.

"So... what do you think? Most people don't want to climb a ladder to get into bed and all that. Are you on your own?"

Martha laughed. "Yes, yes, I'm on my own."

"Good for you. No one will screw you over that way. Anyway, come and look at the garden. It's too much for me, so I need someone who has the time and energy to look after it. That's why I reduced the rent. That and the fact the barn is peculiar. There's no electricity and I'm afraid that the water comes from a hand pump at the back here. We were looking to change all that before my husband went and had his stupid midlife crisis."

She opened a small door towards the back of the barn and more light streamed in from the garden. Martha gasped. It was the garden in the painting. Without abstraction and now very overgrown. But the proportions, the structure of the garden beds, the orchard behind and the way the light filtered through the trees were unmistakable. It was his garden.

"Do you know the person who lived here before you?" she asked.

"No, we went through an estate agent. Another bunch of bastards. I'll never be dealing with them again. They took advantage of the fact we didn't live near here to hide a lot about the state of the cottage. We had it surveyed, of course, but we didn't know that the surveyor was a good friend of theirs. It wouldn't have mattered if we'd stuck to the plan and taken the time to renovate it. Never mind; you know how life gets complicated."

"I think I know the person who used to live here – the one who did all the renovation. I know his work, but I've lost contact with him. Do you know anyone who might know where he is?"

"Why don't you ask in the village? Someone probably knows him at the pub."

Martha nodded. She couldn't believe she'd found the place. His place. It was the closest she'd come to finding him. There was no way she was going to let that go.

"Well, what do you think? Is it something you're interested in?"

Martha smiled and turned away from the garden to face Helen. "When can I move in?"

CHAPTER FORTY-THREE

Stan the barman was happy to talk about Dean. "Yeah, I knew him. Top bloke. He worked here and didn't miss a shift until the accident."

The blood drained from Martha's face and she grasped the bar as she asked, "What accident?"

"Don't worry, love. He's all right now. At least he was when I last saw him." Stan brought her up to speed on the barn, Dean's fall, and his recovery. "Demelza looked after him. He stayed with her until he was back on his feet."

Martha steadied her voice, careful to hide her fear. "Was she his girlfriend?"

Stan laughed. "No – I never saw Dean with anyone, and Demelza was old enough to be his mother, just looked out for him, that's all. She would've been the one to keep in touch with him. You know how lousy we blokes are, once someone moves out of range of the pub."

"Yes, he's a hard man to find, but it sounds like Demelza is the person to ask."

"I'm sorry, dear. She passed on some years ago, around the time Sheila sold the cottage and barn. She had a massive stroke."

"I'm sorry."

Stan gathered up some bar mats, tapping them together to make a tidy pile. "The weird thing was, she looked happy. As happy as she was in life. The paramedics said she probably died in her sleep. I was the one that found her and she looked like an angel, lying on her back with her eyes closed, smiling, as if nothing was wrong. But she was stone cold." Stan saw Martha's face fall, saw her look away. "Sorry. You don't need to hear this, but we miss her. Demelza's death affected us badly, but no one more so than Dean. That's when he quit everything. The dishwashing, of course – I don't know anyone who washes dishes as a career – but also the painting. He stopped painting and helped Demelza's family with sorting out her affairs: the shop, her stuff. And then he was gone, before the new folks at Sheila's cottage even moved in."

"Would anyone else know where he went?" asked Martha.

"No, like I said, Demelza was the one for that. She was the village grapevine, the organiser who kept people connected. The village isn't the same without her and no one will take on that shop. There's no money in it these days."

"I'm sorry..."

"Stan. The name's Stan. And you are?"

"Martha."

"Martha, it's nice to meet a friend of Dean's. He was a good friend to Demelza, and I thought he might move in there, but he just vanished. I think he was heartbroken, losing his friend and his home so close together. He went off like a wounded cat. Cats go off on their own to die, don't they?"

"Do they?"

"God, I'm saying all the wrong things, aren't I? I'm sorry, Martha. I really am. Let me shout you a drink. It's good to know someone will be living in the barn. Demelza said it was a marvel."

"It is, Stan. It certainly is. I'll have a small glass of sherry. Then I'd better bike home, whilst I can still remember my way back."

Moving into the barn was a turning point for Martha. A removal company brought down her boxes from storage and she settled in immediately. She worked outside in the mornings, rescuing the overgrown garden, and painted in the afternoons. Her hands were always busy, but her mind was free to reflect on what Stan had said. She couldn't imagine Dean going off to die, despite his loss of Demelza and the barn. He had dealt with adversity before and came across as a positive person with a love of life, which must have been magnified now that he was free to live how he wanted. Sometimes she faltered. If he was alive, why did no one know where he was? Where would he have gone? What did he have to hide from now? Once again, she drove herself downward, trying to find him in her mind. She had to calm herself and let it go by centring herself in the place. The place that was full of reminders of him, making him real and alive to her. There were dents in the floor where he must have set up his easel too, working where the light from the windows was best. Many more clues to his life were scattered through the barn and garden, magnifying her happiness each time she found one. A shopping list for a trip to Truro was tucked into the kindling basket. When she removed the smothering bindweed, flowers and vegetables sprang from seed in beds he had tended. More flowers grew from bulbs he had planted under each orchard fruit tree.

The summers were perfect, working in the garden and the barn studio, taking days off to bike or bus to the coast for hikes over headlands and swims in the rocky coves. The winter was hard, but the wood stove heated one end of the barn well. She painted in February, wearing five layers and fingerless gloves. She often ate winter lunches in the house, supplying fresh brassicas, herbs, jars of tomatoes and fruit, which Helen transformed into delicious stews and soups. Martha declined the offer of an extension cord for power because she enjoyed being in tune with nature, waking with the dawn, eating her last meal at dusk in the winter, listening to the radio for an hour or so after, before climbing up the ladder to sleep. There were no clients to demand her hours, no dinner parties to endure. The rhythm of the seasons brought more life to her paintings, which became like nothing she had created before. She built up a large body of work, filling the last of the space.

Martha went to the gallery in Truro where she had seen Dean's painting, and they agreed to exhibit hers. They sold well, and the cards sold by the box load. It was enough to live on, and Martha was happier than she had been in decades. She felt close to Dean, connecting through the earth the way trees reach out their roots towards each other. There was peace in the garden and her surroundings. The pain that had dragged her down for years was scrubbed out by her sense of place. It burst through her paintings. She painted the garden over and over again, until it became mere abstraction and feeling. It was light and joy and hope.

She was ready to contact the agent in London again, and pulled out his well-worn card from her purse. When she called him from the Mevacombe phone box, she was nervous. She need not have worried, as his phone number had changed; it rang through twice to someone who cut her off each time. The next time she went to Truro's library, she used its computer to find an email for him, sending him photos she had taken of her work. When she went back to exchange books a couple of weeks later, she was surprised to find a flurry of replies to her email, each one more impatient than the one before. Martha had forgotten that the speed of city life was much faster than the time it took her to read four books. The agent wanted to meet her and for her to bring as many paintings as she could. It was time for her to step back into London on her own terms. She would meet with Robert Avery again, and this time her paintings would make it worthwhile.

Robert's office was in South Kensington, a half-hour walk from Paddington Station. The route Martha had marked in her battered A to Z took her through Kensington Gardens, past the Serpentine Gallery, around the Royal Albert Hall and behind some student flats. She found his address and waited until she was exactly on time before pushing the buzzer.

The door clicked open and Robert's voice crackled over the intercom. "Fifth floor. Can you manage the stairs? The bloody lift is broken again."

Martha was glad she had only brought two canvases, as she stumbled into the office where Robert was waiting with a glass of water.

"Sorry about that. Seems to happen any time I'm seeing paintings, I'm afraid."

Martha hadn't mentioned to Robert that she had approached him years ago. She thought she saw a glimmer of recognition, but he said nothing about it, and she was relieved not to have to discuss the state of her previous portfolio. He looked at the two canvases and swore.

"What's wrong?" Martha watched Robert as he walked up to the canvases, put his reading glasses on and stared intently at each one, before whipping off his glasses to pace quickly around the room.

"You emailed me five photos. How many paintings do you have?"

"I've sold a few at the local gallery, but I haven't given them any since the start of this year."

"Which is how many?"

"Twelve."

Robert swore again.

"Is that bad?"

Robert laughed, hugged her, then stepped back. "Sorry. I know I'm not supposed to do that, but no, it's not bad. It's very, very good. You paint like no one I've seen before. Well, that's not strictly true. I have one client whose work is close, but yours has an edge to it. It'll reach people in the way some people like the sound of breaking glass. It's polarising. Visceral. Goes straight to the heart. My heart." Robert put his hand over his heart, sighed and scratched his head. "I'm rambling, which is exceedingly unprofessional, sorry."

Martha laughed. "Don't apologise. I'm glad you get it. I was afraid to show the local gallery owner. I'm not sure this work is for the tourists who want a souvenir of their holiday."

"No, you're right. But I know people who will absolutely love it. I don't want to rush you, but given the amount of work you have and your maturity as an artist, I think the best way to launch you is with a bang. A big exhibition. After I've circulated some pictures through my network, of course. Would that be okay?"

"Yes, of course."

"Great. I know a chap who works at the Serpentine. A major exhibition he was planning has gone down the gurgler because the artist turns out to be a kiddie-fiddler. He needs another exhibition to fill the slot sharpish, plus he owes me for the sell-out Reuben Erickson exhibition we did recently. He'll still owe me after this one, though, I assure you."

"Really? Reuben's work is hanging in the Tate Modern now. And the Serpentine is a lot higher profile than anywhere I've exhibited before. Isn't it a little risky, for someone unknown in the art world?"

"With these paintings and my connections? No. This is a sure thing. I know one when I see it. It's been a long time coming, but you're definitely it. And if you're prepared to do publicity, we can get you more attention than that other client of mine. I could have made him a superstar if only he'd let me."

"He sounds intriguing. Do you have any of his work here?"

"I'm afraid not." Then Robert rummaged in a drawer. "But I do have some cards: reproductions of his paintings. Here. They don't tell the whole story, of course, but they sell well."

Robert gave her a couple of cards and Martha knew immediately. "These are by…" she stopped herself from saying his name. "Barn Owl, aren't they?"

"You know his stuff?"

Martha knew she had to be careful. There was a reason he wasn't putting his name to his work, why he had been hiding himself away. She didn't want to screw this up now, now that she was so close to finding him. If she scared him away, she couldn't live with herself.

"Yes, I saw a painting of his in a gallery in Truro." She knew that Robert would find out where she was living eventually, so she added, "It happens to be of the garden where I'm living."

"Well, that is a coincidence. I'll have to let him know."

Martha restrained herself and looked at her watch. "I'll have to leave in half an hour. I bought one of those train tickets where if you change it, it costs a fortune. Perhaps you can invite him to my exhibition."

"Of course. I'll do that."

Martha left Robert's office without her paintings, but with a contract to look over and the details of a careful courier company who would collect her canvases and any more she completed in the next two months, assuming her lawyer approved of the contract. Martha was happy with what Robert suggested, apart from contacting a lawyer. She liked Robert, trusted him and didn't want to do anything to jeopardise this new, but tenuous, link to Dean. She would send copies of the contract to Garth, Camille and Frankie, who would all tell her to sign it and make sure they were invited to the exhibition (Garth saying he could fly back for work, call it a research trip, and claim it all back on expenses).

CHAPTER FORTY-FOUR

Martha felt light-headed as she walked towards Paddington. She treated herself to a coffee and a pain au chocolat at the station, before boarding the train. Then she settled into a seat by the window and slowed her breathing. Her hand shook as she picked up the coffee. Dean was alive, which was no surprise – she had always felt that to be true. But now she knew he was working and his agent was hers as well. Which meant that soon he would know she was working too.

He would see her paintings, see her through it, know where she was. And then...

Martha couldn't think beyond this. All her focus had to be on the exhibition. She would work harder over the next two months than she had ever worked in her life, hoping that Dean would see everything, and she would love every minute she was in front of canvas, connecting with him.

She ate her pastry, drank her coffee, and looked out of the window. So, she thought, an agent. I have an agent. I guess that means I'm a proper grown-up artist now. Finally. I wonder what Dean will think of that. She hoped he would be glad to know the path she had taken was working out for her – after too many years of struggle, it was true. He was always with her now when she worked, critiquing her choices, making her find her true self. That self contained the loss of him, she knew. Even Robert had said her paintings had a tinge of melancholy about them, despite the light. It wasn't her intention, but when she painted, she entered another state and channelled something deep inside her.

The train stopped. It wasn't at the station, but it was a busy time and sometimes trains had to give way to let others pass. She gazed out of the window and watched as a London-bound train slowly trundled by.

And then she saw him. It was surely him, because he saw her too and she registered his startled look. The look she had as well. And then he was gone. Martha leapt from her seat and got off at the next station. She had to wait twenty minutes for the next train back to Paddington. Please let him be there, she thought. Please.

But he wasn't. Martha sat on the bench and cried. People glanced at her as they passed. She pulled herself together and waited for the next train home. She had thought about going back to Robert. That could be where he was heading. But if he had wanted to see her, wouldn't he have waited? He couldn't know yet that she had met Robert, could he? Martha's head was filled with questions as she made her way back to Cornwall. Her feelings for him had never disappeared, only been submerged. Seeing him again was like seeing his painting – it had brought all of them back to the surface. Now she was adamant she would not let him go again. If he came to the exhibition, they could talk. She didn't want to think beyond that. She only hoped she would see him soon and that this time there would be no teacher/student relationship that would get in the way.

Dean watched the scenery blur from green to grey. Small stations with a smattering of passengers grew to acres of platforms packed with people shoving their way onto the overcrowded trains. He was coming into the city as most were escaping it. Robert had persuaded him to come up and fill in some paperwork.

"When was the last time you were in London, Dean?"

"1990."

"Ah. The year of your fall. And resurrection, I might add."

"Thanks for reminding me."

"Oh, come on, mate. I've been through worse. Still going through it, in fact. But now that I'm properly single again, you can be my wing man."

"I'll come up, sign the papers and stock up on art supplies, but I won't be anybody's wing man, especially not yours. You can't afford to fall in love again, Robert. Another divorce would bankrupt you."

"Always the voice of reason, Dean. Well, it will be good to see you, even if you are going to behave like a bloody eunuch. I hope you're bringing paintings – I'll need to sell several to pay my lawyer's last bill."

Dean smiled to himself. Robert was a salutary reminder of the advantages of an independent life. A simple life. Thinking for one, without conflict. Though there were things he missed and tried not to dwell on.

The train slowed as it approached Paddington and he looked into the carriages of the outbound train. Grey-faced commuters looked down at their phones, trying to connect with anyone but the people around them.

One woman was looking up, looked at him and held his gaze. With a start, he was transported back to a classroom, facing a new student who had engaged him then, startling him so that he had to look away. He didn't look away now, but his train kept moving and she was gone. It was Martha. He was sure of it. She was older, but just the same to him. The years of yearning to see her were rewarded in an instant; he felt like a drowned man brought back to life by a jolt of electricity.

The train was in the station, and commuters were piling into the precious seats. He grabbed the canvases from behind his seat, fought his way out against the tide and broke out of the doorway to stumble onto the platform.

He was still swimming against the tide of people when he got to the barriers, fumbled for his ticket and was waved through by an impatient guard. He was meeting Robert at his office and running late, like his train. His legs felt leaden, pulling him up short – should he go back? Would she? Then he berated himself. No. Too much time had passed. She would be settled in her life, whatever she had made of it.

He'd put that at risk before; he couldn't do the same thing again.

"These paintings are good, Dean. In fact, they're great and we should plan an exhibition."

"I don't want that kind of attention, Robert, and you know it."

"Okay, well I'll tell you about someone else who's having an exhibition," said Robert, looking at Dean. "A very talented artist who I'm just about to sign. Look at these." Robert showed Dean Martha's two canvases. "Her name is Martha Carson."

Dean knew they were hers before Robert told him. Her style was unmistakable, though more developed now. He saw the light and darkness – chiaroscuro. She had worked with a palette knife to create abstracts of nature. A garden with greens reaching for sunlight, but with a well of loneliness beneath. One was dawn and the other dusk. The giving and taking of light and life left him reeling. Dean sat back in one of Robert's battered club chairs, like a boxer who had barely stayed on his feet for a round.

"Are you okay? You look like you've seen a ghost."

"Yeah. I'm fine. Hey, let's go and get a drink."

"I thought you'd never ask."

Robert waited until Dean was on his second drink before he broached the subject. "My new artist, Martha Carson, would like me to invite you to her exhibition."

Dean flushed red as he took a big swig of wine.

"You know her, don't you?"

Dean put down his glass and studied it carefully, thinking about how an admission wouldn't hurt anybody now. "Yes. I know Martha."

Robert pressed on. "She was your student, wasn't she? She was the one. The reason you left your bloody awful wife. The reason you're mostly happy now. Except for the fact you've never got over her, have you?"

Dean's silence was admission enough.

Robert continued. "She's good, Dean. But you know that. You've always known that. And I'm sure you've been a big part of her development as an artist. She wants you to come to her exhibition. You have to do that. Tell me you will."

"I'll try, Robert."

But it would be difficult. Seeing her work had upset his equilibrium. It put him in an emotional state that he hadn't been in for decades. Seeing her on the train had done the same thing, and to meet her again, up close, surrounded by her work... It would take mental fortitude to do that. He wasn't sure that he had it. Because he wasn't sure he could bear to see what he'd lost, up close.

CHAPTER FORTY-FIVE

Martha channelled all her hopes and dreams into her paintings. She painted from when she got up to when she crashed out to sleep, stopping only when she had to. Helen worried about her, but Martha said it was because this exhibition was the most important thing that had happened in her life. She didn't say it was because of who she wanted to be there. Helen was excited for her and supported her by daily invitations to lunch, which became more substantial when she found out that Martha wasn't stopping to eat at any other time.

When Martha called the courier to collect the finished canvases, she warned him he might need a bigger van than normal. There were eighteen paintings. They were in a sequence from dusk to dawn, expressing the dark soul of the night, punctuated by the movement of the stars, ending exhausted but with the excited anticipation of the day to come.

Robert was delighted with Martha's work, though his friend at the Serpentine had a headache getting it all to fit in the allotted gallery space. He succeeded only by pushing the first two paintings in the series out into the reception area.

"This is going to make me very unpopular – I'm sure I'm breaking dozens of health and safety protocols," said Cameron as he propped open the fire doors.

"It is an opening – let's open everything," said Robert as he uncorked champagne and filled glasses.

"I've never seen you shout for the French stuff before, old boy."

"Just two cases. I want the press to be in a good mood. By the time the cheap stuff comes out, they'll have made up their minds."

Martha couldn't believe how many people had squeezed into the gallery. Her friends and relatives were well outnumbered by the movers and shakers of the art world.

Robert guided her through the room, introducing her to reporters, critics, and buyers. All of them wore bright smiles and her cheeks hurt, attempting to reciprocate. Robert made sure she spent just the right amount of time alone with each person, before coming back to whisk her away to the next somebody she had to meet. When they had done the rounds, he steered Martha into the alcove behind the canapés, where they could view the main room.

"They love you, my dear. Everyone showed except for the guy from *The Guardian*, and he texted me to say he has food poisoning. My phone keeps pinging with interview requests and holds from the buyers – you've sold most of them already."

"That's amazing."

"You don't look amazed. You look like a stunned mullet. We're done with the schmoozing; now it's time to get some champagne into you. Enjoy yourself!"

Robert pulled her back into the room, found her parents and told them how exceptional their daughter was, before leaving her with them to close deals he needed to edge over the line.

Martha's parents hugged her.

"This is quite something," said her dad.

"We always believed in you, but didn't know others would see it too," said her mum.

Her dad was now crying. "Sorry, it's the champagne. It always has this effect on me. Of course, your paintings are lovely. We're so proud of you." He was too choked up to say any more, and her mum put her arm around him.

"Your father is a little tired – it was a long drive up."

Martha suddenly noticed how small her parents looked, surrounded by her friends and strangers. Little lost country mice in the big city. "Shall I get you a taxi to the hotel?"

"Yes!" said her mum, a little over-emphatically, before adding, "We can meet you for breakfast and find out what we missed."

"Of course. You must both be exhausted, and the hotel is lovely. I'm glad Robert is paying!"

Once Martha had put her parents in a taxi, given the driver directions, and paid the fare plus a good tip in advance, she returned to the gallery and scanned the room. The gang from the framing shop she used to work in were hoovering down food and champagne. Helen was in deep conversation with Camille and Frankie. She couldn't see Dean. Then there was a tap on her shoulder and she turned around.

To find Garth holding two glasses of bubbles.

"It's the last of the good stuff, darling. And you deserve it – your paintings are quite marvellous. Where were you hiding your talent all these years?" He put a glass in her hand and gave her a bear hug.

It was then that she saw him.

Dean had just stepped into the gallery. They locked eyes for a moment and then he turned away and was gone. As Garth released her, she dropped the glass, apologised, and ran after him, making excuses as she pushed through the throng. Mere seconds later, she was out of the double doors and in the cool evening air. But he was nowhere to be seen. Dean had vanished again.

Robert pushed the last guests out of the doors and nodded to his friend, who was keen to lock up. "I told you it would be good, Cameron – now you owe me, big time!" Then he grabbed the coats from the cloakroom and walked Martha out. "What are you still doing here? I thought you'd be out celebrating with your buddies."

"I told them I'll be along in a bit. I wanted to talk to you first."

"Sure. Let's talk en route; I'll give you a lift. Where are you meeting them?"

"Notting Hill."

"Too easy. Get in," he said, opening the passenger door of his Audi. "We'll talk on the way."

Robert talked most of the way to the restaurant about the blinding success of the exhibition. "You sold all but two of your paintings, Martha. That's unheard of for a debut artist. Even Reuben Erickson didn't start with that much of a bang. I didn't break even on him until his third year."

"Yes, but he's good, isn't he? We had his work in our gallery until we couldn't afford to insure it."

"Reuben is good, but you're exceptional. And if you love the work and can keep on doing it, you have a bright future. Provided you don't throw it away, of course. I don't see that happening with you. Unlike some of my younger artists, you know who you are and are unlikely to throw your career away for the next shiny object that appears before you. I lost a fantastic chap last year because he decided his talents lay in fashion design. They didn't, and he blew what was left of his money on cocaine. I got him into rehab, but I won't be representing him again. I don't think that's something you'd be likely to do."

"Yes, a couple of glasses of Shiraz are fine for me and I wouldn't know what was fashionable if it bit me on the bum."

"Good woman. In that case, we have an exciting time ahead of us, don't we?"

"Yes. Thank you, Robert. Thank you for organising all of this. I'm so grateful to you."

"But you wanted to talk to me about something else, didn't you?"

"Yes. Dean Finlay. He was going to come to the exhibition –
"

"I saw he didn't show. Don't take it to heart – he's not a big fan of the city."

"No, that's the thing. He did show. I saw him and he saw me and he left."

Robert waited for Martha to continue.

Martha sighed. "He saw me with Garth."

"Your gay friend."

"Yes. He saw us hugging and turned and left. I'm afraid…" Martha crumpled and tears spilled down her cheeks. "I'm afraid I'll never see him again."

Robert reached into his jacket, pulled out a handkerchief, and dabbed at Martha's eyes. "Don't cry, sweetie. You'll ruin your make-up and you need to celebrate your fabulous debut on the national art stage."

"But you don't understand…"

"That you've been in love with my best friend for all your adult life? It's written all over your face, my dear."

The shock of her feelings being articulated by Robert stopped Martha from crying. "How long have you known?"

"I should have known the moment I met you. You and Dean are peas in a pod. It's in your paintings: the way you feel about each other and the world at large. When Dean came in after our first meeting – "

"Second meeting. I first met you a long time before that."

"Ah, I thought so. I have to say it was your style of painting that looked familiar. I'm better with art than with names and faces, I'm afraid. Anyway, when Dean saw your work, I thought he might have a heart attack. It was obvious he knew it, and since you haven't been represented by an agent before, I knew he knew you, too. It didn't take too much arithmetic after that to work out you were the student he had fallen in love with all those years ago."

"He was in love with me?"

"Oh dear, he is useless, isn't he? He could deny it himself, but it was in everything he did from the time he moved to the barn. I'd never seen him grow so much as a tub of cress before that. You were in his head, guiding his new life. He's been carrying a torch for you for bloody decades."

Martha wiped under her eyes. "I'm sorry, but I can't lose him again. I can't bear it a second time."

"You don't have to. I know where he is and I'll tell you." Robert scribbled down Dean's details on a slip of paper, folded it, and held it up. "I'll give this to you on one condition. Tonight is about you and you only. Go out with your friends. It's their time now. Dean can wait until tomorrow, or after that. He's waited long enough for you and another day or so won't hurt. Go out with the other people who care about you. Do you promise me you'll do that?"

Martha nodded, smiled, and took the piece of paper. She put it in her purse and tried not to think of it as she celebrated her artistic success with her friends. Though she got back to the hotel well after midnight, she barely slept, and left a note for her parents so that she could take the first train to Cornwall.

CHAPTER FORTY-SIX

Dean was about to put away the 'Open' sign when he heard footsteps on the gravel path. Bugger, he thought. No one comes all day and now, five minutes before closing, I'm going to have to hang about so that someone can dash up the 142 steps of the lighthouse, look at the lantern room, come back down and buy a postcard or two, before I can shut up shop. He steeled himself, fixing a smile to greet the intruder.

And then he saw her. The late afternoon sun picked out highlights in her hair and he noticed laughter lines crinkling around her eyes as she smiled. She seemed different to the woman he had glimpsed in the Serpentine Gallery, but she was absolutely, unmistakably, Martha.

It was twenty years since she had seen him up close, but he looked the same, save for a few streaks of grey through his hair and creases now crosshatched around his eyes as he smiled. She had played the scene in her head a thousand times about how she would find him, run to him and hold him, but now only her heart was racing as she stood rooted to the spot, watching him walk steadily towards her.

A shaggy grey lurcher bounded ahead and Dean called, "Solomon! Solomon!" He caught up to Solomon, who had jumped up but was now sitting, as Martha scratched his head.

"Sorry, he usually hides from the visitors."

She looked up at him and all the words she had prepared vanished from her head.

He seemed to struggle to find the right words as well, and settled on, "Hello, Martha."

"Hello, Dean."

"This is a nice surprise. How did you find me? No, don't answer that. Robert told you, I assume..."

"Yes. I made him tell me. I saw you at the exhibition."

"Sorry. It was a mistake. I shouldn't have come."

"Yes, you should."

"I was interrupting something. You have your life, your friends and – "

"That's all. Just an average life and some friends, most of whom are average too. You weren't interrupting anything. When you walked in at the exhibition, you saw me with Garth. My ex-flatmate."

"Ah."

"My gay ex-flatmate."

"Sorry. Especially that I didn't see your exhibition. Robert thinks your paintings are exceptional."

Martha came closer. Dean looked at her kindly, but kept his dog between them, as if he didn't trust her. Or himself. "What brings you here now?"

"Really? You have to ask that?"

"It's been a long time, Martha."

"That's not my fault. I've been looking for you ever since you ran out on me."

Solomon picked up on the tension and padded back to the lighthouse. Dean reached out an arm, but Martha stepped back, folding hers.

"I had to leave, Martha. You must understand that now."

"You left me a note. You could've talked to me."

"How would that have changed anything? You were a child. I was your teacher."

"You know it wasn't that simple. And yes, nothing you could've said would have changed how I felt. Or still feel. It never changed, Dean, never. I may have been a child, but I knew who I was, who you were, who we were together. No amount of time changes that. Did it change for you, Dean? Did it?"

Dean didn't answer and Martha carried on. "I've thought about this a lot over the years. How you didn't mean to hurt me, but you did."

"I'm sorry, Martha."

"I know, but I haven't come to hear you apologise. I've been through it all: denial, anger, bargaining, depression... But I could never accept it. Not until I saw you and talked to you. Not until I was done being a student and no one could remember you were my teacher. Not until so many years had passed the age difference wouldn't matter anymore. I'm older than you were when I met you. It doesn't matter. All that matters is how we both feel." Martha looked into Dean's eyes, deep wells of loss now filling with tears. "How do you feel about me, Dean?"

He reached out and pulled her to him, hugging her hard, kissing her forehead and pulling back to say, "Does this answer your question?" He held onto her as if she was the one who'd deserted him.

"Maybe." Martha breathed in his clean, earthy smell and squeezed him back. Then she pushed him away and punched him.

"Ow! What was that for?"

"Trying not to be found. I looked for you all my adult life, Dean. You didn't make it easy."

"I know. I thought I was doing the right thing."

"Have you noticed how doing the right thing keeps messing up your life?"

"People have told me that, yes." He stepped towards her, reaching out his hand to brush her cheek.

Martha looked down, but Dean tilted her face upwards to look at her. "This is the right thing, though, isn't it?"

"Yes, this is the right right thing." She felt Dean pull her in tight, felt his need released. She pushed him away, but gently now. "So don't screw it up by disappearing again."

He laughed. "I won't. I promise. And now you can tell me how you persuaded Robert to break his vow of silence."

"I'll explain, but I'm parched. Any chance of a cup of tea, or are you closing?"

"I'm open for you, Martha. Come in."

Dean made tea as Martha told him how Robert had become her agent, and how he had linked the two of them. She also told him what had happened before. The years of trying and failing to find him, but never giving up.

"Martha, I've never stopped thinking about you, but I was sure you would have made a good life for yourself. The more time passed, the more I felt I couldn't interrupt your life, whatever you had made of it."

"I wish you had interrupted it. I made a mess, Dean, for years I made a mess. But I'm here now. What about you? How did you end up here?"

"It's a long story."

"I've got time to hear it."

"After I left Kristina and the school, I needed somewhere cheap to live. A friend of Robert's had an old barn on the other side of Truro. I lived there for years, even though there weren't what most people would consider basic necessities."

"I'm living in a barn like that now."

"Really?"

"I'll explain later," said Martha.

Dean filled her in on how he had brought the barn and garden back to life, inspired by thinking of her and how she loved plants. He then told her about his accident, the sale of the house and the death of his friend.

"After the barn was sold and with Demelza gone, I went to Spain. I've never travelled, you see. I spent a couple of years in Andalusia – I can wash dishes and paint in any language! But I felt like an outsider and that feeling magnified as I learned more Spanish and more about the culture. Family is everything in Spain. Generations of family and friends and their families meet in the streets – you socialise en masse with everybody else. No one has dinner parties."

"That sounds brilliant."

"It was, for a while. I miss wandering from bar to bar on a balmy night, having a drink and tapas in each one, bumping into people you know only because you keep bumping into them. But I missed the intimacy of in-depth conversations with friends, where language and culture are not a barrier. I was trying to insert myself into a society where everyone has grown up with everybody else. There is almost a communal way of thinking that I found hard to get into. I made friends, and it has a special place in my heart, but I remember the conversations you and I had on paper being deeper. I couldn't bear to read your letters again after I left, but the feelings behind them have stayed with me."

Martha thought about Dean's letters she had kept and how she had practically memorised them with repeated reading. That they were now fragile things, like ancient texts in the British Library but for being stored in a battered biscuit tin. Hidden from a man who never wrote to her, and never went with her to Spain as she'd wanted. "I wish I'd gone to Spain."

"We'll go back. I have wonderful places to show you, and friends who will like you nearly as much as Robert does."

"What did you do when you got back?"

"I found a flat above a pub in Dartmoor. But that meant bartending, not dishwashing, and dealing with the general public drained me. It sapped my artistic soul. Luckily, I saw an advert in the West Country Heritage Trust newsletter. They were looking for a caretaker to live in this place. Someone who was a bit of a handyman, and could be here during opening hours to let in the occasional visitor. That was over five years ago. But last month the Trust had to sell the place. They were short of funds and had to let the least visited properties go. So they sold it last week."

"Oh no! When do you have to move out?"

"I don't. I bought it."

"No way! How?"

"Yes, I was surprised too, but it turns out that five years of caretaking and selling paintings, while having minimal expenses, are enough to buy a decrepit lighthouse. Especially as the Trust knew I was happy to keep it open to visitors. They sold it to me for a lot less than it's worth, I'm sure."

As Martha placed her empty cup on the saucer, Dean took her hand. "I have to show you something. Close your eyes and come with me." Dean led her out of the kitchen door to the back of the lighthouse. They crunched along a path of seashell grit, and then an intense smell of flowers arrested her. He stopped too, put his arms around her waist, and whispered in her ear. "You can open your eyes now." The smell of the flowers and Dean beside her made her giddy, and she leaned back into him. She breathed in deeply, opening her eyes to look out on a beautiful garden. Above her was an archway of jasmine and honeysuckle.

Dean let his arms fall away, stepped back, and asked, "Well, what do you think?"

Martha had tears in her eyes. "How could you think I wouldn't want to be here? With all this? With you?" She laughed. "You are an idiot."

"Come here and say that."

She walked back to him, but before she could utter the words a second time, he kissed her. The same deep, dissolving kiss she had replayed in her mind for so many years. But now it was right and no one could separate them. She had found him, found home, and neither of them was going anywhere.

Martha knocked on the door frame of the studio Dean was building for them at the end of the garden.

He put down the drill. "You look serious. Is everything okay?"

"Everything is very okay. I love this life. I love you. I'm pinching myself each day to make sure I'm not dreaming."

"You're not dreaming, so what's wrong?"

"I need to tell my parents."

"I've been saying that for months."

"Yes, but I can't just pick up the phone and say I'm living with this guy, this amazing guy, and oh, he used to be my teacher."

"You don't need to say it like that."

"Exactly. Which is why we should get married."

"You said marriage was an outdated institution designed by men to show ownership of women."

"Did I say that?"

Dean smiled at her as he leaned on the new door frame and waited for her to continue. Sometimes Martha felt physical pain, knowing that he was here with her and wanted her as much as she wanted him. It was the thought that she might lose him again.

As he often did, Dean read her thoughts. "I'm not going anywhere, you know. The marriage certificate wouldn't change anything for me."

"Nor for me. It's not for me."

"It's for your parents."

"I want them to know how serious this is. How important you are to me. A wedding would signal that to them and anyone who might doubt it."

"Anyone who might doubt it?"

"Yes."

"Okay. But." Dean looked at her sternly.

"But what?"

"We're not inviting Miss Staverly."

Martha picked up a clod of dirt and threw it at him.

Dean ducked out of the way. "Okay, if you insist... But she'll demolish all the champagne."

They didn't invite Miss Staverly, of course. The guest list was tiny: Martha's parents and Amy and Robert, the friends who meant the most to them.

Martha need not have worried about her parents. Once they received the invite, she could barely keep them away from the lighthouse. They were always dropping in on the way to pubs, walks or shops they had never shown an interest in before. And 'on the way' was a stretch, as the lighthouse was on a peninsula at the end of a lane that snaked a good ten miles down from the main road. Dean and her dad clicked immediately, talking about gardening, DIY and all things practical. A shared love of books connected Dean with her mum, and they exchanged many of their favourites before discussing them at length over lunches and dinners. Martha's parents stayed over so many nights she joked she was going to charge for their room as a bed-and-breakfast. In truth, she delighted in their ease with Dean and their acceptance of their relationship.

The September garden hosted the wedding. Flowers remained in the ground in full glory – sprays of cosmos, heleniums, echinacea, and rudbeckia filled the beds, and a backdrop of roses fringed the orchard. The studio and marquee were festooned with trusses of ripe tomatoes and strings of chillies and peppers. The garden also gifted aubergines, corn, and courgettes for the barbecue, with plenty of salad plus blueberries, figs and raspberries that spilled over the pavlova and cake. One of Stan's regulars came to despatch a deer that had been raiding the veggie patch at night. He returned with two guns, a week before the wedding. Dean and Martha helped him kill the rabbits which had reproduced to plague proportions since winter. Venison was barbecued and rabbit was stewed and the garden was freed of its protective chicken wire for the wedding day.

Robert and Amy were best man and woman. Martha was surprised and delighted Amy could make it, given that she always seemed so busy on the farm. She arrived two weeks before the wedding to help, and Martha had to drag her in from the garden each evening at gin and tonic o'clock. She would find her hammering in tall iron stakes and tensioning the wire to make fences to dissuade any more deer from eating the vegetable part of the menu.

"Amy, you don't have to do all this…"

"Are you kidding? Your fences wouldn't keep out an ageing Shetland pony, let alone a sprightly deer. And you should run some electricity through them to teach them to stay away."

"Dean isn't keen on that idea."

"We can set up a small solar power panel to power it. And it wouldn't kill them – it would just teach them a lesson."

"Maybe. I'll talk to him. But you've been out here working since breakfast. You're on holiday – relax!"

"I am relaxing – you two don't get up until seven. We only start out here after a leisurely breakfast. Lunch hour is more like two and I've no kids to home-school and no sheep to worry about. It's bliss."

"I'm sorry your family couldn't come."

"I'm not. Mike is wonderful, but sometimes he forgets I had my own life, my friends, my family. That I gave it all up for him. It's fine – I knew the deal – but it's good to remind him.

He'll be super sweet for at least a week when I get back. And I will be happy to be home."

"Okay. But next time, you'll have to bring them."

"Or you'll have to visit us! I can show you the serious rabbit-proof fence around my garden."

"Let's talk about that with Dean – he's waiting for us by the studio."

"With G and Ts?"

"Yep. And homegrown edamame."

Amy shoved her pliers in her pocket and took off. "My favourite – last one there is a big fat ape!"

Martha laughed and ran after her, making gorilla noises as she reached the deck. She had become quite convincing, as Amy always beat her, with or without a head-start.

When the best man arrived, Dean was surprised to see him creeping up the gravel road in a Prius. "No sports car, Robert? What's wrong?"

"Nothing. Did you know the fuel economy on this is unreal?"

"I did. But it never bothered you before. Are you skint?"

"Far from it. I make quite a decent living on the commission I get from Martha's and your paintings."

"So, a new girlfriend you needed to impress?"

Robert narrowed his eyes. "You are rotten, Dean." He opened the boot of the car. "And correct."

"Come on, mate! Why didn't you bring her?"

"It's early days, and I'm taking it slowly."

"You? This must be how you have a midlife crisis – you're going sensible on us." Dean turned and yelled into the garden, "Martha, Robert's here, and he's all grown-up!"

"Very funny, Dean. Now let's wait for Martha, as I've got something for you both."

"Hey, we said no presents, unless they're drinkable."

Martha arrived and gave Robert a big hug. "Nice car, Robert."

Robert pecked her on the cheek. "Thank you, Martha. Now I've brought you both something."

"We said no presents," said Martha.

"I think you'll want this." Robert handed Dean a package.

"It feels like a picture."

"It is," said Robert. "Open it."

Martha pulled at the string and unwrapped the brown paper. She put her hands to her mouth and tears came to her eyes. "No way!" It was the painting she had seen in the Truro gallery that had rekindled her desire to find Dean. The one of the garden by the barn that had been his home, and then hers.

Dean looked similarly shocked. "How the hell did you end up with that, Robert?"

"When you showed this painting to me, I knew it was important. I couldn't let you sell it to a random tourist. So when I took a photo, I gave copies to every gallery I found in a ten-mile radius of your barn. I told them to call me if the painting ever came up for sale, and luckily, your gallery owner did."

"You are a sneaky bugger," said Dean.

"I had to make sure it ended up in the right hands. And I have, haven't I?"

Martha gave him a massive hug in answer.

"Yes, you bloody have," said Dean. "Now, can I see that speech before you unleash it on our nearest and dearest?"

"No way," said Robert.

"I thought you'd say that," said Dean, "but it was worth a try. Come in and I'll show you your room. It has a view of the garden."

"Is it as good as that one?" said Robert, nodding at the painting.

"Even better," said Martha, as they went inside.

Martha was struggling to zip up the back of her robin's-egg-blue wedding dress when Amy burst into the bedroom, all of a fluster.

"Where is the vicar? We don't have a vicar!"

"You mean 'celebrant'," said Martha.

"We don't have one of those either. I was double checking everything you need to get married and we don't have someone to perform the ceremony. It's a disaster!"

Dean put his head round the door. "Are you two okay?"

Amy yelled, "Get out, get out! You can't see the bride in her dress before the ceremony."

"I'm shielding my eyes. But I saw her when she tried it on in a vintage store – lovely, isn't it?"

"Yes, but get out!"

Dean retreated behind the door. "What's the kerfuffle?"

"Amy is concerned that we don't have a celebrant."

Dean paused and then swore. "I knew we forgot something!"

Amy dashed out of the room. "Who can we call?"

Dean followed her down the stairs and out to the front steps. "Maybe that guy," he said, pointing to a man sauntering across the lawn.

Amy watched the man, dapper in a three-piece suit and bow tie, make his way to the pergola.

"Who's that?"

"Stan. He was a registrar before he became a publican. When I was working with him, he ended many nights with stories about the terrible couples he had joined in unholy matrimony. It only took him a few pints and a slap-up feed with a local councillor to get all his paperwork in order as a celebrant."

"Stan, the scruffy bartender of that pub you took me to?" asked Amy.

"The one and only. He always looks better after a haircut and a shave."

Stan not only looked the part but acted it, as Martha and Dean both vowed to respect, listen to and care for each other in sickness and in health, till death did them part (they had decided that love could not be promised, but would continue if they kept to their vows).

Stan then pronounced them husband and wife, as Martha's dad and Robert cried buckets, and Amy and Martha's mum opened the champagne to continue the celebration.

"You may kiss the bridegroom." Stan nudged Martha.

She stood on tiptoe, was folded into her husband's arms, and felt just as she had at seventeen.

It was a schoolgirl crush that would last a lifetime.

ENJOYED THE KEEPER?

I hope you enjoyed this book. If you did, please help spread the word by leaving a review for it on Amazon, Goodreads, or wherever good people might find it.

Get the The Sustainable Heart newsletter and read a bonus scene to discover what happened between the last chapter and the epilogue.

axwilkinson.substack.com

The password for the pdf download page is "LIGHT-HOUSE", in capital letters.

ACKNOWLEDGMENTS

I'm indebted to the other members of the Super Writing Group, Deborah and Helen, who helped improve my writing, particularly after reading early excerpts of *The Keeper*. Without their encouragement, I doubt I would have ever finished this book.

Thank you also to the readers of the final draft, who helped me improve it immensely: Nicky, Sarah and Jane. Nicky spotted an embarrassing number of glaring errors and pointed out when I was assuming too much prior knowledge (not everyone has had the delight of being in a 2CV, or knows what it means to 'have the painters in'). Jane gave me excellent feedback on the art college, which began as Central St Martin's, but for which I had all my facts wrong. She furnished me with the name of its fictionalised replacement, Saint Hibbert's, as well as Monty, named after her dear departed chocolate Labrador. Thanks, Jane – you are a legend.

Lastly, thank you to Sheila Glasbey, who went above and beyond what is required of an editor. Any mistakes left in this book are probably ones I've made post-edit, and I'm terrified that this last paragraph is full of errors.

A X Wilkinson

* 9 7 8 0 4 7 3 6 7 6 0 7 0 *